SECRET
Indiscretions

 Daisy Jones
1507 S. Curtiss Dr.
Urbana, IL 61802

Also By Trice Hickman

Unexpected Love series

Unexpected Interruptions
Keeping Secrets & Telling Lies
Looking for Trouble
Troublemaker

Playing the Hand You're Dealt

Published by Dafina Books

SECRET
Indiscretions
TRICE HICKMAN

KENSINGTON PUBLISHING CORP.

www.kensingtonbooks.com

DAFINA BOOKS are published by

Kensington Publishing Corp.
119 West 40th Street
New York, NY 10018

All Kensington titles, imprints, and distributed lines are available at special quantity discounts for bulk purchases for sales promotion, premiums, fundraising, and educational or institutional use.

Special book excerpts or customized printings can also be created to fit specific needs. For details, write or phone the office of the Kensington Sales Manager: Kensington Publishing Corp., 119 West 40th Street, New York, NY 10018. Attn. Sales Department. Phone: 1-800-221-2647.

Dafina and the Dafina logo Reg. U.S. Pat. & TM Off.

ISBN-13: 978-1-61773-743-5
ISBN-10: 1-61773-743-7
First Kensington Trade Paperback Printing: August 2015

eISBN-13: 978-1-61773-744-2
eISBN-10: 1-61773-744-5
First Kensington Electronic Edition: August 2015

10 9 8 7 6 5 4 3 2 1

Printed in the United States of America

Acknowledgments

Although acknowledgments appear at the beginning of a book, they're usually written once the story is complete. So after pouring hours, days, and months into this novel, getting to this part of the book feels surreal because it means that God has once again blessed me with my dream come true, which is another published book that will go on my shelf, and hopefully on the shelves of many others. I have a great deal to be thankful for, so here goes.

I thank God for blessing me beyond measure. I'm thankful for all the ups and downs, successes and failures, and the good and bad that I've experienced while writing this book. My life has changed in many ways, and through it all, God delivered me to much better days, and I look forward to what's ahead. Thank you, Lord!

Thank you to my parents, Reverend Irvin and Alma Hickman. Your unconditional love, support, and guidance mean the world to me. I thank God I was born to you! Thank you to my siblings, Marcus and Melody, whom I will always love. Thank you to my cousins, aunts, uncles, and family friends, so many in number that I can't name all of you without leaving out someone, so again I say thanks and I love you!!

Thank you to Todd Terrell Hayes, Sr., Todd Terrell Hayes, Jr., and Eboni Simone Hayes. You welcomed me into your lives and have made mine much richer in the process. I love each of you!

Thank you to my girls, ride or die chicks for sure (☺), who always have my back: Vickie Lindsay, Sherraine Mclean, Terri Chandler, Kimberla Lawson Roby, Barbara Marie Downey, Tiffany Dove, China Ball, Lutishia Lovely, Tammi Johnson, Cerece Rennie Murphy, and Yolanda Trollinger. You women are my sisters and I love you to the moon and back!

Thank you to my wonderfully talented and wise agent, Janell Walden Agyeman. I so admire your commitment, professionalism, and integrity, and I thank you for guiding my literary career. You ROCK!

Thank you to my amazing editor, Mercedes Fernandez, who helps put the patina on each of my books. Thank you to my independent publicist, Ella D. Curry, for being one heck of a promoter and friend. Thank you to all the librarians, bookstore managers and employees, street vendors, and online retailers who sell my books to your customers. I appreciate you all!

Thank you to my alma mater, Winston-Salem State University, for always supporting me and showing me love. I have the best HBCU on the planet!

Thank you to my loyal readers and book club members who, because of God's grace, are growing in numbers with each book! Your support of my work and your willingness to spread the word to your family and friends mean more to me than I can put into words. I appreciate every single thing you do!

Happy Reading!
Peace and abundant blessings,

Trice Hickman

Truth doesn't grow dim because we squint.

—Charles M. Blow

Prologue

I wish I could have taken a picture of the look on Johnny's face when I pulled out my gun and aimed it between his eyes. But then again, I didn't need a picture because that sweet memory will be etched on my brain for the rest of my life. And besides, a photograph would be evidence, and after the time and effort I put into planning this son of a bitch's murder, the last thing I need on my phone is a picture of a dead man.

Usually when someone shows up at a person's doorstep late at night, a booty call is more than likely on the agenda. But because there's no way in hell that was the case between us, Johnny knew right away that this visit wasn't going to end well. I was actually surprised that he opened the door once he realized that it was me standing there, but then again, too much alcohol can make a person do things they normally wouldn't. He smelled of liquor and he could barely keep his balance.

"What're you doing here?" he asked, slurring his words.

They say that the eyes are the window to the soul, and I believe that to be true. From the moment we looked into each other's eyes, Johnny knew that I came here tonight to kill him.

We stared at each other for what felt like a long time, but was only a brief minute. His eyes said he was sorry for what he'd done to me, and to a host of other people, too. But my eyes told him that I didn't give a damn about his remorse, and after what happened a week ago today, he had to have known that he was going to have to pay for his sins. I guess that's why he opened the door for me in the first place.

He quickly sobered up when I pointed my gun between his eyes, and that's when he allowed the reality of what was about to happen to sink in. He didn't put up resistance. He didn't fight. And he didn't plead for his life. He did none of the things I thought he would do, and I was glad because that made my job easier. The bastard actually helped me by taking a few steps back into the kitchen, eliminating the need for me to drag his body out of plain sight once I did what I came to do.

I didn't want to prolong this because I knew I had a set amount of time to get in and get out. But I also wanted to enjoy this moment, savor it, and swallow the sweet taste of revenge. However, I had to use my head, otherwise all my planning would go right down the drain, and I'd end up in jail. I couldn't let that happen, so I lowered my gun to Johnny's chest and smiled as I pulled the trigger.

Chapter 1

GENEVA

If there was one thing Geneva Mayfield had learned in the five years, two months, and twenty-two days she'd been married to Johnny, it was that she knew straight away when he was telling a lie.

A slight hesitation in his velvety smooth voice, a subtle shift in his deep brown eyes, or a placid expression framing his thick, kissable lips were all telltale signs for Geneva that her husband wasn't being truthful. Over the last six months, to her disappointment, he'd added another move to that growing list of signals, and that was the art of avoidance, which he was exercising tonight.

Who does he think he's fooling? Geneva said to herself. Her husband's shenanigans, along with the humidity clinging to the stifling Alabama heat, had frayed the edges of her nerves.

For the last ten years, she'd braced herself each summer for the unrelenting heat that covered the town of Amber, Alabama, practically smothering its residents. She was one of the thousands of African Americans who'd completed the reverse migration to the south—by way of Chicago—in search of a slower pace and more affordable standard of living. She loved Amber because it provided her with the best of both worlds.

With a population of just over 90,000 residents, Amber was small enough to provide a homey feel, but not so small that everyone knew everybody. And given that it was a quaint suburb situated not far from Birmingham, the largest city in the state, Amber attracted business professionals, entrepreneurs, and small companies, which contributed to its growing affluence.

If he thinks I'm letting this one go, he's out of his mind, Geneva quietly seethed. She knew she should've put an end to Johnny's lies several months ago when he'd started feeding her spoonfuls of half-truths. But now that he was boldly pouring lies down her throat, it had become too much to swallow.

As she stood at one end of the couch staring at Johnny, who was reclined on the opposite end, pretending to be transfixed by the sports announcer on ESPN, Geneva was becoming more upset by the minute. She was disturbed and confused about a lot of things that had been happening in her marriage, and she couldn't figure out what had brought about the change. She was still as attentive to Johnny as she had been the day they'd married. She still put time and care into her personal appearance, making sure she looked fashionably chic on his arm. She still cooked delicious meals, kept the house meticulously clean, and made sure she supported him in everything he ventured to do in both his career and personal life.

Geneva knew she was a good wife and helpmate, and as her best friend and coworker, Donetta Pierce, had told her, a hell of a catch. "Most men would love to have a fly, smart, dutiful wife like you by their side," Donetta often said. But for some meritless reason that Geneva couldn't explain, Johnny acted as though he couldn't care less about her or their marriage. And again, Geneva didn't know what to make of the current state that she and her husband were in. But there was one thing she was sure of, and was willing to bet her life on, and it was that her husband was up to no good.

"Johnny, did you hear a word I just said?" Geneva asked.

"Unfortunately, yes I did."

She took a deep breath. "Why're you talking to me like that?"

"Like what?"

"Like you have absolutely no respect, care, or concern for me. Like I'm some person on the street, instead of your wife."

"I answered your question, didn't I?" Johnny said with annoyance. "You're so dramatic."

Geneva shook her head. She knew she was many things, but dramatic certainly wasn't one of them. If anything, she knew that her meek, often reserved manner could stand a tune-up, and tonight was the perfect time to start. She placed her hand at the top of her slim but curvy hip. "I can see that you have an attitude tonight, but just so you know, that's not gonna stop me from getting to the bottom of why you haven't answered my question."

"We've been through this already and I don't feel like rehashing it," he said without so much as a glance in her direction. "Now can you please stop with the interrogation and let me watch the game highlights in peace."

Geneva folded her slender arms across her chest and took deep breaths in her attempt to calm herself. Johnny's behavior had gone from troublesome to alarming, almost overnight. At first it had been subtle: a missed phone call here, an unanswered text there, or a hurried reply message sent hours after she'd originally contacted him. But she'd chalked it up to the pressures and busy schedule that went along with growing his real estate and property management company. However, over the last two months things had worsened, and now their marriage was unraveling like a bundle of yarn.

It seemed as though he flat-out didn't care about her at all, which was apparent by the laissez-faire attitude he now demonstrated in the way he treated her.

Two weeks ago Geneva had waited inside Frank's Auto Repair for more than two hours before Donetta finally came to pick her up, all because Johnny had forgotten that she'd needed a ride home while her car was in the shop. Then last Monday she'd waited at the fertility clinic all alone, hoping and praying that he'd change his mind and join her for a consultation with a specialist that had taken her several weeks to arrange. But to her extreme disappointment she'd had to sit through the visit without him. And now tonight, she was bubbling over with hurt because the romantic dinner she'd prepared especially for him, complete with candles, fresh flowers, soft music, and fine china, had gone cold and untouched, the result of him walking casually into the house nearly four hours after she'd told him to come home early because she had a surprise for him.

"I won't continue to be ignored and disrespected," Geneva said, infusing bass into her voice to signal she meant business. "This little game you're playing needs to end right now." She walked over to where Johnny was sitting, leaned over, picked up the remote that was lying beside him, and pressed the power button.

"What the hell?" Johnny said with surprise. "Woman, what's wrong with you?" Although his words were short and abrupt, his voice and tone was calm, and he never took his eyes off the screen. "Turn it back on, Geneva."

"Not until you answer my question."

"You're pushing it."

"And you're full of it!" Geneva spat out angrily, which was counter to her normally laid-back, even-tempered demeanor.

The sharpness in her voice got Johnny's attention, prompting him to finally turn his eyes to hers. "Why're you trippin?"

"You have some nerve asking me that! I can't believe you," Geneva said. She was so upset she was nearly trembling. "I left the salon early, went to the grocery store across town, and bought a ton of food. Then I rushed home and cooked and baked all afternoon, just so I could make your favorite meal. All I asked you to do was come home at a decent hour because I wanted us to enjoy a good meal and a quiet evening together like we used to. But could you do that? *Nooooo!* You drug in here ten minutes ago acting like everything is fine when you know good and doggone well it's not."

Geneva was pissed off and at this point she didn't care if Johnny knew it, and in fact she wanted him to know just how upset she was.

From the first day they'd met, Johnny had called all the shots and had basically set the tone for their relationship, while Geneva had acquiesced at every turn because she wanted to please him and make him happy. But now she regretted ever taking the first step down a path that was destined for bumps and roadblocks. It was times like this when she knew she should've listened to the advice that both her late mother and Donetta had given her when she'd first started dating Johnny six years ago.

"Baby, don't sit around takin' his mess for too long 'cause before you know it, you'll be layin' down under his foot of demands, and you won't be able to get back up," her mother had told her. Donetta's advice had been more blunt and to the point. "You need to teach that Negro a damn lesson and let his ass know that God didn't stop handin' out dicks when He made Johnny's. Let that fool know that if he acts up, you can get another one just like him, and without the attitude."

Johnny leaned further back into the couch as he spoke. "Geneva, I don't know who you think you're talking to, but . . ."

Geneva cut him off midsentence. "I know exactly who I'm talking to . . . a married man who stays out past midnight five days a week. A man who barely speaks to his wife, and when he does decide to say something, it's laced with sarcasm. And last but most certainly not least, I'm talking to a man who is neglecting his marriage and his home."

"I take care of my responsibilities."

"Now I have to ask you who do you think you're talking to?" she said, looking surprised. "You and I both know that what you just said isn't true."

"I pay almost every bill that passes through that door. I make sure you don't want for anything. I get out there and bust my ass, hustling every day to make a comfortable life for you. Do you know how many women would love to trade places with you?"

Geneva narrowed her eyes. "I'm not concerned about what other women want. This is about me and you."

"All I'm saying is, I handle mine."

"Paying bills and paying attention to your wife are two very different things."

"I don't care what you say. I can name ten women right now who'd jump as high as the moon if their man was holding things down financially like I do."

"I can pay my own bills. I lived independently before I married you. I didn't need you financially back then, and the same is true right now. But what I can't and won't do is continue to be neglected and lied to."

Johnny shook his head. "I haven't lied to you."

"You must think I'm a fool. There aren't that many late evening meetings in the world. And who's showing houses at ten, eleven, and twelve o'clock at night anyway?"

Johnny raised his hands in the air. "Here we go with that shit again. Most women would be happy if they had a man who worked his fingers to the bone day and night so he can—"

"Forget about what most women want," Geneva interrupted. "I'm telling you what I need." But Johnny was on a roll and continued talking as though she'd never said a word.

"Provide for her and make sure she never had to struggle. But not Queen Geneva," he said, staring hard at her. "All you're concerned about is what time I come home, who I've been talking with, and how many meetings I've had. This bullshit is getting old."

Geneva ignored his remarks like he'd just done hers. "Tell me where you really were tonight."

Johnny took a long sigh. "I already told you. I was showing a property to a couple who just had a baby and want to upgrade to a bigger house. Late night is the only free time they have in their busy schedule, and being the professional I am, I accommodated them."

"Yeah, right. Who, or shall I say, what else, are you accommodating?"

Johnny smirked. "You're trying to get a rise out of me, but I'm not gonna let you do it. Now turn the TV back on," he said casually.

"Why're you acting like nothing's wrong?"

"Because it's not. Now for the last time, turn the damn TV back on."

Geneva couldn't understand how Johnny could possibly believe his behavior was acceptable, that is, unless he knew it wasn't. Maybe this was his way of turning the tables to make it seem as though he was a hardworking man trying to build his business, and his unreasonable wife couldn't understand or appreciate him. But whatever mind game he was trying to play, Geneva knew she couldn't let up, not this time. And no matter how much Johnny protested, she was going to get answers. She needed them. "I still don't understand why you couldn't call me back," Geneva said. "If you were really showing a property, you could have called me on the way there, or better yet, before you left, so I would know you'd be running late."

Just then Johnny's cell phone rang. He glanced at the screen and answered the call before it could ring again. "What's up, man," he said in his deep baritone.

Geneva watched intently as Johnny held the phone close to his ear. She could see his thumb pressing the volume key on the side of his smartphone, adjusting the sound level to a volume so low that Geneva couldn't hear what was being said on the other end.

"Okay, yeah, I can leave," Johnny said into the phone as he stood and walked over to the hook near the door and removed his keys from it. "I got your back. I'll be there . . ."

Geneva cut him off midsentence. "Who're you talking to and where are you going?"

"Bernard," Johnny whispered, covering the phone with his hand. "He's having some issues with Candace again. He needs somebody to talk to."

"I don't believe you." Quicker than Johnny could blink, Geneva walked up to him and took the phone out of his hand. "Who is this?" she asked in a hostile tone.

"Um, hey, Geneva. It's Bernard. How you doin' this evening?"

Geneva's eyes hit the floor, and she wished she could undo her bold move. "Oh, hi, Bernard. I um, I'm sorry I interrupted your conversation."

Johnny grabbed the phone back out of her hand. "Man, I'm sorry about that. I'm leaving the house now and I'll see you when I get there."

Get where? To his house? To a bar? Geneva wanted to ask where he was going but she was too embarrassed. She felt bad about what she had just done, and she knew that Johnny was furious.

"See, this is what I'm talkin' about," Johnny snarled. "I work hard, I pay the bills, and I take care of my family and friends. I'm a responsible brother tryin' to do the right thing. But all you can do is nag, complain, and accuse me of shit I'm not even doing. Well, you know what, Geneva," he said, letting out a deep, frustrated breath, "since I'm getting accused of all sorts of things, I might as well go out and make good on some of them."

Johnny slipped on his loafers, retrieved his wallet from the counter, and headed toward the door. "Don't wait up." And with that, he was gone.

Geneva walked toward the front window and watched the taillights of Johnny's SUV as he sped down their street. He'd said he was going to meet his friend Bernard, but he didn't say where, or what time he'd be back. "I can't take too much more of this," she said aloud.

Twenty minutes later Geneva slipped under the cool, freshly laundered sheets she'd put on the bed only hours earlier—when she'd been anticipating a tantalizing romp after a romantic meal with her husband. But instead she was lying on her Egyptian cotton sheets all alone, and it was becoming a regular occurrence. As Geneva stared up at the ceiling, her mind replayed the interaction she'd had with Johnny. Even though she'd heard Bernard's voice on the phone, she wasn't convinced that the call was on the up-and-up. She didn't want to admit it, and she'd been fighting the reality for a few months, but now she had to face what she feared. Her husband was involved with another woman.

Tears streamed from Geneva's eyes. She felt alone and unwanted, and she knew this couldn't continue. Her marriage was on the brink of dissolving right before her eyes, and as she cried until her lids felt tired, she knew that their argument tonight was just the tip of the iceberg to come.

Chapter 2

JOHNNY

Johnny Mayfield was highly impressed with himself. He knew that not only was he charismatic, handsome, and a smooth talker who could think quickly on his feet, he was, without a doubt, smarter, more resourceful, and more creative than most men could dream of being. Johnny didn't consider it braggadocio to believe such things because he knew it took the brains of Einstein, the strength of Hercules, and the trickery of Houdini to consistently fool a woman, day after day, and that's exactly what he'd been doing throughout his five-year marriage, and in particular, the last five months. He'd been deceiving his wife, Geneva, by carrying on the most illicit affair he'd ever been involved in.

But after tonight's showdown with his wife, Johnny knew that his carefree days of coming and going as he pleased would soon be coming to an end. Geneva was fed up with his late nights away from home, as well as the emotional distance he'd put between them, and she'd told him so. She'd even snatched his phone out of his hand to find out who he'd been talking to. Johnny knew that was uncharacteristic of his wife, and that meant she was at the end of her rope.

As Johnny cruised down the highway he hit redial on his phone. "Hey man. I just left the house about five minutes ago. Where you at?"

"Home," Bernard said into the phone. "And that's exactly where your ass should be."

Johnny laughed. "I'm a grown-ass man and I can go wherever I like."

"You playin' a dangerous game, and you need to pull back before it's too late."

Johnny shook his head. He could picture all six-foot, two-inch, two hundred forty pounds of pure muscle that Bernard carried, reclined in his comfortable leather chair, downstairs in his man cave, talking shit. If Johnny were a betting man he'd say that Bernard was probably sipping on lemonade instead of a real drink—brown liquor—thanks to his pushy girlfriend, Candace.

Johnny still didn't understand what in the hell Bernard saw in Candace Taylor. Bernard was a handsome man whose rugged good looks rivaled those of the actor Idris Elba. But Candace, on the other hand, looked as plain as any woman walking down the street. She was so ordinary looking that even after he'd met her, it had taken Johnny several times to remember who she was. But for reasons that still baffled Johnny, Bernard couldn't get enough of Candace, and he acted like she was the only woman who'd ever donned a bra. That's how caught up he was.

Bernard Seymore was Johnny's best friend. They'd grown up on the same street in Southeast Amber, played on the same Pop Warner football team, gone to the same high school, and had been the best man at each other's weddings. The two men were like brothers. But lately, Johnny's extracurricular activities were starting to drive a wedge between them.

"Listen," Johnny said. "I'm handling my business. I'm cool."

"I hope you're not on your way to do what I think you're about to do."

Johnny chuckled low and deep as he drove at breakneck speed. He was on his way to see Vivana Owens—his mistress, or as Bernard called her, trouble with a capital T.

Johnny had been seeing Vivana for five months, and so far they

had been five of the most thrilling, exhilarating, freaky, and adventur-
ous months he'd had the pleasure of experiencing in a very long time.
He grinned as he thought about the mind-blowing sex he was going
to have with the seductive woman whom he couldn't seem to get
enough of. The more he was with Vivana, the more enthralled he became. Her passion was hotter than the late August heat outside. "Man,
it ain't nothin' but a thing," Johnny said slowly to Bernard as he steered
his white Navigator around a sharp curve. "Don't worry. I know what
I'm doing."

"You sure?"

"I can't believe you just had the nerve to ask me that. Of course
I'm sure."

"I don't know," Bernard said. "When your woman jumps on your
phone, you can't be sure of anything."

"I ain't sweatin' that."

"You're standing—on one leg, I might add—on some very dangerous and shaky ground. Shit's gettin' real, fast, and in a hurry. Cut
this off while you're still ahead, and while you still can."

Johnny smirked. *Bernard must be smelling those flowers Candace is
shoving up his ass,* he thought. "I know you're not going soft on me?"

Bernard sighed. "Listening to you, no one would ever think
you're a grown-ass man because you say some simple, elementary
school shit."

"This is real talk. You goin' soft, man."

"This has nothing to do with goin' soft. I'm trying to help you,
brother. When you know better, you do better. What you're doin'
ain't right, and it's not gonna end well."

Johnny breathed in deep. "We ain't Oprah and Gayle, man," he
said with a loud laugh.

"You think this shit's funny? You think it's a game?"

"Damn. Calm the hell down," Johnny said. "You're my boy. I
know what you're trying to do, but I got this."

Bernard sighed on the other end. "When Geneva came on the
line I didn't know what she was gonna ask me."

"Hell, neither did I. She surprised me with that one."

"Keep on, and you're gonna get a lot more surprises."

"Thanks for the encouragement."

"Hey, like you said, it's real talk."

"Yeah, yeah, yeah. For what it's worth, thanks for what you did tonight. Geneva had me jammed up until you called. You called right in the nick of time."

"Save the thanks. If I'd known you wanted me to call so you could get out the house . . ."

"Man, you trippin'."

Bernard huffed loudly, clearly agitated. "I asked you a few weeks ago to stop involving me in what you're doing. I was caught off-guard tonight and pulled into some bullshit that you created. Johnny, I don't appreciate that shit, man. If you want to jump down the rabbit hole, be my guest. But don't drag my ass down there with you 'cause I'm not tryin' to mess up what I got."

Johnny laughed. "Hold up. Now I see what's goin' on . . . you're scared you're gonna get put on lockdown by the warden." He could only shake his head when he thought about the weak excuse for a player that his best friend had become since he'd started dating Candace six months ago.

Bernard had always been a hard-core ladies' man, even when he'd been married. He was the only man Johnny knew, besides himself, who could say he'd bedded more women than he'd actually known, and that was because in many cases he didn't know the women at all. They'd simply been one-night stands. But Bernard had gotten sloppy at the height of an intense affair with a woman who Johnny had never thought was quite worth the risk. Bernard's wife, Suzanne, had caught him cheating, which had happened repeatedly throughout their eleven-year marriage. But this time Suzanne had reached her limit with his constant lies, manipulation, and philandering. Bernard had given her an STD that left her infertile. She filed for divorce, took half of everything he had, and never looked back. That was five years ago.

Bernard had been going through life just fine until Candace came along. Now, in Johnny's mind, it seemed as though his friend constantly caved to Candace's demands.

"Say what you want, but Candace is the best thing that could've happened to me. I don't fear her, I respect her."

"Uh-huh . . . where is she right now?"

"At the hospital; she's pulling a double shift. Why?"

"Just checking." Johnny chuckled. "I'd hate to get you in trouble for talking on the phone past your bedtime."

"Man, fuck you."

"You know I have to mess with you for acting all scared."

"I'm not scared for me. I'm scared for you, fool," Bernard told him.

"You're talking to the man with the plan. It's all good."

"Your plan must not be that good because you're dragging me into it. And for the one hundredth time, I have no interest in being part of what you're doing. Geneva is a good woman."

Johnny reached under his seat for the box of condoms he'd placed there yesterday. He sat them on the passenger seat as he turned onto the exit ramp that would lead him to his rendezvous with Vivana. "I thought you were my boy. You're supposed to have my back, B."

"You say some childish shit. I wouldn't be talking to you like I'm doing if I didn't have your back."

"You the one acting like a little girl."

"Listen, don't question my manhood or my friendship. Just because I don't want to see you mess up like I did, or be a part of it, that doesn't mean I'm goin' soft, or that I'm not your boy. You know I'm the realest cat you got in your corner. So don't come at me with some bullshit just so you can justify your own shit."

Johnny could tell by the tone in Bernard's voice that he was starting to get upset. Johnny had already gotten his friend caught up in a lie that Bernard had to tell Candace last month when Johnny had used him as an alibi for one of his late-night romps with Vivana. Bernard had been livid. "I hear you, partner," Johnny said.

"Good."

"I'm almost there now. I'll be careful."

"Man, you're playing with danger. Vivana is nothing but trouble. If you know what's good for you, you'll leave that alone. But if not, just leave me out of it."

Johnny didn't want to get into it again with Bernard, and he didn't want to ruin what was going to be a great evening ahead by talking to a man who had clearly lost his edge. He knew that just because his friend had messed up it didn't mean he would, too. "Man, I'm about to bounce, but I hear you. We're solid."

"That's all I'm sayin'."

Johnny nodded on his end of the phone. "All right, playa. I'll hit you later."

"Be careful, man."

"No doubt."

"Later."

Johnny steered his truck around to the back of the Marriott Court-yard Hotel. The parking lot was crowded, but he managed to find a spot, which was, unfortunately, right under a bright light. Anonymity was key, so he definitely didn't like the position he was in. "Damn . . . oh well," Johnny said.

Normally, he was a man who loved being the center of attention, but only in certain situations, because despite his seemingly brazen behavior with Vivana, Johnny prided himself on discretion. That was the reason he'd never been caught cheating since he'd been married. He couldn't count the number of women he'd hooked up with, and had secretly photographed and in some cases videoed their sexual exploits for his own private pleasure, all without his conquests knowing. That's just how slick he was. Vivana wasn't his first affair, and she certainly wasn't going to be his last, but she was definitely the most exciting.

Johnny reached for the box of condoms he'd placed on the seat, took out two, and put them in his pocket. He'd always had free reign over his truck and what he put in it because Geneva never set her foot in his vehicle. But after her tirade tonight, and the tone she'd used with him, he knew things were about to change. Geneva was becoming bolder by the day, and the excuses, lies, and deceptive tactics that used to work for him in the past were starting to wear thin on her.

Johnny breathed in deeply and placed the box of Trojans in his glove compartment. *I'm gonna have to find a new hiding place for these,* he thought. He didn't know what had gotten into Geneva tonight. Sure, he'd been out late, and yes, he knew his behavior over the last several months had been suspicious, but she'd always dealt with it, just as he felt any good wife should. Geneva was easygoing and calm about things, which was one of the qualities he genuinely loved about her. She was an old-fashioned, good woman who took pride in herself, valuing her commitment to him. There was a time she'd never have talked to him the way she had tonight, and he didn't like it.

"I guess my excuse for a father was right about one thing," Johnny said aloud. "Shit changes."

He knew he needed to have a talk with Geneva first thing in the morning before her attitude got too far out of hand for him to control. But for now, Johnny didn't want the weight of his best friend's cautions, or his wife's nagging, to sink the cloud he was floating on. He opened his driver's door and began to walk toward the hotel's back entrance, where Vivana stood waiting for him, like clockwork. He pushed his troubles to the side because he knew the next three hours were going to feel like Nirvana.

Chapter 3

VIVANA

Vivana smiled as she watched Johnny step out of his truck and walk toward her. The very sight of him made her panties wet, and she could barely contain herself. With each stride his long legs took to reach her, she lusted with bated anticipation, excited about their night ahead, and if she was lucky, and her plan worked, their good time would spill over into the early hours of the morning.

"Hey, baby," she said with a sexy smile as she opened the heavy glass door and greeted him. "I'm so glad you're here."

"Hey," Johnny said with a hurried smile. He rushed past her like a strong wind, barely looking at her as he entered the building. "Let's head upstairs."

Vivana wanted him to embrace her, hold her close, and kiss her passionately. But instead he'd acted as though she was a casual acquaintance. She'd received a better welcome from the greeter at Walmart this afternoon than from the man whom she wanted more than she cared to admit. But she knew she couldn't allow herself to become upset because of the reality of their situation.

As she walked behind Johnny, looking at his tight behind, the sexy swagger of his walk, and his big, broad shoulders, she reminded herself that she had to be patient. She knew he acted this way for a reason. He was married and so was she, and neither of them could afford the risk of getting caught engaging in romantic behavior in the hallway of a hotel late at night.

Once they walked onto the elevator and the doors closed, Vivana wrapped her arms around Johnny. "I couldn't wait for you to get here, baby. I missed you."

"Whoa, whoa. Slow down. Chill." Johnny quickly unhooked her arms and moved a small distance away from her.

"What the hell?"

"Vivana, they have security cameras set up in these things."

Vivana rolled her eyes. "Cameras on elevators are reserved for top-tier hotels, not the Marriott Courtyard."

"You can never be too careful. That's how people get caught. They slip and mess up."

"Whatever, Johnny. You're acting like you don't want to be with me tonight."

Johnny sighed and shook his head as they stepped out of the elevator. "If that was true, I wouldn't be here right now. It's ten o'clock on a weeknight, and I'm on the outskirts of town with you instead of lying in my bed at home. That should tell you all you need to know."

Vivana wanted to smile at his words, but she kept her hard edge. She liked the fact that she had the power to seduce Johnny away from his wife and probably a home-cooked meal that she'd prepared for him. The very thought gave her a rush. She loved the control she wielded over men.

Slowly, she slipped her card key into the door and then let Johnny turn the handle before pushing it open. After practically ignoring her just moments ago, she knew he was watching her now that they were entering the privacy of their room. *I'll show him,* Vivana thought. She slowly sauntered by him, swaying her wide, curvaceous hips from side to side as she made her way to the chair on the other side of the bed. She purposely chose to sit there. *Sometimes you've got to teach a man a lesson.* If Johnny wanted her tonight, he was going to have to work for it.

"Why're you sitting way over there?" Johnny asked, a slight pout beginning to form at his lips.

"It's a comfortable chair, and right now I feel like sitting up instead of lying down." She reached for the television remote control on the nightstand beside the bed, and pressed the power button. She wanted to laugh when she turned up the volume and saw Johnny's eyes grow wide and then narrow with disappointment. She seductively crossed her thick thighs, giving him a good view of the caramel-colored skin that peeked from beneath the hem of her cheetah-print skirt. She watched out of the corner of her right eye as Johnny removed his tailored shirt and pants.

He's sexy as hell, Vivana thought as she did a quick once-over of her lover. But she refused to let him know that she wanted him, and that he looked more delicious than the raspberry cheesecake she'd had for dessert after polishing off a hearty lunch. From the moment she'd laid eyes on Johnny Mayfield, she knew she had to have him. He'd mesmerized her from their first hello, and she'd been hooked ever since.

She still remembered the chilly, rainy day five months ago when she walked across the lobby of Fortune United Bank, and saw a man who she thought looked like a tall, mocha latte–colored dream. She'd felt an instant attraction to the handsome stranger and knew it had to be fate that brought her to the bank that day. She was a contract employee in the company's IT department. She worked from home and only visited the branch offices on rare occasions. On that particular day the bank's new computer system had gone haywire, requiring her physical presence to help the managers navigate the intranet from their desktop PCs.

Vivana had spotted Johnny and scoped him from head to toe as he stood in line waiting to approach a teller. She could see that he was well groomed, stylishly dressed, and had a physique that could only be accomplished by regular workouts at the gym. She felt a rush of hot excitement as she watched and listened to him talk with the teller. His voice was deep, but gentle. Commanding, yet easy. And it was definitely full of sensual charisma that even made the teller blush. In the time it took him to complete his transaction and turn to walk away, Vivana had already developed a plan to get him.

She was a woman skilled in the complicated art of seduction. All her life she'd been able to draw men to her like bees to honey. Her pretty face and inviting smile made them notice her, and her curvy, plus-size body made them want her. From her melon size breasts, to her round behind, to her wide hips and thick thighs, she knew how to work her assets in a way that made men swoon. But her most alluring feature of all was her walk. She didn't simply put one foot in front of the other, she strutted with a sway that dripped with sexy innuendo. "I like to see you come, but I damn sure love to see you leave," men always told her, referring to the fact that they loved to watch her sashay from side to side when she turned to walk away.

Vivana had used all her crafty know-how to suck Johnny into her web. She'd sauntered by him as he walked back across the lobby, and then boldly smiled, looking directly into his eyes. She held his stare just long enough to let him know what she wanted without speaking a word. She'd even been bold enough to give him her signature good woman/bad girl smile that she knew drove men wild. And not to her surprise, it got Johnny's attention. He stopped her in the middle of the bank and struck up a conversation. The fact that he'd been wearing a platinum wedding band didn't mean much to her because she'd been wearing one, too.

"You look so familiar," Johnny had said. "Have I seen you before?"

Vivana dropped her smile and shook her head. "I know you can do better than that."

"I beg your pardon?"

"A brother as smooth and as fine as you should be ashamed to use that weak line. Retire it, or save it for someone who doesn't know their head from their ass," Vivana said with a serious stare. She leaned on one leg, shifting the bulk of her weight to her red high heels. "I don't look familiar because there's not a woman out here who comes close to all this," she said as she turned her body slightly to give him a good view of her profile. "And you haven't seen me before because if you had, we'd be having lunch right now instead of standing in the middle of this lobby making small talk." She said all that in one seamless breath and then turned on her pointed-toe heels before slowly sauntering away, using the same sexy strut she'd seduced him with on her initial approach.

From that moment forward, Vivana had wrapped Johnny in her web. He wasn't the first man that she'd had an affair with during her one-and-a-half-year marriage to her husband, Samuel, but he was the only one who'd made her want to leave the dull existence she'd been living.

Initially, Vivana had married Samuel Owens for what could be considered the wrong reasons for most women, but had been the perfect cocktail for her. Most women wanted love, first and foremost, as the basis of their marriage. But not Vivana. She knew that fallacy was for weaklings with no ambition. Vivana's objective for marriage was concrete and clear. She was tired of being used and played by men who couldn't afford to take her to a hamburger joint, let alone a nice restaurant. Samuel was refined and educated. He came from money and he'd made a lot of it on his own from an educational software model he'd developed and sold right out of college. The financial freedom he'd achieved from that deal had allowed him to pursue his passion, which was shepherding the education of children. He volunteered in his community and donated money to local charities. In Vivana's estimation, he was a sucker ripe for the picking.

Vivana saw in Samuel a man who was stable and financially solvent, and she used every trick in her arsenal to get him to trust her as she lured him in for the kill. When she'd met Samuel, he'd just completed his doctorate in higher education administration, and had been appointed as the new principal at Sandhill Elementary School. He was easygoing, engaging, responsible, and gentlemanly—all qualities Vivana had never experienced in a man.

She knew she was different from any woman he'd ever dated: daring, vivacious, bold, sexy, and wild. She'd completely enthralled him after just one date. Within a few months he'd proposed to her and she'd readily accepted. Vivana didn't mind that he'd asked her to sign a pre-nup, which basically protected all assets he'd acquired prior to the marriage. She was fine with it because she knew Samuel was the type of man who'd strive to continue to build upon his wealth portfolio, which would net her a substantial pay-off in the likelihood that they didn't work out. They were married within six months of the day they'd met, and over the next year, Vivana had become bored out of her mind.

She'd initially found Samuel's conservative manner, calm demeanor, and homebody ways a refreshing change from the hustlers, pretty boys, and players she'd dated in the past. He was intelligent, practical, thoughtful, and kind. Being an elementary school principal, Samuel had a natural love for children and learning, and an affinity for structure and organization, which Vivana didn't have a clue about.

They were opposites, and the differences that she'd initially found interesting quickly became irritating. She liked to watch TV, he liked to read. She listened to current hip-hop and rap, while he enjoyed classical music and jazz. He was passionate about politics and community activism, but she saw it as a hassle, and she didn't want to be bothered with other people's problems. He was practical with his money, never making purchases he didn't need. She loved spending, shopping, and more shopping. But the number one issue that had become a battle between them, and had surfaced a month into their marriage, was his desire to have children, and her secret wish to have her tubes tied.

They had never fully discussed having children during their whirlwind romance. Vivana had known that Samuel thought she wanted to start a family because he'd brought up the subject a few times, voicing that he wanted at least two kids, preferably a boy and a girl. But she purposely kept her lack of desire for motherhood to herself, for fear that Samuel might have second thoughts about marrying her if he knew the truth—that she saw children as a major annoyance.

Six months ago, after yet another explosive argument with Samuel over having a child, Vivana made steps to take matters into her own hands. She'd met with her doctor and had secretly scheduled an appointment to have her tubes tied, which would put an end to her childbearing years, along with Samuel's nagging about the subject. But a few days prior to the procedure she came down with a bad case of the flu. A month later she'd met Johnny, and had been consumed by him ever since, tossing all else to the side, including her husband. All she wanted these days was to be with Johnny, and become the love of his life that he couldn't do without.

Now as Vivana continued to ignore Johnny, she felt empowered knowing how much he wanted her, too.

"Vivana, come on now," Johnny said in a deep, sexy voice as he walked over to the chair where she was sitting. "Why're you acting like that? You know the deal when it comes to how we have to act in public."

Vivana could see that he was trying to ease back into her good graces, but she wanted him to do a little squirming before she granted him access. She looked at him with a casual glance and nodded. "Yes, I know the deal all too well."

"Your tone ain't right."

"Neither are your actions, so that makes two of us who need attitude adjustments."

"I'm sorry, okay. I just . . . we have to be careful. You know?"

Vivana ignored him again and changed the channel on the TV, pretending to pay more attention to the small screen than to Johnny. He was getting more and more frustrated by the moment, and it made her want to dance with satisfaction.

But he did something next that she hadn't expected. He walked back to the side of the bed where he'd removed his shirt and pants, and began to put them back on.

"I don't need this bullshit tonight," Johnny said, frustration peppering his voice. "I worked hard all day, then came home to listen to my wife's nagging mouth, all because I've been trying to find ways to spend time with you. I even asked Bernard to call me tonight so I could get out the house to meet up with you. But do you appreciate it? No! You run off at the mouth, giving me attitude that I don't need."

Vivana was alarmed when he slipped on his shoes and made his way toward the door, but she didn't move a muscle or act as though she was the least bit affected one way or the other.

Johnny shrugged his broad shoulders. "If I'd known you were gonna act like this, I would've kept my ass home. But guess what, I'm headed back there right now."

Vivana sat up straight in the chair when the heavy door slammed behind Johnny. She wanted to run after him and apologize. She wanted him to know that she'd been looking forward to seeing him all day. She wanted to tell him that she, too, had made sacrifices to see him. Samuel thought she was out of town at a training workshop. She wanted Johnny more than he knew. She wanted to laugh with him, talk with him, and find out how his day had been. And more than anything, she wanted to feel his strong arms wrapped around her voluptuous body while he kissed her passionately, like a man in love.

But she refused to cave. She knew that men respected power, and if she showed the least bit of weakness, especially with an ego-driven man like Johnny, she would lose her edge. She wasn't about to let that happen. But at the same time she wanted him so badly that her desire for him was starting to feel like an obsession. "Calm down," she talked to herself aloud. "Just play it cool. He'll come back. Just watch, he'll be knocking on that door in a few minutes."

Sure enough, ten minutes later there was a knock on the door. She looked out the peephole and there was Johnny, standing on the other side looking deflated. She wanted to jump up and down with excitement, but instead she took a deep breath, adjusted her pencil skirt around her hips, and opened the door.

"Vivana, I'm sorry," Johnny said. He was holding a bottle of wine. "I got this at the store across the street. It's a peace offering. Do you forgive me?"

Vivana stepped to the side. "Come on in."

Within a matter of minutes they were under the sheets, sipping wine from the bottle, about to make love. Vivana was glad she had not given in, and that Johnny had been the first one to concede. She knew that small things, like the disagreement they'd just had, added up in big ways. This was yet another confirmation to her that she had a strong hold on him, and she had absolutely no intention of giving it up.

Vivana set the bottle on the nightstand. "It's time to make up properly," she purred.

Johnny smiled. "I'm all for that, baby."

Slowly, Vivana eased the sheet back with one hand as she stroked Johnny's growing hardness with the other. She slid down until she reached his midsection, kissing his stomach, circling her tongue around the inside of his navel, all while massaging his rock-hard erection. When she opened her mouth and engulfed him, she closed her eyes and enjoyed the sound of his lustful moans. She devoured his thick shaft, taking him further into her mouth until she felt him at the very back of her throat.

Vivana sucked and licked, and teased Johnny as he held her head in place and enjoyed the expert, porn-movie style blow job she was giving him. "Damn, that feels good," Johnny moaned.

When she finally came up for air, Vivana was so turned on that wetness dripped down her thighs. She placed her hand between her legs, swirled her finger inside her creamy middle, and then brought it to Johnny's lips for a mouthwatering taste.

"Delicious," Johnny said with a seductive smile.

"I can't just take your word for it, let me see for myself." Vivana stroked her clit with her index finger before bringing it to her lips.

"You're right," she moaned, and then smiled as she watched Johnny's eyes dance with lust.

"You're so fucking hot," he said.

Vivana sank her finger between her legs again, and then placed it at Johnny's lips as he hungrily sucked it dry. By now he was so hard that she knew he couldn't wait any longer. He reached for the condom he'd placed on the nightstand, quickly put it on, and plunged inside her as he lifted his head and latched on to her right nipple. The forceful yet sensuous rhythm of his mouth combined with the sweet thickness of his manhood made Vivana scream out as he thrusted in and out of her until she orgasmed so hard she trembled. It only took a few more minutes before Johnny joined her.

An hour later as she lay in bed listening to Johnny snore, Vivana thought about her future, and in particular, her future with him. She knew they made a great couple and that they could make each other happy. The only thing she needed to do now was find a way for them to be together without having to sneak around under the cover of night. She was ready to leave Samuel, and from what she could see, Johnny was ready to leave his wife.

Patience wins the race every time, Vivana thought to herself as she watched Johnny sleep soundly beside her. If there was one thing she'd learned in her thirty-five years on earth, it was that people always wanted what they couldn't have. Johnny couldn't have her completely, and that was one of the reasons he was so hell-bent on being with her. She also knew that once a person got what they wanted, they could lose sight of what got them the prize in the first place. But when it came to him, she wasn't about to let that happen.

Vivana smiled as she softly stroked Johnny's shoulder while he slept. She didn't like the fact that before he'd drifted off, he'd asked her to wake him up in thirty minutes so he could get back home. She wanted him to herself and she was tired of sharing him with another woman.

She decided that she needed to follow through with the scheme she'd cooked up earlier that evening, before he'd arrived at the hotel. She smiled to herself, knowing that while what she was about to do was wrong, it would be right in the long run. And that's what was on her mind, the long run, and she once again thought about their future and how bright it was going to be. Now, all she had to do was come up with a foolproof plan to make him leave his wife.

Chapter 4

SAMUEL

Samuel Owens stood in the middle of his spacious chef-style kitchen staring at the refrigerator. It was ten o'clock at night, and he was tired and hungry. He didn't want to eat this late because he knew what kind of damage it could do to his waistline. But long meetings and a demanding schedule had caused him to skip lunch and dinner, and now his body was letting him know that it needed to be fueled. His stomach growled as he looked down at his pudgy midsection that had once been svelte. He shook his head and sighed. "I really need to do better."

A few minutes later Samuel found himself sitting at the solid mahogany table in his breakfast nook. His mouth went dry at the sight of his unappetizing plate of carrots and celery, accompanied by a tall glass of water to wash it down. "I'll be hungry as soon as I finish this rabbit food," he said with a frown.

He rose from the table and went back to the refrigerator, scouring the shelves and even the bottom drawer freezer, in search of something a bit tastier and more filling. But there wasn't a single thing that looked remotely appealing to his eyes or stomach. It was times like this that he longed for his mother's home-cooked food. His wife, Vivana, detested cooking; she didn't even like putting frozen dinners in the microwave. Even though he loved to dabble in the kitchen, his hectic workdays left little time for culinary pursuits. He sighed again, then picked up the phone and dialed Valentino's Pizza. "The usual," he said to the person taking his order.

Samuel knew it was a shame that nearly every restaurant within a ten-mile radius of his home was on speed dial, programmed alphabetically into his phone. "Take-out is better than nothing," he mouthed as he thought about how much he was going to enjoy the buffalo wings and supreme pizza he'd ordered. He walked over to the family room, pulled out a tray table, and sat it beside the couch where he planned to dine tonight.

Samuel hated eating alone. When he and Vivana were dating, they ate together, whether at a restaurant or at his luxury condo downtown, nearly every night. But once they got married, as with many other things, that all changed. These days Vivana seemed to always be gone. Her late-night meetings and out-of-town travel had increased over the last few months. Samuel was happy that his wife had gained newfound passion for her career, but he didn't like that it was coming at a cost to their relationship, putting more strain on their already shaky marriage.

The large rift that had widened between him and Vivana weighed heavily on his mind, and he knew it was something that needed to be addressed and corrected if their one-and-a-half-year marriage was to make it to two. After he placed his delivery order, he put the remainder of his uneaten carrots and celery in a plastic container and set them back in the refrigerator. "This'll be my mid-morning snack tomorrow." He loosened his tie and his belt, taking a long, deep breath as he thought about his long day.

Samuel looked at the clock, noting he had another twenty-five minutes before the delivery guy would be ringing the doorbell with his food. He climbed the large staircase leading up to the second floor, and walked toward his bedroom at the end of the hall. He stood under the crystal-beaded ceiling fan, enjoying the cool breeze it provided. He took another deep breath, closed his eyes, and then opened them as he looked around the luxurious master suite. The rich earth-tone jacquard comforter was the only thing about the entire room that reflected his taste. Everything else was his wife's choice of décor, which dominated not only their bedroom but the entire house.

He'd never felt comfortable or relaxed in his own home, and that was ironic considering the fact that he was a homebody, and spent more time there than Vivana, and that he'd actually been the one who'd picked out their house and put a contract on it the month before they'd gotten married. But even that choice hadn't truly been his.

The only reason Samuel had purchased the large, custom-built brick home in the neighborhood where they lived was because he knew it was what Vivana had wanted.

"You're giving that woman too much control," his brother, Joe, had told him when he'd visited right before the wedding and got a tour of the new house Samuel had just purchased.

"It's what she wants," Samuel countered. "Dad always says if your wife is happy, you'll be happy."

Joe hunched his shoulders and shook his head. "See, that's the problem, li'l bro. I think it's going to take a lot to make her happy. I know you love her, and I don't want to overstep my bounds, but I've got to call it like I see it. I think you're moving too soon. Give this relationship a little more time before you jump straight into marriage."

Samuel raised his brow. "Sounds like you're telling me to call it off."

"I am."

"But the wedding is in a few days."

"I don't care if it's in a few minutes. It's never too late to change your mind. But once you say 'I do,' it's hard as hell to get out of it. Especially if you're the one with all the assets. The more you have, the more you can lose."

Samuel knew that his brother didn't care for Vivana, and that his dislike for her clouded his words. Vivana had been living in a cramped apartment when Samuel met her. And while she wore designer clothes and drove a late-model Lexus, she could barely afford her rent and other monthly bills. She had no appreciable assets, and credit card companies constantly rang her phone demanding payment. Living this way wasn't new for Vivana because it was how she'd been raised by her grandmother, who'd robbed Peter to pay Paul each month a bill was due.

Conversely, Samuel hailed from a privileged background. His parents, Herbert and Sarah Owens, worked hard to give their two children a life they'd never had. His father owned three car dealerships and his mother was his right hand, helping him run the auto empire they'd built. The house where they'd raised Samuel and Joe—located in Prince George's County, Maryland, one of the wealthiest counties of African Americans per capita—was grand by any measure. Samuel was the benefactor of a stellar education by way of Sidwell Friends, one of Washington, DC's most elite private schools. He'd wanted for nothing and lived in the comfort his parents provided.

Prestige, wealth, and material trappings weren't new for him, but they were an unknown world for Vivana, whose rough, hardscrabble neighborhood in Mobile, had shaped her into the gutsy, often brash woman she was today. Samuel knew this, and that was part of the reason he tried so hard to give Vivana everything she wanted and needed.

"Just be careful," Joe had cautioned. "Keep your eyes open and watch her because I have a feeling she's going to put you through some serious changes."

Samuel knew his brother loved him and that he wanted the best for him, but a part of him also felt that Joe was jaded. His brother had suffered two failed marriages and, as it stood, was in a dating slump. "Can't you just be happy for me?" Samuel said. "I love Vivana."

"Why?" Joe asked.

Samuel had to think for a moment before he finally answered. "Because she's fun, and exciting, and she balances me out. She's good for me."

"Do you think she loves you?"

"She wouldn't be marrying me if she didn't."

Joe gave him the side-eye. "People marry for all sorts of reasons. Just like you're doing."

Samuel wrinkled his forehead in confusion. "What are you talk-ing about?"

"You didn't mention love as a reason for marrying her."

"Because that's a given." Samuel could see that he wasn't going to make any headway with his brother so he ended the conversation and the house tour. Now, as he thought back on that brotherly exchange and many others they'd had in recent months, he had to admit that Joe had been right.

"I should've listened to my brother," Samuel mumbled to himself.

Samuel looked at the digital alarm clock on Vivana's nightstand, noting he had only ten minutes before his food would arrive. He quickly undressed and showered, glad to wash away his worries. He emerged smelling good from the expensive bath products he'd used, feeling more relaxed. He walked back downstairs to the spacious fam-ily room wearing baggy gym shorts and a Sandhill t-shirt. A stack of documents lay beside him in a neat pile on the couch. Normally, he didn't mind the extra work his job required, but tonight was different. And just as he didn't want to eat late, he didn't want to work late, ei-ther. But since he was all alone, with no one to share his evening, the tedious paperwork suddenly turned into a welcome distraction until his food arrived.

Samuel's career was one of the bright spots in his life, and he felt blessed to be able to do what he loved. This month made seven years that he'd been the principal at Sandhill Elementary School. When he'd first started, the morale of the teachers, students, and staff had been low, the result of years of sub-par test scores, underperforming students, and a mismanaged administration.

A county investigation revealed corruption in the front office. The principal was fired, amidst scandalous charges of sexual misconduct, bribes, and kickbacks. Samuel happened to be in the right place, at the right time, with the right credentials and the right connections. He was the assistant principal at a large public school in Upper Marlboro, Maryland, and was looking for a change from the grind of city living to a slower pace of life. His fraternity brother, who happened to be a member of the Amber school board, phoned Samuel one night and told him to apply for the position. The rest was history.

It only took Samuel three years to turn Sandhill around from the lowest performing elementary school in the county, to the second highest. Thanks to his steady leadership, the school that had once been marred in scandal now boasted a full enrollment with a waiting list of children whose parents were willing to pay money to get them in.

As Samuel thought about his accomplishments at Sandhill and the new projects he had planned for the upcoming academic year, he felt disappointed and frustrated that Vivana wasn't going to be with him tomorrow night for the staff and volunteer open-house meeting. If it hadn't been for his wedding band, he knew that most people wouldn't even know he was married. And because he'd stopped wearing it several months ago, due to the strain of his and Vivana's lackluster relationship, he knew people would be even more in doubt about his marital status.

Once they said, "I do," things between them had changed. Vivana stopped going out with him. They argued over simple things they used to do, like going out to eat, watching a movie, going to concerts, and any other type of leisure activity he wanted to do. She didn't have many friends and she'd never bothered to introduce him to the few she had. And what made things even more strained was that she didn't involve herself in anything related to his career. She had long stopped attending events at Sandhill and she never showed her face at any of the community meetings or festivals that the school routinely hosted. It was a stark contrast to the kind of relationship he'd watched his parents build since he was a child.

If ever there was a blueprint to follow as an example of true teamwork, Samuel knew that his parents were it. They'd been each other's study partner in college, and after graduating in the top ten percent of their class, they'd both worked long hours, side by side, in training programs to gain business and leadership experience. They scored their biggest accomplishment when they walked down the aisle and became husband and wife. And while their marriage was more a partnership than a love connection, Herbert and Sarah's union was still going strong after forty years, and they remained each other's biggest supporter. Samuel smiled at the thought of his parents and wished he had the same kind of support in his relationship that they had in theirs.

He put his papers to the side when the doorbell rang. The delivery guy, who appeared to be in his mid-fifties, greeted Samuel with a smile and sweat dripping down his round face. "Good to see you, Dr. Owens," the man said.

Samuel smiled back. "Likewise, Paul. How's it going?"

"Can't complain. Just hot as hell out here tonight, especially without the AC working in my car. But fall is around the corner and I'm looking forward to the cooler weather because I don't do well with this kind of heat."

"I know what you mean, man." Samuel was getting damp just standing in the doorway. A few minutes later he returned to the couch, hunched his body over the tray table, and began devouring the wings and pizza as if it were lobster and steak.

As Samuel finished his third slice of pizza, he again thought about his marriage, and how he was growing tired of it all. He was fed up with trying to please someone who acted as though they couldn't care less about him. "Why am I living a loveless existence?" he asked himself out loud.

He'd suggested many times that they seek marriage counseling to improve their relationship. But each time he brought up the subject, Vivana looked at him as if he'd lost his mind before telling him no. Then another argument would ensue before she stomped downstairs where she would sleep for the night.

Samuel was a man of logic and reason, and he knew he had to take the same advice he gave to his teachers and their students: if he wanted different results he was going to have to start changing things up. He'd been passive for far too long, which was contradictory to the bold entrepreneur he'd once been. His logical mind, along with his common sense, gave him the answer about what he needed to do.

"I deserve more. I deserve better," he said, "and if Vivana can't give me what I need, I'm prepared to call it quits."

Chapter 5

GENEVA

"I think he's cheating on me," Geneva said to Donetta as she stood in front of the oval mirror, styling her pixie-cut hair with a generous amount of mousse.

"Of course he is," Donetta said, not holding back. "He's a damn dog who's sneaky as a fuckin' snake."

"I didn't want to believe it, but now I have no other choice."

It was seven thirty in the morning, and Geneva and Donetta were the only two stylists in Hair Heaven, the chic salon where they worked. Rachel Miller, the owner and manager who was a retired stylist in her late sixties, only came by the salon once every other week, which gave the stylists free rein that most salon employees didn't experience. The shop didn't open until eight, which gave the two friends a half hour to talk before the listening ears and gossiping tongues of coworkers and clients interrupted them.

Donetta sighed. "Honey, I'm just glad you've finally come to your senses about that triflin', no-good excuse for a man that you call your husband."

"Me too."

"I hate to say I told you so, but . . ."

"You're going to do it anyway."

Donetta nodded, fingering her long, razor-cut brown hair as she spoke. "Yes I am, 'cause the man's a pussy hound and can't possibly be trusted. I don't know why it's taken you so long to finally realize what I've been saying."

Geneva fluffed her bangs and nodded in agreement as she spoke. "Because of how you are," she said. "That's why it took a while for me to understand."

"Oh, and how am I?"

"I love you, you know that I do. But you're very negative and you've never said a kind word or positive thing about Johnny, or hardly any man, for that matter, since I've known you. You're just bitter."

Donetta blinked her long lashes and paused, as if in deep thought. "That may be true, but it doesn't stop me from being right. And let's face it, I'm right most of the time."

"Yes, I have to admit, you are." Geneva continued to style her bangs, giving them a tousled look before lightly spritzing them with a mist of hair sheen. She took a deep breath and then sat in her chair, facing Donetta. She slumped her shoulders and shook her head. "I've been such a fool. How could I have been so stupid?"

"You're not stupid. What you are is trusting. You loved him."

"Love makes you do some crazy, out-of-your-mind things. I tried giving Johnny the benefit of the doubt. I looked past things that I knew in my heart weren't right. But I wanted my marriage to work. I wanted him to change, and I thought if I tried a little harder, maybe he would. I've supported him and encouraged him. I've taken care of him, and I've tried to satisfy his needs so he wouldn't have to look outside our marriage for fulfillment. But none of that mattered to him. I feel horrible and I wish I could go back home, pull the covers over my head, and cry."

Donetta walked over to Geneva, reached for her hand, and held it tightly. "You might feel like shit right now, but honey, trust me, you'll get over it."

Geneva looked down at the floor. "I don't know, Donetta."

"You're saying that now because everything's still fresh. Give it some time, you'll be singing a different song before you know it."

"I feel unattractive and unwanted."

"That bastard really did a number on you," Donetta said with a hint of sadness. "Don't let him break your spirit or question your worth. Your pretty ass looks like a million bucks. Your hair is fly, your makeup is flawless, and you're working the hell outa those jeans. So hold your head up high, kick that sorry-ass, chicken eatin' Negro to the curb, and start enjoying your life."

Geneva couldn't help but smile. She was thankful for Donetta, and as she looked into her friend's piercing hazel-colored eyes—compliments of Bausch and Lomb contacts—she knew she couldn't ask for a better person to stand by her side during times of trouble. From the day they met in cosmetology school ten years ago when Geneva had relocated, they'd hit it off and been best friends ever since.

Geneva was disappointed that Johnny had never cared for Donetta, which she'd initially thought was because of her friend's alternative lifestyle. But slowly she'd come to realize that his dislike for Donetta had stemmed from the fact that Donetta had sized him up and called him out for being no good. "Watch that sneaky bastard," she'd said from the moment she'd laid eyes on Johnny.

Donetta Pierce, whose birth name was Donald Eric Pierce, looked, walked, talked, and acted like a woman. But when it came to knowing men and their ways, she was one hundred percent male, and one hundred and ten percent right, ninety-nine percent of the time.

Donetta was a transgender diva who spoke her mind and didn't give a damn about what people said or thought about her or her choices. At six-foot-two and 190 pounds of lean muscle, toned arms, and long legs that seemed to extend a mile, Donetta was a well built, striking man who was blessed with smooth, cinnamon colored skin and natural good looks. But with fashionable blond highlights that complemented the chestnut brown weave that hung down her back, neatly arched brows that accentuated her feline-shaped eyes, and perfectly manicured French-tip nails that showcased her slender fingers, she was an equally attractive woman. Today she was wearing a stylish navy and white boatneck shirt and slim-fitting navy capris that made her look as if she'd just stepped out of a Banana Republic ad.

"Thanks for trying to cheer me up," Geneva said with a smile.

"Honey, I'm just speaking the truth. Forget Johnny and his tired, played-out ass."

"You're right, and I shouldn't even be thinking about him. But he's my husband."

"He's a fucking mistake."

"I just can't believe he'd do this to me. I could almost understand him treating me this way if I wasn't good to him, or if I was a horrible wife. But I've done nothing but love him and try to please him. This hurts so much."

Donetta softened her eyes. "What happened that made you finally open your eyes? . . . Did you catch him with someone?"

"Not exactly." Geneva recounted last night's event, giving a blow-by-blow of what had happened. "He didn't even bother to come back home last night."

Donetta shook her head. "That sorry bastard had the nerve to stay out all night?"

"Yes, all night. He finally came home this morning as I was filling my coffee mug. I was so angry and hurt that I didn't say a word to him, and he didn't speak to me, either."

"Y'all just avoided each other?"

"Yes, that's exactly what we did. I looked him straight in the eye but he wouldn't even glimpse in my direction." Geneva shook her head. "Honestly, I wanted to kill him, and if I'd had a gun . . ."

Donetta sucked her teeth. "I wish I'd known; you could've borrowed mine."

Geneva knew her friend was completely serious because Donetta didn't play when it came to exacting revenge. She'd sent more than one lover to the hospital for doing her wrong.

"What hurt so bad," Geneva continued, "was the way he ignored me, like I wasn't even there. He walked straight back to the bedroom, and when I heard the water from the shower, I couldn't get out the door fast enough." Geneva wiped away a small tear that had run down her cheek. "He was probably washing off the scent of the woman he was with last night."

Donetta sat down in her chair, crossed her long legs, and perched her elbows atop her right knee. "Get it out, honey."

"I just feel so empty. So confused."

"It's a damn shame that he did this to you. His sorry ass reminds me of Eric," Donetta said, referring to her ex, who'd ended up in the hospital at her hands after a lover's quarrel that had turned deadly. The only reason the man hadn't pressed charges was because he didn't want his wife to find out that he'd been creeping.

Geneva sniffled and pulled a bottle of Visine from her station drawer. She put two drops in each eye and blinked rapidly. "I've got to pull myself together before those doors open."

"When are you moving out? You know you have to divorce his ass, don't you?"

"It's not that easy, Donetta. We've built a life together."

"No you haven't. You've been a footstool that he constantly steps on. That's not building a life with someone, that's tearing down someone's spirit. You shouldn't be walking around here feeling defeated or shedding a single tear over his sorry ass, 'cause I guarantee you that bastard isn't losing a minute of sleep over what he's done to you."

Geneva knew that her friend was right, and it made her feel even worse. She wanted Johnny to suffer and feel the same kind of hurt she was going through. She wanted him to feel remorse and agonize over what he'd done. She wanted him to regret his actions and come running through the door to beg her forgiveness. She wanted him to do anything that showed he cared. But she knew the reality was that none of those things would happen. The love they'd once had for each other had faded.

Geneva reached back into the top drawer of her workstation and pulled out a mini box of Godiva Gold Ballotins. Godiva was her favorite chocolate, and whenever she felt down she knew the delicious confections could lift her spirits.

"You and your chocolate," Donetta teased.

"It's the one thing I know I can count on."

"You better include me in that mix."

Geneva nodded. "Yes, Donetta, you're right up there with my ballotins and truffles."

Just then the door opened, and she and Donetta both looked toward the entrance at the same time. Geneva half hoped it was Johnny, but it was only Shartell Brown, the nosiest, most gossiping stylist in the entire salon, and quite possibly the entire town.

All the other stylists, including Geneva and Donetta, had secretly nicknamed Shartell "Ms. CIA," because she had intel on everyone in Amber—even folks she didn't know by name. It was a given that if you wanted to know about the hottest scandals, latest break-ups, most recent makeups, and everyone's screw-ups, Shartell had it covered. Whenever she said the four words, "Quiet as it's kept," everyone knew she was getting ready to lay down some serious gossip.

Shartell was outrageous in every way. From her long, auburn-colored weave, to her one inch acrylic tips, to the neon-colored, tight-fitting clothes she stuffed her size-twenty figure into, Shartell was loud, daring, and often brash in her behavior. She was definitely an acquired taste, and regardless of whether people liked her or not, the one thing no one could deny was that her information was always accurate. She never told a lie or exaggerated a situation beyond the facts of what actually happened, which served to make her gossip as solid as steel. If she told you something, it could be trusted.

"Good morning, ladies," Shartell said, her thick Southern drawl oozing like molasses. She stomped her way toward her workstation, which was right beside Geneva's. "I wish we had an elevator in this shop," she panted, out of breath. "The walk up that flight of steps is a workout and a half, and on hot days like this one it can wear you out." She removed her black, horn-rimmed sunglasses from her round face and squinted her large brown eyes. "Did I interrupt something? Looks like you two were having a pretty serious conversation. Is everything all right?" she asked, looking back and forth between Geneva and Donetta.

Donetta leaned to the side and placed her hand on her hip. "Heffa, you nosey as hell."

"Yes, that's true," Shartell said with a big smile, not the least bit offended. "But you still haven't answered my question."

"I can't go there with you right now," Donetta said with a roll of her eyes. "You need to sit down somewhere and mind your own business."

Shartell smirked. "Y'all know I'm gonna eventually find out what's up, so why don't you just go ahead and tell me now."

"Why don't you just wipe that cheap-ass lipstick off your two front teeth and concentrate on setting up your station for your clients, instead of worrying about what the hell we're talking about."

Shartell ran her stubby finger across her teeth and smacked her lips. "Kiss my ass, Donetta."

Geneva stepped in. "Shartell, please give it a rest today. This isn't the time."

Shartell slowly removed her designer handbag from her shoulder. "Oh, my . . . Geneva, you seem a little testy today." She scratched her head and looked Geneva up and down. "Somethin's going on with you, sugar. You're the only person in this whole salon who's always happy, and don't nothin' bother you. But right now you look like somebody just stole your last piece of candy out your precious Godiva box. Yes, somethin's definitely wrong."

Geneva took a deep breath, trying to remain calm. She'd started her morning on the wrong foot and now Shartell was making it worse. "I asked you nicely. Now please, Shartell, give it a rest."

"Are you having problems at home with Johnny or something?" Shartell persisted. "I know that look, and it's got man troubles written all over it. And after all, you are married to Johnny Mayfield," she said, ending her words with a sigh.

Geneva looked as though someone had just told her they could see through her clothes as she wondered what Ms. CIA knew about her husband and his activities. "Why do you say that?" she asked defensively.

"Don't feed into her wicked web," Donetta chided as she looked from Geneva to Shartell. "It doesn't make any sense for one person to be so damn messy. Your mouthy ass always gotta be stirring up shit. That's why people don't like you."

Shartell reached into her station drawer, pulled out an orange smock, and put it on over her hot-pink shirt and bright purple pants. "Donetta, you really need to watch how you talk to me. You're lucky that I'm not the type who gets easily offended, otherwise there would be some consequences and repercussions goin' on up in here."

Just then Councilwoman Charlene Harris walked into the salon with a bright smile on her face. She'd started coming to Geneva a few months ago after her long-time stylist had moved away, and had quickly become one of Geneva's favorite clients. She kept a standing biweekly appointment that she never missed. She was never late, she always tipped generously, and she always had encouraging, uplifting words for everyone. She was kind, smart, loyal, and hardworking, which was the reason why she'd won a seat on the city council one year ago.

Geneva, along with everyone else in the salon, admired Councilwoman Harris. And although Geneva's style was different from her client's, Geneva loved the way the woman carried herself. She was the picture of classic sophistication in her St. John business suits and sensible pumps, accompanied by expensive but understated jewelry, usually consisting of genuine pearls. For a woman who was approaching her late fifties, she looked several years younger than she really was. She was old school, in a classic kind of way, and no matter how much Geneva tried to get the councilwoman to change up her hairstyle, she wouldn't budge. "I know what I like and I'm not interested in changing," she'd always say with a smile. She only wore one of two styles. If her slightly longer than shoulder-length hair wasn't hanging down in layers, it was pinned up in a sophisticated chignon, as it was today. Other than those styles, the councilwoman wasn't having it.

"Good morning, Geneva," Councilwoman Harris said. "And good morning to you, too, ladies." She smiled, offering a polite nod to Donetta and Shartell.

Geneva nodded. "Good morning." She formed her lips into a smile that forced her personal problems to the background of her mind, relegating a vacant space for it to be dealt with at another time. She was a professional, and right now she had to conduct business. "You want the usual or are you in the mood for something different?" This was Geneva's standard question, even though she knew what the answer would be.

"I'm going to switch it up," Councilwoman Harris said.

Geneva, Donetta, and Shartell each took a collective pause as their eyes widened with surprise.

"I want this cut." The councilwoman reached into her bone-colored Chanel handbag and pulled out a picture that looked as if it had been cut from a magazine. She handed it to Geneva and smiled. "What do you think about this? I fell in love with this style when I saw it in my *Essence* magazine last night. Do you think it will look good on me?"

Geneva examined the picture of a woman sporting an asymmetrical bob that was short at the nape and hung down below the chin on one side. The style screamed funky sophistication and could go from classic to glam depending upon what kind of mood one was in. Geneva instantly knew the style would look perfect on the councilwoman. This time the smile that formed at Geneva's lips was genuine. "I love it!" she said enthusiastically. "What do you think about trying a little color? I think some light brown highlights will really make this cut stand out and frame your face nicely."

The councilwoman smiled. "All right, let's go for it."

"Fantastic! You're going to love your new look."

"I have no doubt that I will." She took a deep breath. "Change is good."

"Yes, it is," Shartell said, inserting herself into the conversation. "The only thing that's certain in life is change."

As much as Geneva didn't want to hear Shartell's mouth, she had to agree that Ms. CIA was right. "Okay, let's get started on this new do."

The councilwoman clasped her handbag shut and placed it back on her shoulder. "I'm sorry, but I need to run back out because I just realized I left my cell phone in my car. I'll be right back."

"Okay, take your time," Geneva said as she donned her black smock, kicked off her sexy red heels, and stepped into her comfortable black Crocs.

Once Councilwoman Harris was out of earshot, the gossip began.

Donetta sat in her seat and crossed her long legs. "Something's up with your client, Geneva. There's only a handful of things that will make a woman chop off all her hair and go rogue, and man trouble is one of them."

"She and her husband are getting a divorce," Shartell said. "She put him out the house yesterday morning and he checked into the Roosevelt Hotel down on Bellview Street last night."

"Oh, no," Geneva said. "That's awful. She and Mr. Harris have been married forever. I can't believe it."

Shartell pursed her fuchsia-colored lips. "Thirty-one years, to be exact."

"Damn!" Donetta said. "Okay, I know you have all the ugly details about what happened, so give it to us."

"No, don't say a word," Geneva said, shaking her head. "Councilwoman Harris is probably torn up about this. If they've been married thirty-one years, that means she's spent more than half of her life with that man, and it's got to hurt like hell for this to happen. Plus, because of who she is, the whole town will be gossiping about her soon enough. Lord knows she doesn't need us doing it. The poor woman."

Donetta laughed. "Poor woman? Puh-leeze! Did you see that big Kool-Aid, I-just-won-the-lotto looking smile she had on her face when she walked through the door? I don't know her circumstances, but I do know body language and human behavior. If you ask me, that woman's happy as hell."

"Donetta's right," Shartell said. "Quiet as it's kept, she and her husband been havin' problems for quite some time."

Despite initially not wanting to hear the rumors, Geneva found herself listening with rapt attention as Shartell quickly told them about the details that had led to the demise of Councilwoman Harris's marriage.

Charlene and Reginald Harris appeared to have the picture-perfect marriage, but once the last of their three children went away to college, the trouble began. Reginald, a handsome lawyer with a tongue as slick as his smile, started cheating on Charlene. She forgave him the first time, which provided him cushion for the second, which eventually turned into a third. What Charlene had initially thought was a mid-life crisis that her husband was suddenly going through was actually a long-standing situation that she eventually discovered the hard way.

Shartell shook her head. "That man has taken her through some changes. I guess he thought he could continue to do anything he wanted, but she proved to him that he can't, at least not with her . . . anymore."

"She got tired of his bullshit," Donetta said. "Good for her. At some point a woman has to face reality and make some hard decisions."

Geneva saw the look that her friend discreetly threw her way. She knew Donetta was right, but she couldn't bring herself to offer up much. "I'm sorry to hear that," she said quietly.

"Oh, but here's the clincher," Shartell said, this time with a solemn face. "Their youngest daughter, Lauren, who's a student at Tuskegee, well, she started dating this guy who's in one of her pre-med classes—smart, good looking guy from what I understand. Come to find out, the boy is her half-brother."

Donetta's eyes got big. "Shut the front door!"

"What?" Geneva said.

"Yep," Shartell continued. "The boy is Mr. Harris's son that he had with another woman. Lauren and that boy are only a month apart in age, too. Turns out he been steppin' out for years, but Mrs. Harris didn't know. That's how quiet he kept his shit."

"Leave it to a man who knows the ins and outs of the law to duck and dive," Donetta said. "That kind of mess really pisses me off."

Shartell nodded. "But every dog has his day, and this one is having his. When Lauren told her mama and daddy that she had a new boyfriend, and that she was serious about him, quite naturally they wanted to meet him. That's when the truth came out."

"Lord have mercy," Geneva said.

"Uh-huh, and quiet as it's kept, that's why Mr. Harris's arm is in a cast and his eye looks like he stepped into the ring with Mayweather."

Donetta craned her neck. "What do you mean?"

"He didn't slip and fall off their deck a few days ago. She beat the shit outa him."

"Noooooo," Geneva said, covering her mouth in shock. "Not Councilwoman Harris!"

"Yes, sugar. Turns out Ms. Thang has a mean right hook. After she clocked him dead in his eye, she took out a baseball bat and broke the man's arm. He was pretty banged up and bruised, too."

"How the hell do you know all this stuff?" Donetta asked in amazement. "Did you have hidden cameras planted at their house or something?"

Shartell smiled and winked. "I have my sources."

They all stopped talking when Councilwoman Harris walked back in. "One benefit of coming here that I didn't have at my other salon is that I get a light workout on those steps," she joked.

"You got your phone?" Geneva asked, hoping she didn't look as guilty as she felt.

"Yes, and I hope my temporary absence gave you ladies enough time to talk about my situation with my soon to be ex-husband."

Geneva smiled nervously. She felt bad for the woman. "I . . . um."

Councilwoman Harris nodded. "It's quite all right. I know how things work. The worse the news, the faster it spreads," she said, looking directly at Shartell. "I'd rather you talk now before the salon fills up with people." She paused, and then smiled at Geneva. "I'm ready to go back to the shampoo bowl now."

Two hours later Geneva watched Charlene Harris walk out the door with a new hairstyle and what appeared to be a new attitude. The spring in her step was noticeable, and Geneva had never seen her client look so good. The councilwoman was always well pulled together and attractive. But today she glowed with a polished patina, and that was because she looked happy, just as Donetta had said earlier.

"You know that could be you," Donetta said just loud enough for Geneva to hear as she walked over to borrow some spritz. "What you just saw right there was happiness walking out that door. But that woman had to get pushed into making that leap. I hope you don't let that asshole you're married to tip you over the edge. Let Ms. Harris be an example to you. Don't waste the best parts of your youth, because you've got too much livin' to do."

Geneva knew that Donetta was right, but she didn't have time to think about her troubled marriage. Right now she had to focus on the ten other clients she had lined up today, and then the volunteer meeting at Sandhill Elementary School she was going to attend tonight.

Chapter 6

JOHNNY

It was lunchtime and Johnny was starving. He'd been so busy bouncing from one thing to the other that he hadn't eaten since this time yesterday. As he sat at his desk listening to his stomach growl, he thought about the dinner that Geneva had prepared for him last night. "Damn, I should've packed some of that food for lunch," he said to himself. She'd prepared his favorites: beer-batter fried pork chops, garlic mashed potatoes with gravy, seasoned green beans, and her world-famous sweet potato pie. When he walked through the door last night, he'd wanted to dive mouth first into the food. But Geneva had been angry, and he knew better than to attempt to reheat the food that had gone cold because he'd neglected to come home on time.

"I don't know what's wrong with me," Johnny said aloud as he rubbed his empty stomach. "I'm so tired I can't even think straight. I should've gotten some food out of the refrigerator 'cause a pork chop sure would taste good right about now." But just like yesterday, this morning he'd been too busy to think about eating. His mind had been consumed with the usual: work, money, and what he was going to do about Vivana, all in that order. He knew if he hadn't stayed out all night he wouldn't be so tired, and he would have remembered to pack some food for lunch. Although he'd once desired Vivana like a drug that he couldn't get enough of, she was beginning to cause ripples in his normally calm life.

He hadn't meant to spend the entire night with Vivana—something he had promised himself he'd never do—but after they'd consumed the entire bottle of wine he'd bought as a peace offering, and then made love so hard and heavy that his body felt exhausted, he'd gone to sleep almost immediately after reaching his climax. Just before he drifted off, he asked Vivana to set the alarm so he could wake up in two hours. Geneva was an early riser, but she wasn't a night owl, and she usually had trouble staying up. He'd hoped he would get back home somewhere between her drifting off to sleep that night and waking up bright and early the next morning. But apparently Vivana had been wiped out, too, and she'd dozed off right along with him, forgetting to set the alarm.

"I need to slow things down with ol' girl," Johnny said aloud as he sifted through the papers on his desk. He could tell that Vivana was becoming more attached than he liked. She'd even tried to withhold sex last night because she'd been upset that he hadn't greeted her with a hug and a kiss when she let him into the hotel. But they'd been in public, and as he'd told her from the beginning, he couldn't risk getting caught.

Unlike the other women he'd slept with since he'd been married to Geneva, Vivana had a husband, which Johnny initially thought was going to be a plus in his favor because she had just as much to risk as he did. He reasoned that he wouldn't have to worry about her demanding more from him than he was willing or able to give because she was in the same situation he was. But as he reminded himself from last night's encounter with Geneva, things change. "Yeah, I'm gonna have to cut Vivana back," he mumbled.

Just as he was about to call in a pick-up order to China Express, his cell phone rang. It was Vivana. He didn't want to talk to her right now. He knew he should probably let it roll into voice mail because if he was going to pull back on their contact, this was the perfect time to start. But as he watched her number light up his phone screen, he couldn't deny the urge he had to feel her body next to his and hear her sexy voice moan in his ear. There was something about Vivana that drove him wild, and as annoyingly brazen and temperamental as she could be, he desired her. Against his better judgment he picked up the phone. "Hey you," he said, trying to sound casual.

"Hey back. Are you all right?"

"I'm tired, but good."

"Was she gone when you got home this morning?"

He'd told her that he hoped Geneva would be on her way to work by the time he got home, otherwise things might get nasty judging from the night before. "No she was there."

"Oh . . ."

"She was about to leave for work when I walked into the house. We didn't speak to each other but I could tell she was pissed."

"If you two didn't talk, how do you know she was upset?"

Johnny chuckled. "You know how y'all women do. She gave me the evil eye and a lot of nonverbal attitude."

"Please don't compare me to other women, Johnny."

"That's not what I was doing. I was just making a point. You know what I mean."

"Uh-huh . . . so she was pissed?"

"Of course she was. If you had an argument with your husband and he didn't come home that night, wouldn't you be pissed?"

"Not at all."

"Yes you would."

"No, I wouldn't. You know my situation."

"I guess." When Johnny thought about what Vivana had just said, he realized that he didn't fully know her situation. As a matter of fact, aside from knowing that her husband was a stick-in-the-mud accountant who didn't excite her, she'd given him very few details about her life. But he figured that was a good thing because at this point he didn't want to know anything beyond what she'd already told him, or vice versa.

"You don't have to guess," Vivana responded. "I don't love my husband, just like you don't love your wife, and if there's no love, there's no reason to be mad, right?"

Johnny frowned, but remained silent as he listened.

"That's why I'd be fine if Wilbert stayed out all night," she continued. "Hell, he could stay gone all week and it wouldn't bother me a bit."

This time Johnny responded. "Wow . . ."

"I'm serious. See, Geneva obviously loves you, and that's the reason she's mad. Now my question to you is why do you care if she's mad or not, that is, unless you're still in love with her?"

Johnny's antennae went up. He didn't like the direction in which this conversation was going and he knew he had to quickly change course. "Regardless of who loves who, my wife was mad."

"You didn't answer my question."

"Don't try to turn this into an inquisition." He purposely made his tone sound irritable to let her know he wasn't going to be forced into saying anything that he didn't want to freely tell her. "The bottom line is, I would've made it home last night if you'd remembered to set the alarm like I asked you to." There was a pause, and he knew his statement had made its point.

"I'm sorry, baby. I was so tired that I dozed off without even thinking about it."

"Yeah, I guess we wore each other out."

She purred. "Mmmm, yes we did."

Johnny's mind started to drift back to last night, but he knew he had to refocus. He had to wrap up this conversation before Vivana started asking more questions that he wasn't prepared to answer. "So what's up?" he asked. "You okay?"

"I'm good," she responded. "How're you?"

"Tired and hungry."

"You should be after your performance last night. I wish I could've served you breakfast in bed this morning. That way you'd be satisfied and full."

He could hear the smile and sexy coyness in her voice and it instantly made him horny, and improved his mood. "That would've been nice."

"We could've ordered a big breakfast through room service to feed our appetite," she said in a seductive voice dripping with carnal lust. "I'd love to pour syrup all over your sexy, hard body and lick it off."

Now he was smiling on the other end. Johnny leaned back in his black leather office chair and rubbed his crotch. "Talk that talk, baby."

"You like that?"

"You know I do. Tell me something good." He loved when she engaged in phone sex with him.

"Why don't I come to your office and whisper what I want to do to you in your ear. Then after that, I'll show you."

Johnny leaned forward and sat straight up in his chair. A crease of concern lodged itself in the middle of his forehead. One of the first rules that he and Vivana had agreed upon when they'd starting seeing each other was that they wouldn't meet in public nor would they rendezvous during the day. That meant that sundown, behind closed doors, was the only time they'd be able to spend together. He was perfectly fine with that, and up until now he thought she was, too. He knew he had to nip this situation in the bud. "You know that's off limits."

Vivana laughed on the other end. "After how freaky we got last night, nothing is off limits."

Damn! She's got a point! he wanted to say, but stopped himself. He had to admit she was right. Whatever inhibitions he thought she may have had were thrown to the wind last night. Vivana had proved to be the most sexually charged woman he'd ever been with. She was down for kissing, licking, and sucking every imaginable body part and crevice, which had heightened his pleasure. She welcomed his penetration of every orifice on her body, and when she mounted herself on top of him, she moved her hips in a rhythm that made him shiver. It was clear to him that she enjoyed sex, and she knew how to please a man. She knew exactly how to touch him with just the right amount of pressure that drove him wild.

A part of Johnny wanted her to come over this very moment so he could fuck her from behind on top of his desk, but he knew that would be inviting danger. "Never shit where you work or lay your head," Bernard always told him. It was part of the reason his friend had gotten caught and was now divorced. Bernard had slipped up and gotten sloppy. But Johnny had no intentions of allowing that to happen. "Listen, Vivana, we already talked about this and you know the deal. Maybe we can see each other again in a few days."

"A few days? Why so long?"

"First off, that's not a long time. And second, my schedule is tight and my wife's been asking a lot of questions lately. She's getting suspicious and I need to be extra careful."

The line was silent on the other end. "Hello . . . are you still there?" he asked.

"I'm here."

He could hear the disappointment in her voice, and to him she sounded like a sulking child who couldn't get what she wanted. "I want to see you," he said. "But I can't right now. I've got clients I need to meet with and several properties I need to show. Plus, I have a stack of paperwork sitting on my desk that I need to go through. It's just a real busy time."

Johnny waited for a response, but there was still silence on her end. "Vivana, are you there?"

"I hear what you're saying," she said, frustration seeping into her voice. "But here's what I know. When a man wants to do something he'll make the time to do it, regardless of what's going on in his life."

"You're right, and I won't even try to debate you on that. But it also depends on the man's circumstances. You and I talked about this from the beginning, and I thought we had an understanding, right?"

"Yes, we do."

"So why are you all of a sudden having a problem with our arrangement?"

"I don't have a problem, but things do change. I think we're both different people now than we were when we first met, and that's not a bad thing."

Now Johnny was silent.

"I have needs, Johnny."

"You're insatiable. I thought last night would carry you over for a while. What does it take to satisfy you?"

"For someone so smooth, and sexy, and charming, at times you can say downright insensitive, juvenile things. Sometimes you act like a caveman."

"Thanks for the compliment."

"Don't get sarcastic with me."

He sighed heavily. "Well, what the hell are you talking about?"

"I'm not talking about sex, which is apparently all you seem to have on your mind. I'm talking about being with you, feeling your arms around me, and sharing special time with each other. I just want to see you."

Now he became even more alarmed and he knew he needed to bring this conversation to an end. "Baby, I hate to cut you off but I have a call coming in from one of my clients."

"Wait, did you hear what I just said?"

"I have to take this call. This is business."

"And?"

Johnny couldn't believe his ears. *She's crazy as hell,* he thought. "Listen, Vivana, I'm trying to be nice but you're really pushing it."

"Your client's call probably rolled over into voice mail by now so just deal with them later."

"This isn't how we're supposed to roll."

"Says who? I mean, things are different than they were when we first started seeing each other, wouldn't you agree?"

Johnny was tired and he didn't want to deal with Vivana on an empty stomach. "I have to go."

"So you're gonna leave me hanging?"

"Vivana, I haven't eaten since lunchtime yesterday and I'm so hungry I can't concentrate, let alone have this kind of conversation with you. I was just about to go out to get something to eat when you called."

"Where're you going?"

The curiosity in her voice made Johnny nervous. He hoped she wasn't asking so she could coincidentally show up at China Express when he went to pick up the order he was going to place. "I'm not sure," he lied. "I haven't decided."

"I can bring you lunch if that'll help you."

He moved the phone away from his ear, looked at it, and shook his head. He didn't know if she'd made that statement just to get a reaction from him or if she was serious. Either way, he'd had enough. "Listen, I already told you I have to go. I'll call you later." He hit the end button and ran his hand across his chin.

Johnny rose from his chair and began to pace the floor of his small office. Not only was his stomach growling, his head was hurting and his neck was stiff. He knew his latter two ailments were a direct result of his tense conversation with Vivana.

Suddenly, the untamed desire he'd felt for his sexy mistress fizzled like a soda gone flat. Anxiety mixed with apprehension rumbled inside him as he replayed every detail of their conversation. He could tell from the sound of Vivana's voice and the things she'd said that she was getting too attached for his liking. He'd sensed it last night when she pouted and tried to punish him by withholding sex. At the time he'd brushed it off, thinking she simply wanted some attention, as most women did. But he now knew it had been much more than that. She was starting to develop real feelings for him. For Johnny, that was a scary proposition.

He'd been a player long enough to tell when a woman was going to become a problem, and between her behavior at the hotel, and now her demanding telephone call, Vivana had just shown him signs that a possible catastrophe was in the making. In the span of their ten-minute conversation, she'd gone from someone he couldn't get out of his mind to someone he wanted to forget about. All he kept hearing were Bernard's words. "Man, she's trouble with a capital T."

He was jolted out of his deep thoughts when his cell phone rang again. He hesitated for a moment, and then felt a great sense of relief when he saw that it wasn't Vivana's number flashing across the screen, which he'd programmed into his contacts under the name Michael. He was thankful that Bernard's name appeared instead. "Man, I was just thinking about you," Johnny said. "How's it goin', brother?"

"It's all good. Just holdin' it down here at the office."

"You handlin' things," Johnny said with a nod.

Bernard was the senior manager of security at Crane Technical Community College. He'd worked his way up through the ranks and now enjoyed the comforts of a large office, a secretary, an assistant, and a staff of twenty-five that reported to him.

"So, you said you were thinking about me?" Bernard said.

"Yeah . . . I uh, I keep hearing what you told me about Vivana."

"Did something happen?"

"A lot happened in a short amount of time. I gotta cut that shit loose, and quick."

"Damn, what did she do?"

Johnny told Bernard about the conversation he'd just had with Vivana, and about the way she'd acted last night. "I thought she was cool. We were just kickin' it, and everything was fine. But something changed, almost overnight. It's crazy and I have a bad feeling about it. I have to find a way to end things with her."

"I agree. You've got too much to lose. Does she know where you live?"

"I'm sure she can look it up. I hope she's not crazy enough to try to come by my house."

"She just might. I don't put anything past anyone, especially a woman who's on a mission."

"You're right about that," Johnny said with a heavy sigh.

Bernard cleared his throat. "I hate to even ask you this, but does she know who Geneva is? I mean, does she know her real name?"

Johnny was silent.

"Damn, you told her Geneva's name?"

"I've been seeing Vivana for five months, so of course Geneva's name has come up."

"But you know the rules of the game."

"Yeah, I know I could've made up a name like I've done in the past, but for some reason I didn't. Besides, Vivana told me her husband's name and I even know what he does for a living and where he works. He's a boring-ass accountant, and with a name like Wilbert, what can you expect."

Bernard laughed. "I ain't never heard of no brother with a name like Wilbert."

"Tell me about it."

"You sure that's his real name?"

"It was hard for me to believe, too, and I even told her so. It wasn't until she Googled him on her laptop one night, right in front of me, that I believed her."

"Damn, she's bold to do something like that."

Johnny shook his head. "You don't know the half of it."

"How much information did you share with her about Geneva?"

"Actually, I lied about what she does."

Bernard sighed with relief. "Ever since I straightened out my life, I no longer condone lying. But in this case I encourage it, and I'm glad you did."

"Me too. I told her that Geneva works in the healthcare field. I didn't tell her where she works or what she does, just that she's in healthcare."

Bernard cleared his throat. "Don't go gettin' Candace mixed up in your lies. We don't need that shit."

Johnny couldn't believe how pussy-whipped his friend had become. Although the thought had crossed Johnny's mind to use Bernard's girlfriend as an alibi if needed, especially because she was a nurse who worked odd hours, he had no intention of involving Candace in his business, mainly because he knew she wouldn't comply.

"Calm down," Johnny said. "I wouldn't do that."

"Good. The less information Vivana knows the better, and don't tell her anything else about your home life either."

Johnny's mind started racing. "I hope she doesn't start acting crazy and do some dumb shit. I can tell from our phone call that she's starting to get in her feelings."

"If that's the case, you're definitely gonna have to end it, and you'll probably have to let her down gently if you don't want any problems. But even then she might act a fool."

"I should've listened to you last night because now I'm wishing I'd kept my ass home."

Bernard breathed heavily into the phone. "The important thing is that you've come to your senses and you're gonna end it. When do you plan to tell her?"

"As soon as possible."

"Good."

"I just have to figure out how I'm gonna do it, 'cause like you said, I need to break it off gently because Vivana's so damn volatile. If she was afraid of getting caught, I'd have some leverage, but from what she said on the phone, it's almost like she wants her husband to find out. She comes home late and sometimes not at all, and then she catches an attitude if he asks her about where she's been."

"That's fucked up, man."

"Tell me about it. I couldn't and wouldn't stand for that."

"That's what you do to Geneva, and it's what I did to Suzanne. Sometimes things come back to bite you . . . I'm just sayin'."

"I get that, but still," Johnny said with frustration, "that's not how I want things to roll."

"She sounds pretty bold. Do you think she has violent tendencies?"

Johnny paused and then sat down in his chair as he thought about Bernard's question. Even before last night and this afternoon he'd recognized subtle things about Vivana's choice of words and behavior that had led him to believe she was the kind of woman who could get physical if she was pushed to a certain point. "Probably so. Anyone can go there if they get mad enough."

"True," Bernard said. "But it usually takes a lot to push a woman to the point of physical violence. When a woman's pissed, and I mean really mad, she might curse you out, give you the silent treatment, or show her ass and get loud with you. But most won't take it to a physical level unless they're completely out of control."

"You think Vivana's gonna do something stupid?"

"Like I said, I don't put anything past anyone. I've seen it all working in security. After you cut things off, she'll be a woman scorned, and you know what they say about that."

"Yeah, I do."

"I'm not trying to alarm you, but from everything you've told me about Vivana, you better be very careful. I've had a bad feeling about her and this whole situation from day one. Watch your step, man."

Johnny rubbed his chin and leaned back in his chair. "Up until last night she's been cool, and things were going fine. Then all of a sudden she starts acting strange, wanting to meet during the middle of the day, questioning me about whether or not I love my wife . . ."

"Oh, yeah," Bernard said. "She's more than just in her feelings, she's caught up. And if she doesn't give a damn about her husband, well, she really has nothing to lose and she might try to hijack your shit."

Johnny shook his head in frustration. "Ain't gonna happen. I've made up my mind and I'm putting an end to this before that has a chance of happening."

"You can't just cut her off cold. You gotta be smooth about it or some shit'll really jump off."

"I know, and I will."

"And listen, I got your back, man."

Johnny smiled. "I appreciate you, brother. You could've said I told you so, but you didn't. Trust and believe me when I say I've learned my lesson." Johnny meant every word that he'd said. Bernard was the one friend whom he knew he could always count on, and Johnny was glad that Bernard always looked out for him.

"No problem. That's what real friends do. We're brothers, you know that."

"Yes, we are. Thanks again. I needed this call."

Bernard laughed. "You got so much going on and we got so wrapped up in your situation that I almost forgot why I called you."

"What's up?" Johnny asked.

"After we got off the phone last night, Candace came over because her shift ended early. She spent the night and I wanted you to know in case you told Geneva you stayed over here. 'Cause, man, you know how things can happen, and if Geneva runs into Candace and decides to question her about where you were last night, the gig's up."

"You're right about that." Johnny didn't tell Bernard that was exactly what he'd planned to do.

"And, playa, I'm tellin' you now, Candace ain't gonna lie for you, so you better hope she doesn't run into Geneva."

"I really have to figure something out fast."

The two friends talked a few more minutes before Bernard had to take another call. After Johnny hit the end button on his phone, he sat back and thought about his bad luck. He knew he should've been very worried, just like he was only moments ago, but for some reason he wasn't. Then he realized it was because putting an end to his affair with Vivana was going to free up his time, his money, and his anxiety.

But he also knew that breaking up with Vivana was going to be a little tricky. She was hotheaded and aggressive, and he knew she wouldn't be pleased about him rejecting her. But she was a professional woman, and was married to a professional man, who apparently had a level head. Although she talked a tough game, Johnny hoped that Vivana wouldn't do anything crazy or far out in left field. If there was one thing he knew about her, it was that she was rooted in material trappings, and she wouldn't want to jeopardize her comfortable lifestyle. She might be angry at first, but he knew she'd get over it.

As Johnny sat at his desk and thought more on the matter, he decided that he was going to gradually stop returning Vivana's phone calls, responding to her texts, and limit their physical contact. "Yep, things change," he said to himself. But right now he couldn't let his mind get bogged down worrying about his mistress. He had to handle things one step at a time, and that meant first things first. He called China Express, placed his to-go order, and then walked out the door.

Chapter 7

VIVANA

"He must've forgotten who the fuck he was talking to," Vivana said in an angry tone. She'd just gotten off the phone with Johnny and she could feel her blood pressure rising from his conversation with her. "I can't believe that son of a bitch hung up on me!" she fumed. "He must be out of his freakin' mind."

Vivana had sensed when she called Johnny that things wouldn't go well, but she didn't think he'd dismiss her, as if he had better things to do than engage in a few minutes of conversation. "I knew something was up with him," she said to herself. "Now I need to find out what the hell is going on."

Vivana could tell something was wrong by the way Johnny had acted when they awoke this morning. She'd been lying beside him, pretending to be asleep, when he opened his eyes. The minute he realized the sun was out, he sat straight up in bed as if gunshots had been fired.

"What time is it?" he'd asked in a panic. "The damn sun is out!" He looked past Vivana's naked body encased under the sheet and peered at the digital alarm clock on the nightstand. "Shit! It's seven o'clock," he yelled. "Did you set the alarm?"

"Well, good morning to you, too," Vivana said with sarcasm.

Johnny ignored her and bolted out of bed. "Why didn't you set the alarm? Shit, I can't believe I've been out all night. Geneva's gonna have a damn fit!"

Vivana was so put off she could have spit right in Johnny's face. Here it was she'd just given him the best sexual experience he'd probably ever had, and all he could think about was the fact that he'd stayed out all night, and that his boring nag of a wife was going to be upset. She thought he should've been on cloud nine but instead he was bitching and moaning about something as simple as oversleeping.

"Why didn't you set the alarm?" he asked again.

She watched as Johnny hurriedly pulled his pants up his muscular legs and searched the floor for the sky-blue dress shirt he'd worn yesterday. Even when she was mad at him, which was an emotion she definitely felt at the moment, she still found him irresistible. That undeniable, electric chemistry was one of the reasons she knew she loved him. Normally, if a man pissed her off she was through with him. But with Johnny, it was just the opposite, which served to make her want him even more.

Vivana didn't set the alarm on purpose, and that was because she wanted him to oversleep so they could spend the night together. She wanted him to stop asking her about it because, although she had no problem lying to him to cover her real intent, she didn't want to begin the day that way. They'd just spent their first night together and she'd wanted nothing more than to lie in his arms and start the morning off by making love. But instead they brought in the day with Johnny's obvious disappointment about spending the night with her, which prompted his rush to get back home. She couldn't help but feel hurt from his actions, and what he did next added salt to her fresh wounds.

"Aren't you going to get dressed?" he asked as he fastened his leather belt around his taut waist.

"I don't have a curfew," she responded. She sat up in bed, letting the thin white sheet fall to her stomach, revealing a set of heavy triple

D's that she knew Johnny couldn't resist. But to her dismay, he didn't even look twice.

Johnny sat on the edge of the bed and quickly pulled on his argyle socks before slipping his feet into his stylish Brooks Brothers brown calfskin loafers. "Your husband wasn't expecting you back home last night?"

"No, he thinks I'm out of town on business. But even if I wasn't, we sleep in separate bedrooms most of the time."

Johnny paused and looked into her eyes for the first time since he'd woken up. "I didn't know that."

Vivana wanted to shake her head. She wondered how much Johnny paid attention to the things she told him. During one of their early conversations a few months ago she'd let him know that she and Samuel rarely slept together.

Over the last six months it had become a normal occurrence for her to doze off in her home office, or the couch in the family room, or the sectional in the basement, and she wouldn't come upstairs until the next morning, well after her husband had left for work. She'd intentionally slipped this information into a conversation she'd had with Johnny so he would know that she wasn't sleeping with her husband, let alone having sex with him on a regular basis. But instead of reminding him of that important detail, she decided to use it as an opportunity to satisfy her curiosity about his situation at home. "My husband and I don't have that kind of relationship," she said, sounding nonchalant. "When the love is gone it's hard to lie beside someone at night. I'm sure you know what I mean."

Johnny was silent and didn't say a word. Not only did he not comment, he still hadn't shown the least bit of interest in how sexy she looked, baring her hefty breasts that he normally loved to touch, suck, and lick. Instead of engaging her, he suddenly became as quiet as a mouse. Vivana wanted to come right out and ask him what the hell was up. But instead, she continued to play it smooth. "Even though we overslept, last night was special because for the first time in a very long time I didn't have to sleep alone." She waited for him to say something, hopefully the same thing, but instead he clasped his Patek Philippe to his wrist and walked toward the door.

"I've got to get home. I'll call you later," Johnny said.

Vivana's eyes got big. *Oh, hell no!* she wanted to scream. *I know this Negro ain't gonna leave up outa here without giving me a kiss, or a hug, or something!*

Johnny must have sensed the drama that was about to ensue because just as Vivana was about to go off, he turned and walked back to the bed where she was lying. "Last night was incredible, baby," he said as he looked into her eyes. He kissed her deeply, touched her right breast, and tweaked her nipple between his fingers until she moaned.

She wanted the moment to last, but just as quickly as he'd kissed her, he pulled away and was out the door.

As Vivana replayed the scene in her head from this morning, and then thought about the conversation she'd just had with Johnny, she got more and more upset. She couldn't understand why her lover was suddenly acting as if he didn't have time for her—and for what? . . . So his wife wouldn't be upset with him? The very thought made Vivana so angry she wanted to hit something.

She looked down at her cell phone and stared at the pictures she'd taken of him last night after he'd fallen asleep. His strong, naked body was a work of art, and his face looked peaceful as he rested. She'd taken several shots of him with the sheets draped over his chest and then a few with them gathered around his waist. She'd even snuggled beside him and switched the camera to front-facing mode so she could take a few selfies. As she admired the pictures, the thought of Johnny lying in bed next to anyone other than her made Vivana feel a kind of anger that frightened even her.

"Johnny's wife doesn't know how to take care of him the way I do," she said aloud. "If she was handling her business, he wouldn't be with me," she said to herself with conviction. But deep down, Vivana questioned whether her declaration was entirely true. After all, he didn't comment about his sleeping arrangements at home, and he'd rushed off this morning for fear that his wife would be mad at him for staying out all night. Then, as if that wasn't inconsiderate enough, he avoided giving her an answer when she'd made the point that if he didn't love his wife, why did he care whether she was upset with him or not.

"Yeah, something's definitely wrong," Vivana whispered to herself. "It's time for me to find out what the hell's going on."

Vivana pulled her compact out of her cosmetics bag and reapplied her bronze colored lipstick. She looked at her reflection in the mirror and wondered what Johnny's wife looked like. A few clicks of her mouse had given her more accurate information about Geneva than Johnny had. Vivana discovered that Geneva was a hair stylist, not a healthcare worker as Johnny had told her, and according to Geneva's five-star Yelp rating that was complete with rave reviews, she was excellent at what she did. But because Geneva was a low-key kind of person, she wasn't active on a single social media site, and there were no pictures of her to be found.

Lately, Vivana was becoming more and more curious about Geneva, and now she knew she was going to have to make it a point to see the woman for herself. But in the meantime she focused her concentration on Johnny.

"Since he's acting funny I'm gonna have to make sure I keep an eye on him." Vivana placed her dark sunglasses on her face and watched from where she was parked across the street as Johnny walked out of his office building and climbed into his spotless SUV. She waited a minute or two before she pulled out, making sure to stay several car lengths behind him. "Here we go," she said with a smile.

Chapter 8

SAMUEL

Samuel should have felt tired, frustrated, angry, and disappointed, but instead his mood was brighter than the sun that had been shining all day. It was seven p.m., and he was standing at the entrance of the school auditorium, smiling as he greeted the teachers, staff, and volunteers who'd assembled for Sandhill's open house meeting.

He'd called Vivana last night to remind her about this event, and because she was due back in town by midday, there was no reason why she wouldn't be able to attend. It was the first scheduled event of the school year, and he'd even managed to get a local television reporter to cover the evening's festivities. Although he knew it was unlikely that Vivana would actually make an appearance, he still felt it was worth a try. But Vivana hadn't bothered to call him back, and now he was glad she wasn't there tonight because after the disrespectful way she was treating him, he knew they'd have heated words that could turn ugly.

Vivana had recently begun the neglectful habit of not bothering to respond to him when he called, texted, or emailed her, and it pissed him off. Not only was it rude, it was unsafe. Last night he'd been concerned because she was traveling alone on business to the bank branch in Clinton, which was a two-and-a-half-hour drive away.

But what worried him most and made him uneasy was that he didn't even know the name of the hotel where she was staying. If something happened he wouldn't know where she was. It was a dangerous world and anything could happen.

Samuel was becoming more and more frustrated by his wife's behavior, which was eroding the love he'd once had for her. But he knew he had to put those worries out of his mind until he got home tonight, when he planned to address it once and for all. Right now he had to make sure he exercised the type of focused leadership that would motivate his staff and volunteers and build excitement about the new projects he'd planned for the upcoming year. He thanked God for his job because at this moment, it was a ray of sun among the clouds.

Samuel was drawn away from his thoughts when he saw a welcomed and familiar face. "Hello, Mr. Saddler," Samuel said with a smile and a firm handshake. "How are you?"

"I'm doin' great, Dr. Owens," the older gentleman said, returning Samuel's smile. "How you doin' this evenin'?"

"I'm feeling well, and I'm excited. The summer's just about over and the new school year is here. It's hard to believe this is my seventh year at Sandhill."

"Time flies."

"Yes, it does, and each year I look forward to all the great things we do for the kids."

Mr. Saddler nodded. "Keep that enthusiasm long as you can. You done made a mighty big change here and I'm proud of you, son."

Samuel nodded. "That means a lot to me coming from you. You're an institution."

"I can't believe this gon' be my last year at this here school. I had me some mighty good times walkin' these halls, mighty good."

Mr. Saddler had been working at Sandhill for fifty years. He'd started as a custodian and over the years he'd worked his way up to become head of maintenance. He was a hard-working man who loved the students and teachers at the school just as much as he did his actual job. All four of his children had graduated from the school, as well as several grandchildren and a smattering of nieces and nephews. He was a genuinely kind man who helped out in any way he could, offering advice to some, support to others, and guidance to anyone who needed it. Whatever problem arose, Mr. Saddler was always there to the rescue.

Samuel was going to miss the old man, not just because he was one of his most loyal and trusted employees, but because he'd become a personal friend and confidant. Mr. Saddler had taken Samuel under his wing during Samuel's tumultuous first year at Sandhill, helping him navigate the school's social and political waters. He was without a doubt the greatest mentor Samuel had ever had. And outside of work, Mr. Saddler had listened, without judgment, to Samuel's troubles at home, offering honest and caring advice. And with what Samuel could see as new problems on the horizon, he was going to miss Mr. Saddler more than the old man knew.

"I don't know what Sandhill's going to do without you," Samuel said, "or me either, for that matter."

"You gon' be just fine, son. You smart, ambitious, and you got a good heart. You know what you doin'."

"Thanks," Samuel said. "But knowing what to do and knowing who to trust are two different things. With all the changes I want to implement this school year, that's going to be my biggest challenge."

Mr. Saddler nodded. "Trust in God. He won't steer you wrong."

"Amen," Mrs. Johnston said.

Samuel and Mr. Saddler both smiled when they saw Mary Johnston standing beside them. She was the school secretary and had been working in the front office for twenty-five years. Aside from Mr. Saddler, she was Samuel's favorite employee. She knew where the bodies were buried, and she always had Samuel's back.

"You need to listen to this man," Mrs. Johnston said. "God will always guide you in the right direction. Lead with your heart, because that's where He resides."

"You a smart woman, Mary," Mr. Saddler said.

"Well, thank you kindly."

"I do trust and believe," Samuel said with assurance. "I know that change is good and when you're trying to change things for the better, it will all work out."

Mrs. Johnston smiled. "That's right. And this is going to be one of the best school years yet. Enrollment is at capacity, test scores are up, students and parents are happy, and new volunteers are coming in by the droves."

Samuel was about to agree, but he temporarily lost his train of thought when his eyes caught sight of a woman standing at the registration table. She was medium height and slender, with luscious curves in all the right places. Her erect posture reminded him of a dancer, down to the way she stood with one leg slightly in front of the other, as if she were striking a pose. Her jeans hugged her tight, but not in an obtrusive way, and the strappy red heels she wore gave her a sexy look that pulled him in. She was completing the volunteer form, and Samuel immediately wondered who she was. He knew most of the parent volunteers, but he'd never seen this beautiful woman before.

"I see someone has your attention," Mrs. Johnston said, following the trail of Samuel's eyes.

Samuel laughed nervously, embarrassed that he'd been caught ogling a woman in public. "Well, um, uh," he stammered, trying to form his words. "I was trying to figure out who she is." He quickly averted his eyes from the woman. "I don't remember seeing her at any of our events last year. She must be new."

Samuel couldn't help but glance in the woman's direction again. Her smooth, nut-brown skin looked as though it was glistening and her smile lit up the entire area where she was standing. He watched as she politely handed the pen and clipboard back to the volunteer coordinator and smiled as they chatted. He wanted to walk over and inspect the information she'd provided on the form, and personally welcome her to Sandhill. But given the state of his nerves, he knew that probably wouldn't be a good idea.

Samuel felt a rush of heat engulf his body. He couldn't remember ever having this kind of reaction to a woman on first sight, not even when he'd met Vivana. Then a thought came to him: *I wonder if she's married?* Almost immediately he wanted to kick himself for allowing the idea to enter his mind. Whether the beautiful woman was married or not didn't matter because, regardless of her status, he had a wife, and although his marriage was in serious trouble, and deep down he knew it was just a matter of time before it came to an end, he knew he must still act like a married man.

He looked in the woman's direction again and took a deep breath when he saw her walking straight toward him.

"Looks like you gonna find out 'zactly who she is," Mr. Saddler said, "'cause she comin' this way."

Samuel's nerves had initially been rattled, but now he was excited. This was the first time in a long time that he'd felt the kind of carnal desire that only a woman could elicit. He paid close attention as she walked toward them. He noticed that she carried her large black handbag in the crook of her arm, like the models in magazine ads. She looked hip and trendy, yet elegantly classic, and that turned him on even more. Her head was held high, her back was straight, her shoulders were squared, and her body language emanated a strength that was at once sexy and powerful.

"Hello," the beautiful woman said. "The volunteer coordinator said I should come over and introduce myself." She smiled brightly, letting her eyes land on Mrs. Johnston and then on to Mr. Saddler, before finally settling on Samuel. "My name is Geneva Mayfield, and I just signed up to volunteer with the morning reading program," she said, exposing white teeth that made her smile appear even more radiant.

She extended her delicate, well-manicured hand in the same order that she'd greeted them, first to Mrs. Johnston, then to Mr. Saddler, and again ending with Samuel. When her hand touched his, he noted the softness of her palm and the warmth it carried. He wondered what she did for a living.

"Nice to meet you, young lady," Mrs. Johnston said. "Thank you for volunteering. What grade will your child be starting this year?"

Geneva smiled as she shook her head. "I don't have children."

"Oh, please excuse my assumption," Mrs. Johnston said.

"That's quite all right, it's a normal question. I love children and I've wanted to volunteer for the longest time, but my busy work schedule has made it difficult. Then a few weeks ago I saw an ad in the newspaper for volunteers, so I decided to sign up, because if I keep putting it off I'll never do it. I'm always going to be busy, but the opportunity to volunteer might not always be here."

Mr. Saddler smiled. "Well, young lady, I need to correct you on two things. One, you won't always be so busy, least I hope not, 'cause er'body needs a break. And two, as long as Sandhill's doors is open, you gon' always have a opportunity to volunteer."

"That's right," Mrs. Johnston chimed in.

Samuel was silent. He wanted to coattail on what had just been said, but he couldn't find his voice. In less than ten minutes he was going to take the stage and speak to an auditorium full of people, but looking at the woman in front of him, he couldn't manage to form a single word. *What the hell is wrong with me?* he asked himself.

Geneva smiled. "In that case, I'm looking forward to a busy but great school year."

Samuel felt her enthusiasm and he knew he had to figure out something to say in response. "Yes, likewise. I mean, I am, too."

One would never suspect he'd won the National Spelling Bee his senior year in high school, or that he knew the definition of nearly every word in Webster's dictionary, because right now he couldn't string together a single word that contained more than two syllables. He knew he wasn't impressing Geneva, and he wondered what she must think of him. He wanted her to know that he was smart, and capable, and funny, and quite charming when he was his normal self.

The next few minutes passed with Mr. Saddler and Mrs. Johnston carrying on a lively conversation with Geneva while Samuel listened and interjected—again, no more than two syllables at a time—when he could.

Then suddenly something amazing happened. Samuel got up the nerve to look directly into Geneva's piercing eyes, and when he did, he saw attraction mirrored back at him. She gave him a bashful smile, which confirmed that he was right. Both Mr. Saddler and Mrs. Johnston excused themselves to go mingle with the crowd, leaving Samuel and Geneva standing together.

Samuel searched for something to say. "I'm glad you responded to the ad, Ms. Mayfield. We're always in need of good volunteers and we're honored you chose us."

She nodded and smiled. "Thank you, but the honor is mine. I feel blessed to be able to do something meaningful, and I'm looking forward to working with the children and teachers."

Samuel listened not only to the words that Geneva spoke but to the sincerity in her voice. Working as closely as he did with a very diverse range of people had made Samuel a good judge of character—not to mention the lesson in deception he'd come to learn through his wife— and he could see that Geneva was a genuinely sweet woman with a giving heart, which made him even more attracted to her. As they stood next to each other, he could feel a natural chemistry starting to develop between them.

"I admire what you do," Geneva said. "Educators, especially in administration, have an important but difficult job. The passion you have for what you do is commendable and I can tell you love it."

"You can . . . how?"

She smiled and glanced back at the volunteer table before aiming her eyes back on him. "I watched you while I was filling out my form, and you looked happy and excited."

The fact that she admitted she'd been watching him excited Samuel, and further confirmed what he'd read in her eyes. He knew it was a gamble to say what he was about to tell her, especially in the setting he was in, but everything about this moment told him to trust his instincts. He waited for a short pause in order to give his words more weight. "You're right, but I must confess that half of my reactions came from watching you, too."

She blushed and smiled with a sexy innocence that made her even more irresistible to him. Samuel couldn't believe that he was straight-up flirting with a volunteer, which he knew was inappropriate. But at the same time his gut told him that everything about this was right. Just then Mrs. Johnston walked up to them, breaking the mood.

"Dr. Owens, it's time for you to take the stage now."

Samuel nodded, then smiled at Geneva. "Please excuse me, I have to make my speech now." He cleared his throat. "I hope we get a chance to speak again before you leave."

Geneva smiled. "I'll make sure of it."

Later that night as Samuel lay in his king size bed all alone, he replayed the evening's events in his head. He'd been on a natural high after the success of the open house. Even though he didn't get a chance to speak to Geneva at length as he'd wanted to because of the rush of parents, volunteers, and teachers who took up his time after his speech, he was glad that she'd waved good-bye to him through the crowd before she left the building.

Geneva's beautiful smile had him floating on a cloud until he walked through his front door, but he became pissed as soon as he saw Vivana. She was sitting in the family room, tapping away on her laptop, sipping on a glass of wine.

"We have a serious problem," he said.

"And what's that?" She never bothered to look up from her screen.

He walked up to her and closed the top of her computer.

"What the hell are you doing?"

He could see that he'd startled her. Normally he'd let her go about her business of whatever she was doing, but he'd had enough. "I'm trying to talk to you, so I need your attention," he said with a hard edge in his voice. "We don't have a marriage anymore. We don't communicate, and I feel like what we had is gone. We're broken, Vivana."

Vivana rolled her eyes. "If this is about me not going to the open house . . ."

Samuel cut her off. "It's about everything. It's about how we've grown apart. It's about how we don't even speak a word to each other for days, and then when we do, it turns into an argument."

"Like now," she said sarcastically.

Samuel shook his head. "I'm not arguing with you, I'm trying to have a conversation, Vivana." He looked into her eyes the way he'd peered into Geneva's tonight, but as he focused in on his wife, what he saw reflected back at him was emptiness. He knew he was wasting his energy and his time trying to find or build anything, a love that wasn't there.

"What?" Vivana said with irritation. "Are you gonna just stand there and stare at me, or are you gonna talk?"

Samuel knew when to cut his losses, so he told Vivana good night and went upstairs to salvage what was left of the great evening he'd been having up until he'd come home. Once he was out of her presence, he was able to refocus his mind, and take pleasure in knowing that tonight's event had been the most highly attended, well organized open house he'd experienced since coming to Sandhill. Not only did everyone have a good time, the energy and spirit of the school was showcased in a clip on the late night news, which was set to rebroadcast tomorrow. But above all the accomplishments of the evening, the one thing that stood out to Samuel was the woman he'd met: Geneva Mayfield.

Geneva had captured his interest and managed to hold it, even during his presentation to the open house attendees. He'd found himself glancing in her direction and each time he did, her kind smile and nods of approval made him feel like he'd just been handed a winning lottery ticket. After he left the stage, she'd found him and let him know that his speech had inspired her. He wanted to tell her that she was equally inspiring, but he couldn't find the words.

Samuel reached over to his nightstand and cut off his light. He didn't mind that Vivana hadn't asked him how the open house went when he came home, and it didn't bother him that she was asleep on the couch downstairs, at this very moment, where she'd be spending the rest of the night. He wasn't concerned, because Geneva had taken his mind off his troubles and had replaced them with possibilities. He smiled at the thought.

Geneva was like a breath of fresh air, and he couldn't wait to see her when she came to volunteer at Sandhill this Monday.

Chapter 9

GENEVA

"Thank God it's Monday!" Geneva said with a smile.

Unlike most people who dreaded Mondays, it was Geneva's favorite day of the week. Monday was the universal day off in the salon world, and it was the one day she didn't have to worry about demanding clients, overbookings, shop gossip, or standing all day until her feet and legs hurt. Monday was her day to relax and do absolutely nothing if she so chose. But because Geneva was active and liked to keep herself busy, the one simple luxury she allowed herself was to sleep in until nine o'clock. Once she rose from bed, she split her time between cleaning up around the house, washing clothes, cooking and sampling new recipes, and running errands. After her many tasks were complete, she'd round out her day by getting lost in a good book until she fell asleep.

Reading had been her passion since she was a little girl, and today she was going to merge her love of books with her love of children by volunteering at Sandhill Elementary School.

She'd been floating on a cloud since the open house event last week, and she couldn't remember the last time she'd felt this happy. She was energized with the kind of inspiration and purpose that made her feel as if all the worries and problems she'd been going through over the last few months were behind her. Not only was volunteering at the school going to help the children, it was going to fuel her spirit.

"What dress should I wear?" she said to herself as she stood in front of her neatly organized closet. She looked to her right and her eyes landed on a brightly colored sundress draped on a black velvet hanger. "Canary yellow," she said with a smile as she ran her hand across the dress's soft fabric. The color matched her lively mood and the material had just enough stretch to give the garment a wow factor.

Geneva pulled the delicate sundress from the hanger, reached for a pair of sandals from her shoe rack, and then combed her eyes through her hanging jewelry organizer to select the perfect earrings and bracelet that would complete her outfit. As she admired her ensemble, she felt a small glint of guilt, knowing that the reason she wanted to look extra special today was because of another man. She'd been thinking about Samuel Owens since their intense conversation last week. They'd made a definite connection, and she hoped she would see him this morning when she read to the first-graders on their first day of school.

She walked back out to the bedroom and paused for a moment when she saw that the bed was empty. The sound of water running in the master bathroom, music blasting on the radio, and Johnny's voice accompanying the beat in perfect harmony, made her roll her eyes. It was a small miracle that he was home at all. Most of the time he'd rise early and be out of the house before Geneva opened her eyes, relegating their time spent together to the few moments she'd see him before she drifted off to sleep after he came in late at night or the wee hours of the morning.

Johnny had apparently awoken while she was standing in her closet, and hadn't even bothered to say good morning or let her know that he was up. He'd just rolled out of bed and gone straight to the shower, no doubt to wash off the scent of whatever he'd gotten into last night when he came dragging into the house shortly after midnight.

Normally, Geneva would have been upset and hurt by her husband's inconsiderate, low-down behavior, which had been going on for months. But ever since last week her attitude had changed, and surprisingly, she was beginning to care less and less about his misdeeds or on whose pillow he laid his head.

Last week when he'd stayed out all night, she'd been so furious the next morning that she couldn't speak to him. But later that evening, after she'd come home from Sandhill's open house, her entire outlook on things had changed. Samuel Owens had spoken with her in a way that made her feel valued. He'd looked into her eyes when they talked, and she felt a comfort and attraction that gave her goose bumps. The fact that she'd flirted with him had surprised her, but then again, he'd flirted with her, too, and it felt so natural that she welcomed it. When he'd stood in front of the auditorium full of people to deliver his speech, he'd glanced at her every so often, making her feel as though she was the only person in the room. She was mesmerized as he talked about setting goals, pursuing dreams, helping others, and being a good steward of the community. She'd been so beaten down by Johnny's disrespect and neglect over the years that she'd forgotten what it was like to feel empowered, stimulated, and encouraged by a man.

"What's that smile for?" Johnny said, startling Geneva from her thoughts.

He was standing in the•bathroom doorway wearing a mischievous smile that accompanied a rock-hard erection. Droplets of water still clung to his sculpted, naked body as he walked toward her. "I know how I can make that smile even wider," he said, planting himself in front of her.

There was a time, only several days ago, in fact, that Johnny's words and actions would have made Geneva tingle with excitement. But looking at her handsome husband, standing before her in all his rugged, naturally sexy, tantalizing glory, she didn't feel anything at all, not even a tiny spark. The only urge that rose inside her at the moment was the overwhelming need for him to move out of her way so she could go to the bathroom, take a shower, and get dressed so she could leave for Sandhill.

"Can you move, please," Geneva said, looking past her husband, focusing her eyes on the bathroom door.

Johnny smiled and tried to sidle next to her. "What's wrong, baby? Don't you want none'a this?"

She wanted to say no, but instead she decided to be diplomatic. "I have to take a shower and get dressed."

"What I have in mind doesn't require showering, and you definitely won't need any clothes," he said in his deep voice that sounded as though he was still singing. "Come on." He tugged at her nightgown. "You know you want this."

"Stop playing around, Johnny. I have things to do."

He gave her an incredulous look. "What could be more important than making love to me?"

"Believe it or not, my world revolves around more than just you."

Johnny stepped back. "This is the kind of bullshit you do that drives me crazy. First you complain about me not coming home at a certain hour that you think I should, and then you nag and whine that I don't show you any attention. But when I'm here, looking into your eyes, ready to be with you and telling you that I want you, you don't want to be with me."

Geneva couldn't believe his nerve and enormous ego. "You didn't say you wanted to be with me, you said, 'Don't you want none'a this.'"

"It's the same damn thing, Geneva."

If she weren't so irritated, his self-indulged attitude would have been funny. But she was more than irritated, she was pissed. He'd changed her mood from sunny to overcast in a matter of minutes. She was none too pleased, and she was ready to let him have it. She looked at him with steely eyes as she delivered her words. "You have some nerve acting like you're a dutiful husband whose nagging wife won't cut him a break. I complain about you never being at home and not showing me any attention because that's our reality. You stay out in the streets seven days a week, and now because you decided to come home, and late, I might add, I'm supposed to be impressed? Sorry, but I'm no longer operating on your time."

"I've been making an effort lately, but you don't give me credit."

"Ha! Who do you think you're fooling? You drug in here and slipped under the covers last night a few minutes shy of midnight after being out with Lord only knows who. Then you hurried out of bed this morning and took a shower so you could wash off whoever you were with. And now you expect me to be grateful that you want to screw me after the fact? Please! If there's anything I need to do, it's change these sheets," Geneva said as she glanced at the bed.

"I don't have to listen to this bullshit," Johnny boldly said. He walked over to his chest of drawers and removed a pair of boxer briefs and a t-shirt. He pulled them on as he spoke. "I might as well get dressed and get out of here, too."

Geneva was glad that he'd moved out of her way. She knew he was expecting her to apologize and beg for his understanding, but that wasn't going to happen today.

She walked past him without saying another word and headed straight to the bathroom. She looked at the wet towel that Johnny had left on the floor. "Typical." She rolled her eyes and sucked her teeth at the sight. Normally, she would have picked up behind him and put his things in the hamper, but instead she simply kicked his towel to the side and turned on the hot water.

Geneva stood under the large shower head and took deep breaths to calm herself as the water cascaded down her body, loosening her tense muscles, making her feel more relaxed. *I can't and I won't let him ruin my day,* she repeated to herself. By the time she toweled off, she felt brand new again. She looked at herself in the wide mirror above the vanity and smiled. "I'm going to make this a great day, no matter what," she said with confidence.

She walked back into the bedroom and was startled to see that

Johnny was still seated on the edge of the bed, clad only in his t-shirt and boxers. Although he didn't say a word, the look on his face let her know exactly what was on his mind. His eyes and the tilt of his head expressed a mixture of anger and confusion. Her dismissal of him was a foreign situation, and Geneva knew that if it was slightly surprising to her, it had to be downright unbelievable to him.

"Geneva, I don't know what's gotten into you," Johnny said with frustration, "but we need to talk."

She wanted to tell him that she'd been begging him to talk to her for months, and she wanted to scream in his face and let him know that she was fed up with his treatment and lack of respect for her and their marriage. But doing those things would put her back in the place she'd been before she stepped into the shower and cleaned away her worries, and right now she had no intention of revisiting those feelings. She looked at Johnny and shook her head. "I don't feel like talking to you right now." She walked over to her dresser, pulled out her underclothes, and proceeded to get dressed.

"Hold up. How you gonna just tell me that you don't want to talk. I'm your husband."

"I didn't say that I didn't want to talk. I said I didn't want to talk to you. There's a difference."

Johnny stood up and gave her a hard look. "Why you trippin', Geneva?"

She didn't say a word. She knew he was stunned, but she also knew that he was purposely trying to get under her skin. She decided to do what he'd done to her so many times she couldn't count. She ignored him. She walked over to her side of the bed and slipped her beautiful yellow dress over her head. She walked over to the full-length mirror that sat in the corner and admired how the material of her dress graced her soft curves as though she'd been born in it.

Geneva could see that Johnny was watching her closely, and the more he stared her up and down, the more perplexed he became. But she could honestly say that she couldn't care less. She pushed her gold hoop earrings into her lobes, slid her gold bangle bracelet over her wrist, and slipped her strappy sandals on her feet. She didn't even look behind her or tell Johnny goodbye when she walked out of the room and headed out the front door.

Geneva smiled to herself as she steered her car into the Grove Park shopping center to get a mint–chocolate chip Frappuccino from Starbucks before heading to Sandhill. She felt nervous, excited, and a little apprehensive all at once. Here she was, a married woman, rushing out of her house, dressed to impress another man.

"I should be ashamed of myself," she whispered as she pulled up to the drive-through window at Starbucks. She couldn't believe how she was acting, and she imagined this was the kind of feeling Johnny had when he left the house to meet up with whomever he was seeing on the side. But she knew there were a few differences between her behavior and that of her husband. She felt a little guilty, and he, no doubt, didn't. And unlike him, she had no plans to act out the fantasies she'd conjured in her mind.

She was pulled from her thoughts by the call coming in through her car's Bluetooth system. She smiled when she saw it was Donetta. "Hey, girl, what're you up to this morning?" she asked.

"Chillin' on my sofa, enjoying a cup of English breakfast tea with my blueberry scone."

Geneva shook her head and laughed. For Donetta to be as loud, unruly, and often brazen as she was, she believed in refined luxury and made sure she bathed herself in that lifestyle. Most of her paycheck was spent on decorating her beautiful home and pampering herself with luxuries.

"It's a thousand degrees outside and you're drinking hot tea?" Geneva teased.

"Honey, it's never too hot to drink tea, and this shit right here, it's the bomb."

"I'm sure it is."

"And what're you up to, sounding all giddy?"

"I just got my Frappuccino and I'm headed to Sandhill to read to the kids. This is my first volunteer day. I'm so excited."

"*Uhhhh-huhhhh.* I bet you are."

"Why do you say it like that?"

"You know why."

Geneva knew exactly what her friend was talking about, but she wasn't going to say a word.

"I don't know what's got you more excited, the children or that principal."

"Oh, stop it."

"You stop it. You know I'm right. You had a twinkle in your eye when you talked about that man last week. Go 'head and admit that you're interested in him."

"I'll admit that I do find him attractive. But being interested in someone and being attracted to them is two different things."

"Well, at least you admitted that you're attracted to him. That's a start. And there ain't nothing wrong with that, honey."

"Exactly. It's not like I crossed any lines."

"Yet!" Donetta said with a giggle.

"Didn't I tell you to stop."

"Why? This is fun. And it's time you had some fun in your life. That bastard you're married to has practically sucked all the joy out of you. I'm just glad to see you excited about something."

"Yes, I'm excited, and helping the kids is going to help me. It's something I've wanted to do for years and now I finally can."

"What are you wearing?" Donetta asked.

"A sundress and sandals."

"Which one?" Donetta was a fashionista and had borrowed so many of Geneva's blouses that she knew the contents of Geneva's closet as if it were her own. "My yellow one," Geneva replied.

"*Huuunnnneeeee,*" Donetta squealed. "That dress is fierce. It's the right combination of modern class and sexy sass, and it looks gorgeous on you! You gonna have that principal reciting his ABCs and counting to a hundred!"

Geneva laughed. "I can't fool with you today!"

"I'm just sayin', I ain't mad atcha'. Work it out and do your thang."

"I told you, it's not even like that," Geneva said. "I'm going to meet with the home room teacher I'm assigned to, read to the kids, and then go home and enjoy the rest of my day. If I happen to see Mr. Owens, that'll be great, but if I don't . . ."

"Oh, but you will," Donetta said with a chuckle. "And when you do, don't hold back."

Geneva shook her head. "I just pulled into the school parking lot, I've got to go."

"Have fun and do everything I would do . . . and then some."

All Geneva could do was smile as she hung up the phone. She put her car in park, turned off the engine, and drank the last of her Frappuccino. "I needed that boost," she said, placing the empty cup in her console. She ran her hand across the soft fabric of her dress and once again admired its vibrant color. "What am I doing?" She looked at the large brick building in front of her and inhaled a deep, cleansing breath as she thought about the children inside and the real reason she'd decided to wear the beautiful sundress she saved for special occasions. The truth was that she wanted to look good for Dr. Samuel Owens. She wanted to impress him. And deep down, she was scared of what that meant.

As Geneva thought about Samuel Owens, she suddenly began to have second thoughts about Sandhill. "This is how trouble gets started. I can't do this." She turned the key in the ignition and started the engine. "I'll have to find another school where I can volunteer." Just as she was about to drive away, she saw Samuel walk outside the building. He stood in front of the entrance talking to a well-dressed man. She watched him closely, noticing his friendly smile and the self-assured body language that had drawn her to him last week. Before she knew it, she was smiling, as if it was she with whom he was having a conversation. She continued to watch him as he and the man shook hands before Samuel turned and walked back into the building.

"I don't know if what I'm about to do is right, but I know what I feel is real, and I can't deny it," she whispered. Geneva turned off the engine again, opened her door, put one foot in front of the other, and walked toward new possibilities.

Chapter 10

JOHNNY

Johnny sat motionless on the edge of his bed trying to figure out what the hell was going on with his wife. He knew that Geneva was upset with him, and that she was still carrying a salty attitude from last week when he'd stayed out all night. But he thought the way she'd treated him this morning was uncaring, uncalled for, and completely out of character from the woman whom he knew his wife to be.

Johnny rubbed his chin and fell back onto the soft comforter on the bed. He looked up at the ceiling, closed his eyes, and then let out a deep breath filled with frustration. "Here I am trying to do the right thing by coming home, and she's still giving me attitude," he said as he thought about Geneva. "I can't win with that woman."

Over the weekend Geneva had avoided him, keeping her distance wide and her words short. She normally bugged him about attending Emmanuel AME Church with her every Sunday, but yesterday she'd dressed and was out the door without saying one word to him. He didn't mind her silent treatment at first because it had been better than hearing her nag and complain, as she usually did. But when the afternoon rolled around and there was no home-cooked after-church meal on the table, Johnny's jaws became tight and his stomach longed to be fed. Geneva had been so mad a few nights ago that she'd thrown away the leftovers from the dinner she'd made for him, and she hadn't cooked a thing since.

Johnny knew he needed to do something to get Geneva back in line before things got out of hand, so last night he cut his date short with Vivana so he could get home at a decent hour. In addition to trying to work his way back into Geneva's good graces, he knew that spending less time with Vivana would help him gradually end their affair without drama.

Last night was the first time he'd seen Vivana since they'd over-slept at the hotel last week. She'd been texting and emailing like a mad woman, bugging the shit out of him with demands about when they were going to hook up again. She'd gotten on his nerves worse than his wife, but he knew he had to play it cool with her. He'd come to see a new side of Vivana that she'd never shown him, and he didn't like it. He couldn't risk her hijacking his marriage, as Bernard had said she might.

Last night he'd agreed to meet Vivana at a luxury hotel in down-town Birmingham, just a fifteen-minute drive away. Johnny was glad the days were getting shorter, and that nighttime was coming faster, which would give him an excuse to leave early. On his drive to meet her, Johnny had already started developing his exit strategy. They would order room service, watch an in-room movie, and by that time Bernard would call, a little after nine p.m., as Johnny had asked him to do. He planned to tell Vivana that the call was about an emergency at one of the properties he managed, and that would be his ticket out.

Things would have worked out perfectly had Bernard remem-bered to call him. His friend had been too wrapped up in a romantic dinner with Candace, leaving Johnny to make up a flimsy excuse on his own. After fussing with Vivana for two solid hours, he'd finally left the hotel at eleven thirty p.m., which was just enough time to make it back home before midnight.

"If I'd known Geneva was gonna act like this I would've gotten laid last night instead of rushing back here for some bullshit," Johnny said in a huff. Slowly, he rose from the bed and walked to his closet.

He carefully selected a tan linen suit, crisp white shirt, and a money-green tie. After he finished dressing, he looked at himself in the full-length mirror and smiled, knowing he looked good. Then he thought about Geneva again. She'd stood in front of the same mirror less than ten minutes ago, and he had to admit that she looked good, too. Damn good, in fact. Her yellow dress complemented her curves and made her brown skin glow.

There had been a time when Geneva used to turn him on at the mere thought of her. But those days were well behind them. She'd transformed overnight from the hot girlfriend that he couldn't keep his hands off of into a mundane housewife who no longer excited him. Their sex life had become as routine as paying bills, and because Geneva wanted children right now instead of waiting a few years like he wanted to, sex with her had become pressure, not pleasure.

Johnny longed for the thrill of the chase. That was why he didn't feel as guilty about the adulterated lust and hot sex he found in other women whose standards in bed were more relaxed than his wife's. That was one of the reasons Vivana had been able to ensnare him in her web. But that relationship had run its course and now he was ready to move on to other things.

Now, as Johnny slipped on his dress shoes to head out the door, he put his wife and his mistress out of his mind so he could begin his day.

An hour later, Johnny found himself sitting in the Whole Bean Café, waiting to have a late morning meeting with a new client, who had been referred to him by Mark and Marjorie Thomas, whom he'd helped find their ultimate dream house. They'd been so pleased with his top-shelf service that they'd sent him a bottle of champagne as a thank-you, and had been referring as many friends his way as they could.

Johnny looked at his watch and sighed. "I can't stand it when people waste my time. This woman was supposed to be here twenty minutes ago," he grumbled. Had it not been for the fact that the woman was loaded with money and connections, and came highly referred, Johnny would have left the café by now. He was a stickler for time because every second equaled dollars, and the potential to make more money. Johnny looked at his watch and sighed again. "I don't care if she's the Queen of England, she has five more minutes and then I'm outa here," he said as he scrolled through the calendar on his phone.

"Hello, you must be Johnny Mayfield."

Johnny looked up when he heard his name and felt a surge of energy. The voice, which carried a distinctly northern accent, belonged to none other than Councilwoman Charlene Harris. Johnny took notice that she was much more attractive in person, than in the photos he'd seen in the local paper from time to time. She was a stylishly well-dressed woman, well built, who smelled of expensive perfume. She wore success and confidence as comfortably as she did the designer shoes on her feet. He was instantly attracted to her.

Councilwoman Harris extended her hand. "Mr. Mayfield, please forgive me for being late. My office assistant didn't synchronize my calendar."

Right now, Johnny wouldn't have cared if she'd been an hour late. The pleasure that she was giving his eyes made up for her tardiness. He rose from his seat and took her hand in his, giving her a gentle shake. Another surge of energy ran through him when she returned his gentle shake with a firm grip. "That's no problem, Councilwoman Harris," he said with a smile.

She glanced down at his ring finger, saw that it was bare, and smiled back seductively. "Please, call me Charlene."

He returned her smile. "Only if you call me Johnny." Five minutes into their conversation Johnny knew he could have Charlene Harris if he wanted her, and he wanted her in the worst kind of way. With a troubled marriage at home and an overbearing mistress whom he was trying to distance himself from, the esteemed councilwoman was exactly what he needed right now.

"Okay, Johnny," Charlene said with a flirtatious smile on her face and in her voice. "I'll get right down to business."

"Please do."

She smiled even wider as she uncrossed her legs. "I'm only interested in high-end properties. Money isn't a concern because I have plenty of it, but I'm price-conscious just the same, and I want to stretch my money as far as it will go. I've gone over some of the comps in the area I'm looking in, and it appears that inventory is high, which will work to my advantage."

Johnny nodded. "A smart approach. Beauty and brains look good on you, Charlene," he said slyly. "And I'd expect nothing less from a woman of your obvious success." He could tell that she was flattered because she actually blushed.

She took a small sip of her coffee and cleared her throat. "My children are all grown, living in different states, and since it's just going to be me at home I'd like to downsize."

Johnny thought Charlene was married, but apparently not, given what she'd just said. This information made him even more interested in her.

"I want the same craftsmanship and details that I enjoy in my current home," Charlene continued, "but on a smaller and more manageable scale. I'm a busy woman on a tight schedule, and I'm not a fan of wasting time, which equals money, so I'd like to find something within the next thirty days."

"That's doable. Now that I know what you're looking for I'll run my comps and I'll have a few properties that we can take a look at as early as tomorrow if your schedule will allow."

She nodded. "Sounds good. Mark and Marjorie told me that you did a fantastic job helping them find their dream home, and I'm sure you'll deliver great results for me as well. With any luck I'll be closing on my new home next month."

Johnny leaned forward and lowered his voice to a sexy whisper. "I like your approach, and I can definitely make that happen . . . along with anything else you might desire."

When he saw a faint smile slide across her perfectly lined lips, he knew he'd read her like a book, and he was a hundred percent sure that he could get her in bed before the sun went down today. He couldn't believe his great luck! This was perfect, because he knew that if they started seeing each other he wouldn't have to deal with the problems from her that he was experiencing with Vivana. Charlene was older, mature, and direct. She was no nonsense, no muss, no fuss, and she wouldn't demand his time because she was busy handling her business. He could tell by the look in her eyes that she was a woman on a mission, and if there was one thing that Johnny loved, it was the challenge and the thrill of conquering a new conquest.

Johnny enjoyed the way Charlene not so accidentally allowed her leg to touch his under the table, and when she drank the froth from her cappuccino, she licked her lips with her tongue in a motion that let him know she was ready and willing to lick other things, too. But for the sake of business he went through the motions. He talked with her long enough to assess her needs in terms of square footage and amenities, and to have her sign a contract retaining his services.

A half hour later, Johnny was breathing heavily on top of his new client as he thrust in and out of her, enjoying himself more than he'd imagined he would. For a woman her age, Charlene's body was still in excellent shape, and she knew exactly what to do with it to make him feel good. The queen-size bed they were lying on, in one of the vacant units of a small condo building he managed for one of his wealthy clients, had served Johnny well over the years for his midday escapades.

He didn't know if it was Charlene's age and life experience that made her so good, or if it was the fact that she was one of the most stylish, sophisticated, and accomplished women he'd ever been with, but what he did know was that this wouldn't be their last rendezvous. Johnny felt like he'd hit the jackpot. Not only was Councilwoman Harris someone he could do business with, she was someone who could give him immense physical pleasure. He was attracted to her even more because she'd made it clear that she wasn't looking for anything outside of finding a house and an occasional fuck when she needed it. She'd even come prepared with her own condoms. "I'd rather have them and not need them than need them and not have them," she'd said when she removed them from her handbag.

Johnny wanted to take a quick nap to recharge his battery, but he

needed to get back to the office to go over paperwork for two clos-
ings that would take place tomorrow. As they slipped their clothes
back on, smiling at each other from the pleasure they'd both received,
Johnny made up his mind that he was going to continue to hook up
with Charlene every opportunity he could. She was coming at the
perfect time to fill the void once he got rid of Vivana.

Chapter 11

VIVANA

Vivana was so mad she couldn't see straight. She fought to control her anger as she sat in her car, parked across the street from the condo building that Johnny managed for one of his clients. "I can't believe that son of a bitch is cheating on me!" she said through clenched teeth.

"I need to find out who that bitch is," she said. Vivana had taken one look at the woman's clothes, accessories, and the sophisticated way she carried herself, and knew that she was someone of importance. Jealousy surged through her veins, enraging her even more.

Vivana wondered how long Johnny had been seeing the woman. She knew it couldn't have been too long because his behavior had changed only recently. It was clear that the woman was the corporate type, given the stylish business suit she wore and the expensive, high-end handbag that was draped on her arm. Vivana even wondered if the woman was from the area at all because she seemed much too cosmopolitan for Amber. As questions swirled in her head, Vivana knew one thing for sure: even though the woman looked good, she had some age on her.

Vivana glanced at her reflection in the rearview mirror, comparing her looks to the mysterious woman Johnny was with. "I look damn good," she said, appraising her profile. She felt she was holding up well for a woman in her mid-thirties, and, in fact, she knew she looked younger than she was. Her eyes sparkled, her skin was smooth, and her lips were the perfect shape and size for creating what makeup artists called a luscious pout. "What the hell does he want with that old bag when he's got all this?" Vivana huffed.

The more she thought about Johnny cheating on her, the more upset she got. "That old bitch is the reason he's been avoiding me since last week," Vivana fumed. "He's been plotting to see her this whole time!"

Vivana had been tracking Johnny's movements ever since last week when she'd asked him if she could come by his office and he'd said no. Her womanly instincts told her that he had something to hide. She was determined to find out what he was up to, and was prepared to do what was necessary to uncover the truth.

Each morning, rather than sleeping in late as she normally did, she rose early so she could park her car in the vicinity of his office building, well before he arrived, then she'd keep a close watch all day on his comings and goings.

But this morning she was running late, thanks to her annoying husband. He'd kept her up well past midnight because he'd wanted to talk about his plans for Sandhill. When she told him she didn't want to hear his long, boring, drawn-out ramblings about the school, Samuel became uncharacteristically argumentative and even aggressive. He told her that he wasn't happy, and that he refused to continue living that way.

"The love that used to be there is gone," he'd said. "I've tried to make this marriage work, but I can't do it by myself. And honestly, at this point, nothing less than counseling is going to help us, or persuade me to stay."

Vivana shook her head. "You want to waste good money to go and talk to someone about our problems, who probably has problems of their own? That's just foolish."

"This is hopeless. We have a real disconnect going on here. If it wasn't for the fact that I've told people I'm married, no one would know. You're never by my side. We never go out together or spend time talking like a husband and wife should. We don't even sleep in the same bed anymore."

Vivana rolled her eyes and huffed. "First you wanted to talk about the school, and now you want to talk about our marriage. I think you just want to argue, because that's what we do best. I'm tired, it's late, and I have a busy day tomorrow. I'm going to bed."

Vivana knew that Samuel was right. Their marriage was on life support, but she needed to hold things together until she was able to get Johnny away from his wife, and whatever was currently distracting him so she could have him all to herself.

"I'm tired, too," Samuel said, "and I'm not going to continue on like this. I can't do this anymore."

Vivana knew she needed to keep her cool. "What are you saying?"

"Exactly what you think I'm saying." He'd delivered his words and then marched upstairs to their master bedroom and slammed the door.

A small wave of panic rose up inside her. She didn't want their marriage to end until she was ready, but it looked as though Samuel had other plans in mind. She needed the financial stability he provided and the comfort of a nice home. Vivana knew she had to start treading lightly if she wanted to keep Samuel in place long enough to make sure she broke up Johnny's marriage. Once she accomplished that goal she didn't give a damn about what Samuel thought or wanted.

She'd stayed up a good part of the night worrying about how she was going to hold things together, and she'd been so tired she overslept. Little did she know that arguing with Samuel and staying up late turned out to be a blessing in disguise. She'd been so sleepy this morning that she needed coffee, so she drove straight to the Whole Bean Café instead of to Johnny's office. When she parked her car across the street from the coffee shop, she saw none other than the man of the hour strolling inside.

As soon as she saw Johnny enter the shop she got excited. She thought about how nice it was going to be to finally do something with him as simple as share a cup of morning coffee. But in that same instant, something inside her cautioned her not to make a move. For once, she listened to the little voice in her head and stayed in her car, securely fastened in her seatbelt.

She watched Johnny through the coffee shop's large glass window, noting how he kept looking at his watch, as if he was expecting someone. Her antennae went up when she saw an attractive, well-dressed woman approach him. Her eyes zeroed in on them as Johnny talked and laughed with the woman. At first glance one would have thought the two were old friends, given the way they interacted with each other. But Vivana knew better because she could read the expression written on both their faces.

She watched them the entire time they were inside, right up until they left the café, still smiling and laughing. Johnny walked the mysterious woman to her car, opened her door, and then pointed to where he was parked on the same side of the street. Once he got into his truck, the attractive woman pulled out right behind him, following every turn he made. Vivana was hot on their trail, driving at a safe distance so she wouldn't be detected. "That bastard is up to no good!" she screamed from behind the wheel.

Vivana was crushed when Johnny's truck reached the apartment building where she and he had met up for their first tryst five months ago. She wanted so badly to punch something, but that would serve no purpose. She knew she had to use her head, stay calm, and figure out her next move.

There had been many things in the history of Vivana's turbulent love life that had hurt, dismayed, angered, and disappointed her over the years. From falling in love with numerous men whom she eventually ended up despising, to marrying a good man whom she had no feelings for, Vivana had been through trying relationships. But the emotions she now felt were so heated and intense that she was having a hard time controlling her anger. "I knew his ass was up to something," she said in a low, venomous roar. "I knew it!"

Ever since Johnny had blown her off last week, Vivana had been anxious, pissed off, and worried about what was going on with him. She'd initially thought he might be having second thoughts about his marriage, given that he'd remained silent when she hinted about his sleeping arrangements at home. That, coupled with the fact that he didn't want to upset his wife by staying out all night, had made Vivana start to wonder if Johnny was beginning to lose interest in her. That was something she couldn't bear.

Although Johnny had never told her that he planned to leave Geneva, Vivana hoped it was just a matter of time before he did. But now that he was acting so strangely, that meant one of two things: either he wanted to give his marriage another try, or he'd found another woman. She had decided that the only way to calm her fears was to start tracking his moves to see what he was doing, and with whom he was doing it.

No man had ever affected Vivana the way Johnny Mayfield did. Even though he had some annoying flaws, she still craved him like a drug. He was conceited, ego-driven, selfish, and not altogether honest, as was evident by the very existence of their relationship. But she couldn't hold him to task for those foibles because she shared some of the same traits, and that's why she knew they were meant to be together.

But sitting in her car—knowing that Johnny was across the street, in a vacant condo that only contained a bed and a table, screwing another woman whom he'd obviously arranged to meet—was making her more furious by the minute. "He won't even be seen with me during the day, let alone in public," she shouted, "but he has the nerve to meet that old heifer in broad open daylight, at a coffee shop. This shit is wrong on so many levels!"

Vivana couldn't take it any longer and she refused to be wronged or cheated on ever again. She unbuckled her seatbelt, removed her chandelier earrings, which dangled at her lobes, and her bracelets from her wrist. She rummaged through her leather bag in search of a scrunchie, then gathered her long weave into a tight ponytail, making sure to tuck in any loose strands that might make it easy to latch on to.

Before she knew it, Vivana was standing inside the nicely decorated entrance of the building. She was prepared to start walking down the small hallway and knock on every door she saw, in her search for Johnny and his new side piece. But she didn't have to take another step. She watched as the two came walking out of a door to her right. They were no longer talking and laughing as they'd done earlier at the café, but what they were doing now was much worse. Their bodies were in sync as they stood beside each other. They both sported the satisfied look of lovers who'd just experienced ecstasy.

By the time Vivana walked up to them in the middle of the hall, it was too late.

"Vivana?" Johnny said with surprise. "What the—"

He wasn't able to get out the rest because her right hook knocked his head to the side and left his jaw slack. The attractive woman knew what was coming next so she instinctively turned and started to run. But she wasn't quick enough to match Vivana's speed. Vivana snatched the woman by her arm and wrestled her down to the hard cement floor.

"Urrggghhh," the woman screamed as her body made contact with the hard floor beneath her. Vivana drew back her fist and was ready to give her a helping of what she'd just served Johnny, but the force of her would-be blow was stunted by Johnny's large hand. He grabbed her by her wrist so hard that his grip caused a mark on her skin.

"Stop it right now!" he shouted as he restrained Vivana. "What the hell's wrong with you!"

The woman scrambled to her feet, struggling to pull her tailored skirt down her legs. Her eyes widened with astonishment and she trembled with fear. "If you put your hands on me again I'm going to call the police!"

"Not if I kill your old ass first!" Vivana shot back as she lunged forward. She tried her best to hit the woman, but Johnny's hold was too strong.

"This is insane. What the hell are you trying to get me involved in!" the woman yelled, glaring at Johnny as if she, too, [...] sault him.

Vivana could see Johnny's eyes widen at the site of his new [...] face covered in confusion. The woman had the bad luck of not [...] choosing to fuck the wrong man, she'd fucked with the wrong woman [...] man.

Vivana ignored the woman's obvious distress because right now her attention was focused on Johnny. "You low-down, dirty, sneaky, deceitful, lying, no-good, son of a mutha fuckin' bitch!" she rattled off, so mad she wanted to hit him again. "You've been blowing me off so you could hook up with some other bitch, and an old one at that!"

Johnny glared at her. "You better calm your ass down right now."

"Or what?" she said boldly. "What're you gonna do, call the police like that old bitch just threatened to do?" Vivana's hands were on her hips, a direct indication that she was about to show out. "You know as well as I do that you don't want them out here because a police report will only mean more trouble for you if your little wifey gets wind of it."

"She's not your wife?!" the attractive woman said, looking startled as her eyes shifted from Johnny to Vivana.

Vivana smirked. "No, I'm not his wife, bitch. I'm his woman!"

"*Nooo,* you're crazy!" the woman said, adjusting her skirt again. She reached down, grabbed her expensive handbag, which had been thrown to the floor, and gave Johnny an angry stare that could have sliced him in half. "I feel sorry for your wife," she said with venom, before glancing over at Vivana with a look of pity on her face, "and I feel sorry for you, too, you poor, stupid woman." She turned and hurried as fast as her legs would carry her out the front door of the building.

Vivana and Johnny looked on as the woman disappeared from sight. Vivana was madder than ever, and she wasn't going to hold back. "That bitch did have a point," she growled. "You screwed Geneva over, and now you're screwing me over."

"Leave my wife out of this!" Johnny spat out, looking as though he could hurt her.

ace. "You better not even think about
[could have you up on charges?! You

'm not afraid of shit. I haven't put my
ave, and you better be glad that this is a
it it's during business hours and people
of these tenants would've called the cops
ead as he delivered his next words in a
slow hiss. "You'd be the one they'd lock up for assault!"

"I don't give a shit about what any of these people might try to do, or the police, for that matter," Vivana said. "They haven't walked in my shoes and none of them know the kind of hell you've put me through over the last few days."

"What're you talking about?"

"You've been avoiding me!" she shouted. "I thought you might be trying to get back with your wife. But *noooo*, your cheating ass is trying to get you some more pussy on the side. You're a bitch-ass mutha fucka."

Johnny took a deep breath. "You need to calm the fuck down 'cause if you say one more word, I swear to you . . ."

"What?" Vivana yelled, standing so close to his face she was breathing on him. "What're you gonna do except threaten me?"

"I'm walking away from this bullshit." Johnny adjusted his tie and tried to straighten out his clothes. "Now I know without a doubt that I'm making the right decision. Your ass is crazy, and I don't need this bullshit and drama in my life. You and I . . . we're done." He turned to walk away.

His words made Vivana's heart race faster than it already was. He was breaking up with her, and although she was mad enough to kill him, she also didn't want to be without him. "Why did you do this to me, Johnny?" she asked.

Johnny began to walk away as if he hadn't heard a word she'd said, and that only made Vivana feel even more desperate. "I always gave you exactly what you wanted and needed. I pleased you in every way I could. And I made sure that whenever we were together I gave you my undivided attention. You had it all, so why did you have to go out and screw another woman?"

Johnny turned around and faced her. "I wasn't screwing that woman. She was a client. We were here conducting business."

"Business my ass! You two were in there fucking."

Johnny paused for a minute and scratched his head. "How did you get here anyway? Have you been following me?"

Vivana avoided his question. "How could you do this to me?"

"How could *you* fuckin' do this to *me!*" Johnny spat back. "I came here to show a client a potential rental unit, and here you come from out of nowhere, acting like a damn crazy woman. Man, this shit is for the birds. I'm out."

Johnny walked out the door with Vivana fast behind him. Once they reached outside, she noticed him surveying the surroundings, probably checking to see if the woman he'd said was his client was anywhere in sight. There was no sign of her, and he looked relieved, but Vivana didn't care.

"I don't ever want to see you again," Johnny said as he walked toward his truck. He stopped and faced her. "Forget that you know my name and lose my number."

Vivana felt as though the wind had been knocked out of her, and even though they were standing outside in the open, she felt closed in as she fought for air to breathe. "I can't lose you," she sobbed. "I can't."

Johnny didn't say a word. He continued to walk until he reached his driver's side door.

"Johnny, please!" Vivana moaned as if she'd been struck by a sharp object.

"Calm down," he hissed in a low voice, looking from his left to his right. "You're gonna cause a scene."

"Just listen to me, please."

"Stop it. It's over."

"You were avoiding me, baby, and I didn't know what was going on. I went to the Whole Bean Café to get some coffee, and when I saw you come out with that woman, I lost it."

Johnny shook his head. "Did it ever occur to you that she was a client? That I was conducting business with her?"

Vivana searched his eyes, and felt lost in the hypnotizing seduction of their brownness. He sounded so sincere, as if he was wounded by her accusations. Her mind raced trying to determine what was real and what wasn't. Maybe it was only business like he'd said. "You two were coming out of that vacant unit, Johnny. There's only a bed and a table in there," she said. "It's where we first hooked up, so why would you take her there?"

"Operative word is vacant, Vivana. Vacant! That unit has been sitting empty for months and I've been trying to rent it for my client. I got the opportunity to show the place and I took it. This is business."

"Why were you two in there for so long?" she asked.

Johnny drew in a deep breath. "At this point I don't owe you an explanation, but because I'm a good brother, and because I have nothing to hide, I'll tell you." He paused, pulled out a folded wad of documents from the inside pocket of his jacket, and looked directly into her eyes as he held it in front of her. "This is the agreement she signed for me to represent her as her real estate agent." He opened the documents and quickly flashed them in her face. "She's a professional and meticulous woman and she had a shitload of questions that she wanted to ask me about everything under the sun. I wasn't going to rush her because I believe in providing quality service, so it took us a while."

Vivana listened carefully to everything he'd said. She had to admit it was all very plausible, if not actually believable. But she also knew what she'd seen at the coffee shop. The way they'd been acting appeared way too friendly for a business meeting.

Johnny shook his head. "Vivana, this is really fucked up. I've been so busy trying to juggle work, you, and home; how in the hell would I have time for anything or anyone else?"

"Men find time to do whatever it is that they want to."

"Yes, most men do, and we've had this discussion before."

"Only because you've given me reason to bring it up."

Johnny rubbed the hairs on his chin. "Do you honestly think I'd be stupid enough to cheat on the woman I'm cheating with? What kind of man do you think I am?"

Vivana was silent.

"Vivana, I'm trying to conduct business, not screw around. And in case you didn't notice, that woman's a little too old for my taste." He hesitated, and then zeroed in on her breasts as he spoke. "I like my women like I like my fruit, fresh and ripe."

Vivana's eyes softened as she looked at him. "Baby, do you promise nothing was going on between you and that old heifer?"

"I already told you the deal, Vivana. Like I said, I have absolutely nothing to hide. If I was only here to screw that woman, why would I have a signed contract in my hand?" he asked, holding up the documents again. "And why would I bring her to the place where we first got together?"

"Men screw around all the time."

"But I don't. I told you, you and me . . . this is a first-time thing. I'd never cheated on my wife until you came along."

Vivana looked into Johnny's eyes again and noticed the slight shift that could only mean he felt as hurt as he sounded. A placid look framed his lips, which told her that he was sincere. In that moment she forgave him, and she felt terrible for what she'd done. "I'm sorry," she eked out.

Johnny looked away and lowered his head. "I can't do this anymore, Vivana. After what happened here today . . ."

"Please don't, Johnny. I'll make it up to you, and this will never happen again."

"I know it won't because we're through. You showed me a side of yourself that I didn't know was there. I can't have that kind of drama in my life."

"I only did it because I was so hurt, and upset, and the thought of you being with anyone else made me lose it." Vivana knew she needed to play on Johnny's sympathy and convince him of how hurt she was, so even though she hadn't cried over anything since she was a teenager, she dug deep down into her emotions and willed a tear to fall from her eyes. "I love you, Johnny."

After appealing to him a few more times, rubbing her body against his, Johnny agreed to meet her tonight at the Courtyard where they'd rendezvoused last week. Vivana knew she'd just dodged a bullet, and now she was going to do everything in her power to make sure nothing like this ever happened again.

An hour after she left Johnny, she drove to B&B Electronics, where she purchased an array of digital equipment she was going to need for her next project. Vivana prided herself on the fact that she was more than just a mere contract IT specialist, she was a seasoned hacker, programmer, and Internet sleuth, and now she was going to put her training and knowhow to good use. She smiled as she thought about how she was going to ensure that Johnny Mayfield would be hers, and she knew the only way to make that happen was to keep a closer eye on him.

Chapter 12

JOHNNY

Johnny sat at his desk, tilted his head back, and took a long swallow of the Hennessey he'd poured into his glass. He let the smooth taste of the brown elixir roll over his tongue and slide down his throat as he enjoyed the warm feeling it sent through his body. He reached for the ice wrapped in a towel that he'd set on his desk, and firmly pressed it against the knot that had formed on his jaw. "This is fucked up," he said as he thought about what Vivana had done.

He'd known last week that he needed to end things with his increasingly erratic-acting mistress, and after this morning's incident, there was no doubt in his mind that he had to find a way to break off their affair as quickly, and in as pain-free and drama-free a way as possible. But in order to do that, he had to develop a plan, and in order to develop a plan, he needed help. He took another long swallow of his drink, followed by a deep breath of frustration that caused him to shake his head. "Thank God she didn't recognize Charlene," Johnny whispered aloud. This was one time that he was glad she worked from home and never immersed herself into the community. "I need help." He picked up his phone and called Bernard.

"What's up?" Bernard said in an unusually upbeat voice.

"You sound like you just hit the lotto," Johnny joked.

"Nah, man. What I got goin' on is better than hittin' the lotto."

"What's better than money?"

"Two things. First off, I got a promotion at work. You're talking to the new director of security at Crane Technical Community College."

Johnny's lips formed a smile. "Congratulations. I'm happy for you, brother!"

"Thanks, man."

"You deserve it. You're a hard-working man and you've made big changes on that campus."

"I appreciate you saying that, and it's good to be acknowledged."

"No doubt," Johnny said, and then paused. The sound in Bernard's voice was one that Johnny had never heard, and if he didn't know better he would say that his friend sounded almost giddy, which made him wonder about the second part of Bernard's good news. "Okay, so, the promotion is good and everything, but it ain't better than the lotto," he said with a chuckle. "If your ticket hit, you wouldn't even need that job. So what's your other news?"

"The love of a good woman."

Johnny paused again. "What the hell? . . ."

"Don't start," Bernard said, " 'cause there's nothing you can say that's gonna bring me off this natural high I got goin' on. Last night Candace and I reached a new level in our relationship. I popped the question, man. I asked her to marry me, and she said yes."

Johnny raised his glass to his lips and finished the rest of his drink in one long gulp. He knew that Bernard was whipped, but he had no idea that his friend was crazy, too. He was at a loss for words so he sat on the phone in silence.

"Another round of congratulations would be nice," Bernard finally said.

Johnny shook his head. "Honestly, I'm just stunned. I mean, you've only known Candace for what . . . six months?"

"At this stage in my life, and after all the shit I've been through in relationships, I know what I want and I definitely know what I need. Candace has improved my life in more ways than I can tell you, and she's made me a better man," Bernard said with conviction. "She's given me balance and a sense of peace that I've never had. She supports me and believes in me. She encouraged me to go to the VP of my department and demand the promotion I just got. She's the reason I'm in this position. She makes me feel like I can do anything, and with her by my side, I know that I can."

"Just because she encouraged you to ask for a promotion, that doesn't mean you have to marry her," Johnny urged. "I respect what you're saying, but as you know, marriage is a big step."

"And I'm ready to take it."

"Sounds like you've got your mind made up."

Bernard laughed. "Man, I still haven't heard congratulations from your ass. You ain't hatin', are you?"

"No. I'm not hatin' the fact that you're happy, I just think you're rushing in. You're my boy, and I don't want to see you make a mistake." Johnny's words were only half true. It was a fact that he loved Bernard like the brother he'd never had, and that he wanted to make sure his friend was making the right decision for the right reasons. But it was also a fact that he didn't care for Candace, which was a big part of why he wasn't thrilled about Bernard's news.

Johnny didn't like that Bernard had changed so much since becoming involved with Candace—and not in a good way. From the day Bernard had met the woman, Candace had transformed him from the fun-loving, party-going player whom Johnny had always known into a dull, sit at home, hen-pecked shell of a man that Johnny now barely recognized. He could remember a time, not too long ago, when Bernard used to run the streets with him, hang out all times of the night with him, chase women with him, and was down for any kind of mischief they could get into. But Candace swooped in and changed all that.

These days it seemed all Bernard wanted to do was make himself available at Candace's beck and call. If he went out for a night of dancing and fun, it was with Candace. If he went to the movies or even a sporting event, Candace was there. If he went to a restaurant, she was sure to be sitting by his side. Everything he did revolved around that woman, and in Johnny's experience, it wasn't healthy to make your woman your world. One woman could consume a man and that's why Johnny preferred to spread himself around, between several.

"Why can't you just be happy for me?" Bernard said. "Everybody else is encouraging and positive about my relationship with Candace except you. What's up with that? You're supposed to be my best friend."

Johnny had to brace himself to keep from falling out of his chair after hearing Bernard's remark. He thought it was a damn shame that his friend had turned as soft as a piece of cotton, sounding like a whining little girl—all over a woman. He didn't have time for Bernard's drama be-cause he had drama of his own, which drew his mind back to the reason he'd called Bernard in the first place. He wanted advice about how to handle the situation with Vivana.

Even though Bernard had lost the ability to make good decisions in his own life, Johnny knew that when it came to advising others about their problems, his friend was always spot on. And right now, Johnny was desperate and he needed help. So he put his feelings aside about the fact that he thought Bernard was making a huge mistake, and sweetened up so his friend could help him.

"I'm happy for you, man," Johnny said, lying through his teeth. Although what he'd just said was a lie, his next statement was heartfelt and true. "I just care about what happens to you, and I want what's best for you."

"Candace is what's best for me."

"Okay, well . . . congratulations."

"That sounds about as sincere as a damn three-dollar bill."

Cotton ball! Johnny thought. This time he mustered the strength to sound genuine. "Bernard, if you're happy, I'm happy for you. And that's the truth."

Bernard paused for a moment, then cleared his throat. "Thanks, man."

"I got you."

"So does that mean you'll be my best man at the wedding?"

Johnny fought the urge to cuss, and was proud of himself when he managed to pour out a "yes" while sounding scarily convincing. He wanted to applaud himself for being such a good liar, but he had to focus because it was time to get down to business. "While you're planning a walk down the aisle, I'm planning an escape route."

Bernard coughed. "You're gonna ask Geneva for a divorce?"

"Hell, no! I have no intentions of leaving my wife. I'm talking about Vivana." Johnny proceeded to tell Bernard about what went down an hour ago, but he was sure to leave out the fact that the woman he was with was none other than Councilwoman Charlene Harris. He knew that Bernard would hit the roof and never let him hear the end of it for pulling a respected member of society into his drama.

"Damn, that's some wild shit," Bernard said. "But I'm not surprised. I knew she was trouble. Fuck that plan about easing out of this slowly, you gotta cut this shit off now. That woman is dangerous."

"Who you tellin'? When she walked up and cold-cocked me, and then jumped on ol' girl, I knew she was crazy for real. I've been jammed up in some sticky situations in the past, but that was when I was young, in my twenties. I'm too old for this shit now. Grown women fighting and carrying on . . ." Johnny poured more Hennessey into his glass as he spoke. "You're exactly right, I need to cut this off now."

"Before someone ends up six feet under."

"I need a plan because I've seen what happens when I cut her off cold turkey. The next thing I know she'll be popping up at my house, and I can't have that."

"No, you can't," Bernard agreed. "And your first line of defense is to defuse and then dismantle."

Johnny perked up, ready to listen to what his friend had to say.

Despite what Bernard had said about Candace being the reason behind his promotion, Johnny knew that Bernard had earned that promotion because of his good judgment and strategic thinking, and it was that thinking that was going to help him develop a plan.

"You don't need to piss her off any more than she already is right now because she's holding most of the cards. So even if you don't want to see her crazy ass, you need to fake it—until you can quickly remove her from your life."

"I'm already on it," Johnny responded. "As soon as I realized how truly crazy she is, I pulled back from break-up talk because I knew that would only send her completely over the edge. I even told her that I'd see her tonight."

"Tonight?"

"Yeah. After she showed me what she's capable of, I didn't want to chance what she might do next. So when she asked if I'd meet her tonight, I told her I would."

"Okay, good point and good move."

Johnny rubbed his swollen jaw. "But when I think about it, maybe I shouldn't go. Maybe I should play up my injuries like they're more serious than they really are."

"I thought you only had a swollen jaw."

"I do, but she doesn't have to know that. As far as she's concerned I have a broken jaw and whiplash."

Bernard laughed as though someone had told a joke. "Man, are you sure you didn't hit your head on the floor, 'cause you're talkin' like you got brain damage."

"This isn't funny."

"I know it's not. This is some serious shit and you're talking crazy."

Johnny breathed hard. "Listen, it's the perfect way to ease out of this situation and make her feel so bad and guilty about hurting me that she's too ashamed to even dial my number."

"A woman who will stake you out like a detective, and then

whup ass like a prize fighter, all in broad open daylight, has no shame. That plan's not gonna work."

"I guess you have a point."

"And, I have a news flash for you. If your jaw had been broken you wouldn't have been able to move your mouth well enough to have a conversation with her. I'm not even gonna address the whiplash."

"I can't see her tonight. I just can't do it."

Bernard paused and then sighed. "Now that I think about it, you're right. You shouldn't do it. But I do know what you should do."

"What's that?"

"Come clean with Geneva. Tell her everything, and pray to God that she'll forgive you."

Other than announcing his engagement, Johnny thought what Bernard had just said was the most ridiculous thing he'd heard in a long time. But instead of giving voice to that thought, he kept his opinion to himself and carefully guarded his words. "That's not gonna happen. Give me another choice."

"Wait a minute, hold up. Just give it a thought."

"I'm not even gonna entertain it. I have no intention of ever telling Geneva."

"Then take it from me, if you want to keep your wife, you need to stop fuckin' around with all these side chicks who can't hold a candle to a good woman like Geneva. You need to come clean with her, beg like hell for her forgiveness, and then go to couples counseling if you have to."

Johnny wished he had more Hennessey in his bottle because if he did, he'd pour himself another glass. "I can't believe you, man. What you're talkin' is crazy."

"No crazier than what you're doin'. Trust me, you can't keep this up. You're already coming to the end of your rope, and today was a sign of that. I've been down the road you're traveling and I'm telling you now, get off because it's only going to lead you to a dead end."

"Telling Geneva that I've been fucking another woman is like of-fering my head up on a platter. She'll never forgive me."

"The type of woman she is . . . she will, if you come to her in honesty. But I can guarantee you she won't forgive you if she actually catches you."

"I'm not gonna get caught."

"How're you gonna explain the golf ball you said you have on the side of your face?"

"I'll think of something," Johnny said as he shook his head and rubbed his jaw. He sighed and let a moment pass before he spoke again. "I'm not going to tell Geneva."

"All right, suit yourself. Since you're determined to do this, here's my advice."

Finally, Johnny thought.

"Go to the hotel and meet Vivana like you said you would. You don't have to stay long, and you can use your jaw and headache as an excuse. When she sees that despite your physical pain, you still came out to see her, that might put her in a better state of mind so that you can reason with her."

"Yeah, that's what I was thinking, too."

"After you get her nice and calm, lay a guilt trip on her so that she's eating out the palm of your hand. That'll give you a day or two to start investigating her. You need to have something you can use as leverage to back her off of you."

Johnny nodded. "You're right, but damn, I'm so busy I barely have time to breathe, let alone spend time investigating her."

"I'll put in a word with a guy I know who works in fraud pre-vention here at the college. He's a whiz at identity investigations. It might take a few days, but if you can give me some basic background on her, I'm sure he can dig up enough information to find something that you can use against her that might back her off. She may not care if her husband finds out, but if there's one thing that life's taught me it's that everybody has something to hide and something to lose."

Bernard had said some questionable things during their conversation, but Johnny was thankful that his friend had come through in the end. After they agreed to meet for drinks tomorrow night, they hung up the phone.

As much as Johnny didn't want to admit it, he knew that things with crazy Vivana were going to get worse before they got better. She was proving to be too unstable, and he knew that an unstable woman was like a tropical storm: she'd pick up speed before she hit landfall.

Chapter 13

GENEVA

After signing in and securing her visitor's badge, Geneva followed Mrs. Johnston, the school secretary whom she'd met last week, down a long hallway that led to the classroom where she'd be volunteering this morning. The smell of crayons and glue, mingled with the slightly pungent aroma of floor cleaner, made Geneva think of her own school days, which brought a smile to her face as she peeked into the classrooms they passed on their way. She was excited and anxious, and she half expected, and hoped, she'd run into Samuel Owens before she left today.

"You've been assigned to Ms. Redmond's class," Mrs. Johnston said. "You'll love her. She's one of our best first grade teachers. Very kind, patient, and smart as a whip. Plus, she knows how to handle the parents just as well as she does her classroom."

"She sounds like a wonderful teacher."

"Yes, she is. You two are going to get along very well, and if I'm not mistaken, you're about the same age." Mrs. Johnston quickly glanced at Geneva. "You're in your twenties, right?"

"That's the best compliment I've received in a while, and I'll gladly take it. But I'm thirty-four."

"Honey, you look great."

"Thank you, ma'am."

They turned the corner and stopped just outside a classroom filled with the sound of tiny voices erupting in laughter. Geneva smiled when she heard the exuberant giggles of children having fun.

"Here we are," Mrs. Johnston said as they entered the room.

In the short time that Mrs. Johnston had spoken about Ms. Redmond, Geneva had formed an image of the teacher in her mind. But as she looked straight ahead, the person she'd visualized in her mind didn't match up to the woman she saw standing in front of the classroom. Mrs. Johnston had said that Ms. Redmond was Geneva's age, which she'd thought was early twenties, however, Geneva could swear the matronly looking teacher was in her mid-forties.

"It's a pleasure to meet you," Ms. Redmond said with a warm smile. "I'm Stella Redmond, and you must be Ms. Mayfield."

"Yes, I am. It's good to meet you," Geneva said, returning the woman's smile.

A student came up and tugged on Ms. Redmond's blue polyester pants.

"Ms. Redmond," the cute pigtail-wearing little girl said, then pointed her tiny index finger toward Geneva. "Is she gonna read to us?"

"Yes, Hillary," Ms. Redmond answered. "Ms. Mayfield is the nice lady I told you about who's going to read to the class today, and we'll start in just a little while."

"Yea!" the chubby cheeked little girl squealed before running back to her seat.

"As you can see, they're ready for you," Ms. Redmond said cheerfully. "You're going to be great with these kids. I can tell."

"Thanks, I hope you're right."

"Is this your first time working with children?"

Geneva nodded. "Yes, does it already show?"

"Not at all. I only guessed because you have that fresh, excited, I-want-to-make-sure-I-do-a-good-job kind of look in your eyes." Ms.

Redmond leaned forward and whispered, "Give it a month and you'll have that I–need–a–stiff–drink kind of look all over your face," she teased.

Mrs. Johnston shook her head. "I'm leaving on that one." She winked at Geneva. "Have fun, and don't forget to check out at the office before you leave." And with that, she was gone.

Geneva was glad that Ms. Redmond had put her at ease, but she hoped the woman's joke wasn't a glimpse of what was to come. After giving Geneva a quick tour of the classroom, Ms. Redmond gathered all the children to the reading section in the back of the room. Geneva's heart raced with anticipation as she walked toward the reading seat, which was an old rocking chair that Ms. Redmond had painted white and filled with soft, green cushions for comfort.

"Class, say hello to Ms. Mayfield," Ms. Redmond said in a voice enveloped with genuine enthusiasm. "She's going to read a story to you and after she's finished, you'll have time to discuss it and ask questions."

Geneva felt a mixture of happiness and regret as she looked at the smiling, adorable faces of the eager six-year-olds gathered in the small space. She was happy to have the opportunity to do something meaningful, and hopefully make a small difference in the lives of the children. But she also felt the weight of regret tug at her heart for the absence of a child she could call her own. She knew she couldn't dwell on negative thoughts. She had to appreciate and be thankful for the moment she was in, mindful to make the most of it.

Slowly, she opened the pages of the book she'd selected, titled *Betty the Butterfly*, and began to read. Geneva amazed herself as she heard each word flow from her lips. She was more involved in this simple children's book than she was the juicy novel she was currently reading. She allowed the inflections in her voice to rise and fall with each step of Betty's amazing journey, from starting life as a tiny egg, to hatching into a fuzzy little caterpillar, to shedding her skin and cocooning herself so she could grow, and then finally emerging as a beautiful butterfly whose expansively strong wings and vibrant colors were a sight to behold.

A half hour later, after laughs, questions, and interesting comments from the precociously smart children, Geneva found herself not wanting to say goodbye to the classroom of first graders who'd just stolen her heart. Several of them asked when was she coming back. All Geneva could do was smile because she was already looking forward to seeing them again next week.

After hugging several of the children goodbye, Geneva followed Ms. Redmond down the hallway and back to the front office while her teacher's assistant settled the children down.

"You did a great job," Ms. Redmond said. "You're a natural with the children. They loved you, Ms. Mayfield."

Geneva smiled. "Please, call me Geneva."

"Okay, but only outside the classroom," she said. "And Geneva, you must call me Stella."

"It's a deal."

The two women chatted for the length of the short walk back to the office, and hit it off as though they'd known each other for years. Geneva even opened the calendar on her phone and scheduled Stella for a much-needed color and cut the following weekend.

Once they reached the office, they stood outside the door as Stella gave Geneva a quick run-down on the inner workings of Sandhill. "Even volunteers get dragged into the quicksand of academic politics," Stella said. "Make sure you stay clear of it by limiting your contact with too many folks while you're here. There are a few teachers and parent volunteers who're still resistant to the changes that Dr. Owens has made to the school. And with his new plans for accountability this year, I can see some major push-back on the horizon."

The mention of Samuel Owens's name sent a tingle through Geneva, and she wanted to learn more about him, but she knew she had to be discreet about her interest. "Do you think Dr. Owens's changes will help?"

"Oh yes. Since coming to Sandhill he's made tremendous inroads, and now this school is the pride of our district. He's a good administrator and he genuinely cares about making a difference in the lives of families through education. He's the real deal."

"He sounds like a good person."

Stella winked. "Between you and me, if he was single I'd jump on his wagon and ride into the sunset."

Geneva raised her brow.

"Hey, you asked." Stella chuckled. "He's a handsome man, don't you think?"

Geneva didn't know what to say, so she simply smiled and nodded. "I met him briefly during the open house last week and he seems to be all those things you said."

"Like I said, he's the real deal."

Geneva's mind quickly went back to last week. She distinctly remembered looking at Samuel's left hand when she'd met him at the open house, but she didn't recall seeing a ring on his finger. "Did you say he's married?" she asked.

"From what I understand, he is. But it's a weird situation."

Geneva's brow went up again. "How so?"

"Well, for starters, his wife never attends any school events, and no one ever sees the two of them out together."

"Really?"

"Yes, ma'am. Mrs. Johnston is the only person I know who's actually met his wife, and that was by chance when she had to deliver some papers to Dr. Owens's house last year when he came down with the flu and was out for a whole week."

"That's, um, interesting."

"Tell me about it."

After a few minutes of quick and harmless gossip, Geneva hugged Stella goodbye and told her she'd see her over the weekend for her appointment at the salon. She walked inside the front office, turned in her visitor's badge, and thanked Mrs. Johnston for her kindness before making her way toward the front entrance to leave the building. She was a little disappointed that she didn't get a chance to see Samuel beyond the quick glimpse of him that she'd spied from the parking lot this morning, but she was grateful for the information that Stella had shared, and for the rewarding moments spent with the children.

Just as she was about to walk out the door she heard someone call her name. And it wasn't just any someone, it was the someone she'd been hoping she'd get a chance to talk to since last week.

Geneva turned around slowly and smiled when she saw Samuel Owens walking toward her. She'd been thinking about and hoping for this moment, but now that it had arrived she felt nervous, especially when she thought about how she'd flirted with him. Ironically, like the book she'd just read, Geneva felt small butterflies dance in the pit of her stomach. "Hello, Dr. Owens," she managed to pull from her tongue. "It's good to see you, again."

He smiled. "Likewise. How did everything go with Ms. Redmond's class?"

She was impressed that he knew which class she'd been assigned to, but it also made her wonder how a man as busy as he was, running a fairly large school, could possibly know the assignments of the volunteers at Sandhill. Then a small voice told her that maybe he didn't keep up with every volunteer. Maybe he was only keeping up with her. "It went well and I really enjoyed it," she said.

He nodded. "I'm glad you did, and I'm sure the children, as well as Ms. Redmond, equally enjoyed you."

"I hope so," she responded, feeling bashful. "None of the children fell asleep and they actually asked questions."

"First graders are an interesting mix. They're not newbies like the kindergarteners but they're still raw and somewhat delicate."

"Yes, and they're not afraid to ask questions or speak up."

He chuckled. "Not in the least. They're bold and unafraid of anything. That's what makes them so special."

Geneva wondered if he and his wife had children, and beyond

that, she was curious to know the real state of his marriage. Was he happy but private, or was he like her, existing in a troubled situation while going about everyday life? But she once again remembered the flirting and warm smiles they'd shared the week before, and she thought she had a general idea of his present state. "Children are amazing," she offered.

"Yes, they are, and they soak up everything around them." He looked deeply into her eyes. "I'm sure you left an impression on them."

Geneva smiled nervously, feeling warm from the way his eyes seemed to read hers. She discreetly glanced down at his left hand, and just as she remembered, his ring finger was bare. They stood in silence and surprisingly, the longer they were next to each other, the more comfortable Geneva became.

"Ms. Mayfield, I have a few tasks to complete this morning, but while I have a free moment, may I walk you to your car?"

There was something about Samuel that made Geneva feel a kind of excitement she hadn't experienced in a long time. She liked the way he paid attention to her and asked questions that showed he was genuinely interested in what she had to say.

Just a short time ago she'd longed for this type of feeling from Johnny. But today, in this very moment, her husband was the farthest thing from her mind. As she walked beside Samuel, admiring the strong carriage of his gait, the gentleness of his spirit, and the calm presence and confidence he exuded, something inside her told her that her path was getting ready to change in ways she couldn't have dreamed of just a week ago. When they reached her car she was both disappointed and relieved.

"Thank you for walking me to my car," Geneva said with a smile.

"It's my pleasure, and it's the least I can do in return for your generous gift of time and service to Sandhill."

"Volunteering with children is something I've wanted to do for a very long time, but as I said last week, my schedule has been so hectic that it's been hard to take on extra activities. But I'm glad I finally took the plunge because I knew it was time for me to find a way to do things that give my life more meaning."

Samuel smiled. "That's inspiring and such a wonderful way to look at things. You're seizing your moment."

"I guess I am."

Samuel smiled again and looked down at the round solitaire on her left hand. "I remember you said you don't have a child at this school . . ."

"I don't have children . . . period."

Geneva was surprised when Samuel's facial expression didn't change. Usually when people found out that she wasn't a mother, their reaction was often one of surprise. She knew that as a woman in her mid-thirties who'd been married for several years it was an unusual situation to be in, and one that she'd never thought would be her reality.

"That makes your volunteerism even more meaningful," Samuel said. "And again, I thank you for your time, Mrs. Mayfield."

She noticed that he'd now called her Mrs. instead of Ms., after looking down at her ring finger. She felt a battle going on inside of her head, but one thing she knew for sure was that she needed to correct him as she'd done with Stella. "Please call me Geneva."

"That's a beautiful name," he said and then paused. "It suits you."

She blushed. "Thank you. And how about you? Do you have children?"

"No, I don't." Samuel's smile quickly faded. His eyes fell to the ground, and it was clear that he was uncomfortable. He opened his mouth but nothing came out. His relaxed shoulders had stiffened and his overall body language had changed. But then, within a matter of seconds his mood seemed to shift, returning to its relaxed state. Geneva wondered what was going on in his head.

Samuel crossed his arms and leaned against Geneva's driver's side door. "Actually, my wife and I are estranged. We've had problems in our marriage for a long time, practically from the beginning, and now things have come to a head."

"I'm sorry to hear that," Geneva said, surprised by his candor.

"It's okay. It took me a long time to realize that no matter how hard you try, some things just can't be fixed."

Geneva blinked rapidly, not knowing what to say. She studied Samuel's face, and his assured expression let her know that his mind was made up. She knew that because it was the same expression she'd had on her own face when she looked in the mirror this morning, and that knowledge put her even more at ease with the feelings stirring inside her. And because he'd taken the first step to open up about his private life, she wanted to know more. "So you don't think there's a chance of working things out?"

Samuel shook his head. "As you know, marriage is work, and it takes two people who're willing to put forth the effort to make it successful. At one point, very early on, I was willing, but not anymore. Too much has happened and my feelings have changed."

Geneva nodded because she completely understood.

"I can't believe I just told you that," he said. "We've only met once before, and I barely even know you. But I feel very comfortable talking with you, and despite how clichéd this might sound, I feel like we've known each other much longer. It's such a relief to be able to share this with someone."

Geneva nodded again and this time she smiled, letting him know she felt the same way, too. Then, without another thought, she began to unload her own burdens. "It doesn't sound clichéd, and I know how you feel about your marriage because I'm in the same situation."

Geneva and Samuel stood in the parking lot, under the late summer morning sun and shared snippets of their personal stories.

Samuel gave her a look of knowing when Geneva told him that her husband had basically checked out of their marriage by neglecting her feelings and taking her for granted. "He stays out late, six nights a week, and on the rare occasions when he's home, he barely holds a conversation without it turning into an argument," she said, releasing the burden of loneliness she'd been carrying. She shifted her weight from one foot to the other. "Like yours, my marriage has been troubled from the beginning. I've tried my best to make it work, but as you said, it takes two people who want to put forth the effort, and that's not and won't be happening in my case."

"I don't mean to sound harsh," Samuel said as he wiped a small stream of sweat from his brow, "but your husband is a fool. You're a beautiful woman, not just physically, but also in character, which is most important. The thoughtfulness you've demonstrated just by volunteering says a lot about who you are, and it's a shame that he doesn't appreciate you."

"Thank you," Geneva said.

They continued to share their most private experiences, and with every small detail they revealed, and each minute that passed, it became clear to Geneva that something special was happening between them.

Samuel looked up at the bright sky and smiled. "This is the best conversation I've had in a very long time."

"Me too. This time last week my mind was in a very different place. I was unhappy and frustrated, and I wasn't sure how I was going to move forward. But today I feel completely different. I'm refreshed and focused," she said, speaking with the conviction of a woman on a mission. "I know I deserve better, and I'm gonna make sure I get it."

Samuel tilted his head, unfolded his arms, and looked into Geneva's eyes without blinking. "I believe we'll both get what we want, and when we do, we should celebrate . . . together."

Her ears could barely believe what she was hearing, but his tone and body language, which were both decidedly serious and sensual, let her know that it was real. Geneva's heart raced fast. She was beginning to see that not only was Samuel a man of great intellect, he had an understated sexy side that was direct and honest, and it made her even more attracted to him.

"I'm curious," he said, breaking her from her thoughts. "What do you think made you finally decide that enough is enough?"

Geneva brought her right hand to her chin and pondered the question as if trying to answer a riddle. He'd just asked her about something that she'd been avoiding the answer to for a very long time, and it was in that moment that for the first time she admitted the hard truth of what she'd always known deep in her heart. "I got tired of my husband sleeping in other women's beds." She shook her head and let out a deep breath. "I've turned a blind eye and deaf ears to the truth for years, but now I can't do it anymore. Last week he stayed out all night and didn't even come home. That was the proverbial straw."

"Some grown men are really just boys in disguise, and it sounds like your husband is one of them."

"My girlfriend, Donetta, would give you a high five if she heard you say that."

"It's true."

"How about you? What made you come to your decision?"

He began to speak without hesitation. "The night before the open house I was sitting in my den, eating dinner alone, as I'd done countless times, and I knew right then that my marriage was over, and that there was something better for me. The next day I felt the same way and later that evening my feelings were confirmed."

"What happened?"

Samuel paused for a moment and then smiled. "I looked across the room and saw you."

The blazing sun and stifling humidity couldn't match the heat that Geneva felt from Samuel's words. She was taken aback and didn't know what to say.

"I'm doing it again," Samuel said, "telling you things that I wouldn't normally dare mention, but what I just said is completely true. And I have to confess that after the open house I read over your application"— he winked—"because I wanted to know more about you."

1 217 554 6733

"Really?" She was flattered, and she found his open admission irresistible.

"Yes. I was confused about your marital status. You were wearing a ring like you are now, but you left the space for name of spouse blank, and you wrote your friend's name down as your emergency contact."

Geneva looked down at the embellished jewels on her sandals, trying to focus on anything other than the desire and excitement she felt building inside her. Samuel had just told her that she was the reason he felt hopeful, and alive, and free. He hadn't said those exact words, but she knew that was how he felt, and again, she knew because she felt the same way.

"I hope I haven't offended you," Samuel said quietly. "You're a volunteer, and I apologize if I'm putting you in an uncomfortable position. I just felt compelled to express this to you."

"No," she said softly. "I'm not offended at all, so please don't mistake my silence for discomfort. Actually, I feel quite the opposite."

"Now it's my turn to say, 'really?' " Samuel said with relief.

The fact that he was still smiling made Geneva feel comfortable, and more at ease. Even though she was riding high on the excitement of her and Samuel's connection, she was cognizant enough to know that the parking lot in front of the school wasn't the best place to have the type of soul-revealing conversation that her brief chat with Samuel had turned in to.

"Thanks again for walking me to my car," Geneva said. "I'm glad we were able to talk, and on that note, we should probably end our conversation, because from what I've been told, there are probably teachers looking out their classroom windows right now, wondering why you've been outside talking to a volunteer this long."

"Excellent point, and you're right."

After he closed her door, Geneva rolled down her driver's side window and fastened her seatbelt. "I enjoyed our conversation, Samuel."

"So did I." He reached into his jacket and pulled out a business card. "Please keep in touch."

Geneva took the card and placed it in the outer compartment of her handbag. "Thank you, Samuel. I definitely will."

As she drove off and headed down the street away from the school, Geneva had a smile on her face that she could hardly contain. But little did she know that before the sun went down tonight, her smile would be turned upside down along with life as she'd known it.

Chapter 14

SAMUEL

Samuel walked back into his office with purpose in his step and a happy look on his face that he hadn't felt since becoming principal at Sandhill. It was amazing to him how one person could make such a huge difference in another person's life. He knew it was a stretch to say that Geneva Mayfield was the sole reason why a wake-up call had sounded loudly in his head and heart, giving him the impetus to make a long-overdue change in his life, but the plain truth was that she was a big part of why he was sure that it was time to end his marriage.

As Samuel sat at his cherry wood desk, trying to concentrate on the small mountain of paperwork that had already accumulated in the far left corner, his mind fought to stay focused on his tasks at hand instead of on Geneva. He was disappointed when he confirmed that she was indeed married, but it didn't deter him, especially given what she'd told him about her situation at home. Her marriage seemed just as bad as his, and he knew by the look in her eyes that she was determined to make a drastic change. She hadn't gone as far to say that she was going to leave her husband, but she didn't have to. The subtle words she'd spoken let Samuel know what she intended to do, and unless he was very wrong, he also knew that she was interested in him.

He replayed their conversation in his mind and smiled to himself as he remembered the joy he'd seen in Geneva's eyes as she described her experience reading with the children this morning. The fact that she didn't have children of her own was puzzling to him because she was clearly the caring, nurturing type, thus the reason she was volunteering at Sandhill. Everything about her excited him. He'd taken notice of how sexy she looked in her vibrant, yellow-colored sundress that hugged her in all the right places, and how her short, shiny black hair was perfectly coiffed, giving her a stylishly edgy look. When she smiled, it felt brighter than the sun that had beamed overhead, and it made him want her right there in the parking lot.

"Damn," he whispered to himself. He was aroused just thinking about Geneva. Samuel looked down at his crotch and saw the bulge forming in the front of his cotton twill pants. The effect Geneva was having on him was undeniable. "If she can make me feel this way from one conversation, I'm in trouble."

Samuel shook his head, baffled by how a womanizing idiot like Geneva's husband was lucky enough to marry a beautiful, smart, and kind-hearted woman like her. Conversely, he was equally baffled by how a nice guy like him had ended up marrying a disengaged, cold-hearted, and emotionally unavailable woman like Vivana. "My wife and Geneva's husband should get together because they deserve each other," Samuel said.

He thought about how his brother had tried to warn him, and again, he wished he'd listened. But he knew he couldn't continue to lament about the mistake he'd made. What he needed to do was correct it, and that meant asking Vivana for a divorce.

Samuel pushed back from his desk and scrolled through the contacts in his phone until he found the number he was looking for. He called Jerry Butler. Jerry was the parent of a former student and had become a close personal friend over the years. He and Jerry golfed, played poker, and made an annual trip to see their favorite team, the Dallas Cowboys, play each year. Jerry was also a family practice attorney, and had offered his services to Samuel on more than one occasion after seeing what type of marriage he and Vivana had.

Jerry picked up on the first ring. "Hey buddy, how are you?"

"I can't complain."

"Margie and I were just talking about you last night while she was getting Chris's things ready for school. If it hadn't been for you, my son wouldn't be the student he is today. I can't believe he's in middle school now."

"Wow, time sure does fly," Samuel responded. "They grow up fast."

Thinking about his friend's son made Samuel reflect back on the first time he'd met Jerry. Jerry and his wife, Margie, had attended an open house at the school the year after Samuel had become the principal. The two men hit it off right away, and became quick friends. Years later, after Samuel married Vivana, he'd hoped that being around the Butlers would inspire his new wife to join him in his desire to start a family of their own. But Vivana never took a liking to the blond-haired, blue-eyed family. Samuel reflected back on the disastrous outing he'd arranged for all of them to go hiking in the mountains at a retreat that catered to families.

Vivana had ruined the entire weekend. She'd pissed Jerry off with her constant complaining about her disdain for the great outdoors. She'd alienated Margie by making snippy comments whenever the woman tried to engage her in polite conversation, and she'd frightened little Chris by yelling at him for playing with bugs along the hiking trail. A few days after they'd returned from the trip, Margie confided to Jerry, who in turn told Samuel, that she'd caught Vivana flirting inappropriately with one of the hiking tour guides, and that she'd even given him her number. When Samuel confronted Vivana, she'd flown into a rage, claiming that Margie had made up the story out of jealousy. From that moment forward, Vivana wanted nothing to do with the Butlers.

"So what's going on?" Jerry asked. "I hope you're not calling to cancel on me."

"No, no. I'd walk through a hailstorm before I did that. It's not every day that a man gets complimentary tickets on the ten yard line to see the Cowboys play at home, courtesy of his well-connected lawyer friend," he said with a laugh. "What I'm calling about is a bit more serious."

Samuel proceeded to tell his friend that he'd finally had enough, and he wanted to end his marriage. He explained how Vivana had grown increasingly distant and cold and that she was hardly ever home. He even confided that he and Vivana rarely slept together, or did anything else as a couple. "Vivana and I were fine until we said 'I do,'" Samuel told him. "I don't think I ever really knew who she was, and by the time I found out, it was too late."

"I've seen this a million times," Jerry said. "And I've got to ask, do you think she's having an affair?"

Samuel switched the phone to his other ear as he breathed out heavily. "It's possible."

"Now let me ask the same about you."

"No, I'm not." Samuel instantly thought about Geneva and the very real feelings stirring inside him. "For now, I'm good." He knew that Jerry would catch his drift.

"Okay, this is good information to have. We need to talk more at length, but from the little you've told me we can file under grounds of alienation of affection, indignities, and abandonment, which will pretty much get you out of paying alimony. Hopefully she won't try to contest it, but if she does, we can subpoena character witnesses on your behalf."

"I knew I did the right thing by calling you, even though I wish it was under different circumstances. I tried to make it work, but I can't anymore."

"I can't say that I'm surprised," Jerry said. "You hung in there a lot longer than most would have."

"Too long. But I'm about to change that."

"Well, you've come to the right place and you know I'll help you."

After Samuel scheduled an appointment to meet with Jerry this Friday, he hung up the phone and leaned back in his chair. He knew that divorces could be messy, and he also knew that Vivana had the kind of personality that was ripe for drama. That mixture alone could cause problems, not to mention the headache and distraction it could present. But he didn't think things between them would become contentious because deep down he knew she would likely welcome the chance to break free of being married. The only thing she'd want was money, which if he had to pay, he saw as a small price in exchange for his happiness.

The determination he felt earlier when he walked into his office was now multiplied by ten. He was a man on a mission with a new goal. His first order of business was to get through the rest of what was already shaping up to be a hectic workload. After that, he planned to find a way to speak to Geneva again before the day ended. He didn't want to let the sun go down without hearing her voice because he'd made up his mind that he wasn't going to waste another day living with regret.

Samuel felt a combination of excitement and lust rush through his body. He'd gotten his mojo back and he was ready to put it to use. The calm, steady, and reserved part of him was still there, but the strong, fearless, and daringly bold side of him was ready to make an appearance. "Just hold on, Geneva," he said to himself. "I'm coming for you."

Chapter 15

JOHNNY

What the fuck is wrong with this crazy bitch? Johnny shouted in his head as he looked at Vivana. He was pissed, but he didn't want to show it because he wasn't sure what his soon-to-be ex-lover was going to do next.

"Baby, isn't this resort beautiful," Vivana said as she pressed the pages flat inside the latest issue of *Brides* magazine. She was admiring a two-page spread featuring a tropical resort. "I've done my research and this Cancun resort is the best one I've seen. I've never been to Cancun, have you?"

"Uh, no, I haven't," Johnny answered, telling her a bald-faced lie. Cancun was where he and Geneva had spent their honeymoon in grand style in the presidential suite of one of the city's most exclusive and expensive luxury hotels. Ironically, the resort that Vivana was looking at was the very one where he and Geneva had stayed.

Johnny wanted to slap himself for not taking Bernard's advice to go home instead of meeting Vivana at the hotel tonight. When he arrived an hour ago she'd been overly apologetic about how she'd acted earlier today. "I'm so sorry about your jaw," she'd said at least twenty times, touching his face with each apology.

You should be sorry, he thought, but stopped himself from saying. Instead, he milked the sympathy she fed him and the fact that she was willing to get extra freaky in order to make up for the damage she'd done. And because he was going to break up with her anyway, he thought he should at least get one last tryst out of the deal before walking away and never seeing her again. So he unzipped his pants and welcomed the expert blow job she gave him, followed by a pounding penetration that he delivered inside her wet middle, before turning her over for a little backdoor action that culminated in a heart-pumping orgasm, which he felt he deserved after the long, hard day he'd had. Afterward, he was as satisfied and relaxed as a baby who'd just been fed, burped, and put down for a nap.

But his relaxation was short-lived when ten minutes into his post-orgasmic high, Vivana pulled out a magazine with a smiling woman on the cover who appeared to be dressed in a wedding gown. He strained his eyes to get a closer look, and he nearly jumped out of bed when he saw a bouquet of flowers in the woman's hand and a big caption that read *Brides* in bold letters.

Now, as he lay next to Vivana, who was snuggled close to him, all he could think about was how he was going to get out of bed and flee the scene without causing another incident like the one he'd experienced this morning.

Vivana tilted her head to the side, sweeping her long locks behind her right ear. "Well, since you've never been to Cancun and neither have I, it'll be a new adventure for both of us." She looked at Johnny and gave him a sly smile, then folded down the top corner of the page to earmark it. "I was thinking we could go in a few months; that way we can celebrate the holidays in a tropical paradise. What do you think?" she asked, giving him another sly smile.

"I'm not so sure that's a good idea."

"Why not?"

"Because . . ."

"If you're worried about the cost, don't. I know it's expensive, but

I'll go in half with you. And when you think about it, there's no price you can put on spending eight days and seven nights of pure bliss and pleasure with the one you love," she purred.

Love? Who the fuck said anything about love, he thought. Johnny had never used the L word with Vivana or any of the other women he'd fooled around with. "That's not the point. We both have other obligations."

"Johnny, neither one of us has to report in to a nine to five every day."

He blinked his eyes in disbelief. "That's not the obligation I'm talking about. In case you forgot, we're both married. I had hell to pay when I stayed out for one night. Imagine what my wife would say if I was gone for a whole week. And how about your husband? I know you said that you pretty much come and go as you like, but a week? That's pushing it."

Vivana was quiet. Slowly, she rose from the bed in all her naked glory and walked over to the window without saying a word. She leaned on her left leg, placed her hand on her hip, and craned her neck. Right then and there Johnny knew trouble was about to erupt. He'd dealt with enough women to pick up on the subtleties of certain body language. A roll of the eyes meant someone was frustrated as hell and completely over a situation. Sucking of the teeth meant someone was getting ready to be told off. And a strategically placed hand on the hip, coupled with a crane of the neck, meant someone was about to get their ass kicked. The pose that Vivana had just struck sent a wave of worry through him.

Johnny knew he was in a vulnerable position because he was lying in bed, butt naked, still in a little pain from his swollen jaw, and tired from a combination of his rough work day, crazy drama this morning, and rigorous sex this evening. He was in no condition to defend himself, let alone fight, but if he had to, he would. He slowly slid his legs toward the side of the bed in case he had to move quickly to get away from Vivana. He glanced over at his clothes and regretted that they were scattered across the floor instead of in one neat pile that he could grab in the event he had to make a mad dash.

Vivana turned around to face him. "I haven't forgotten that we're both married," she said. "But that's a situation that can easily be fixed."

He didn't want to ask, "How?" because he knew the answer, and it was something he had no interest in pursuing. All he could do was look at Vivana with a vacant stare.

She let out a huff. "We can both get a divorce. When two people feel the way we do about each other, they should be together, no matter what. We were made for each other."

Johnny remained silent.

"We have undeniable chemistry," she continued, "which is hard to find. You understand me and I totally get you. We've filled a void in each other's lives, and no matter what happens we're there for each other. What happened today is a perfect example."

Johnny squinted his eyes. "How does what happened this morning equate to us being there for each other? You followed me and then tried to beat the shit out of my client and me. Your stunt cost me valuable business and left me with a swollen and bruised jaw. Excuse me if I don't see how that's being there for each other." Johnny had meant to keep quiet, so as not to escalate the situation, but Vivana's outrageous comments were more than he could take.

Vivana shook her head and waved her index finger while making a *tsk*ing sound. "Now, now, now, don't get all upset and bent out of shape. What I meant is that in spite of the fact that we had a big misunderstanding this morning, we're back together, stronger than ever. I needed you tonight and you needed me, so here we are."

Johnny didn't say a word, determined to stay quiet this time.

"And what's even more proof of the fact that we're meant to be is that, ironically, we're in the same room we shared last week," she said with a big smile. "From now on, three nineteen is going to be our lucky number. Hell, I might even play it for the lotto."

Johnny hadn't even realized they were in the same room as last week, and he honestly didn't care. All he wanted to do was get the hell up out of there.

"So you see," Vivana continued, "we're getting all kinds of signs that we should be together and that we can weather any storm."

Johnny looked at her with a blank stare. *She's lost her motherfuckin' mind!* he thought. If he was uneasy before, he was downright nervous now. Vivana had gone off the deep end. He knew he had to use his head to scale back the situation brewing, and the only way to do that was to pretend that the pain in his jaw was becoming unbearable, requiring him to go home so he could take the prescription pain meds that the fake doctor at his fake appointment this afternoon had prescribed, which was the story he was going to tell her.

But before Johnny could put his plan of lies into motion, Vivana walked toward the bed—breasts swinging, hips swaying—and sat down in the spot next to him where she'd been lying moments before. She leaned over, placed her head on his shoulder, and smiled. "I'm going to ask my husband for a divorce tonight and I want you to do the same when you go home to Geneva."

The sound of his wife's name coming from Vivana's mouth left Johnny feeling cold. He pulled away from her and groaned loudly as he rubbed his jaw. "Urrgghhh, this pain is intense. I need to take the meds that my doctor prescribed." He eased out of bed, still holding his jaw. He quickly pulled on his pants, stepped into his loafers, and then walked over to the corner and put on his shirt. He was missing his belt but he didn't have time to search for it because he knew that his window of opportunity to leave in one piece was getting shorter by the second. "My medicine is at home so I really need to go."

Vivana raised her brow. "When did you visit the doctor and then have your prescription filled?"

Johnny had to think quickly. He didn't know if Vivana had continued to follow him the rest of the day or not. He couldn't afford to make a slip that could cause her to go off. "I didn't go to the doctor or the pharmacy today," he said. "I have a prescription I got filled a while ago. I still have some pills left over, and it's a good thing I do because I need them right now."

Vivana sat straight up. "Don't leave, baby. Stay here and I'll take care of you. I know exactly how to get your mind off your pain."

"I really need to leave before this pain gets any worse."

Vivana stood up and walked toward him. She planted her feet in a stance that one would use if steadying for a fight. Her arms hung down by her sides and her fists were formed into balls. "I said don't leave!" she growled.

Up to now, Johnny had been passively dismissive of Vivana's increasingly aggressive tone. But his ego-driven, alpha-male bravado wouldn't allow him to continue to be talked to or threatened in the manner in which she was doing. He stared back at her, eyes blazing with anger. "I guess you didn't hear what I just said. I'm in pain!" he shouted. "Pain that you fuckin' caused. Now I'm gettin' the hell outa here!"

"Dammit, Johnny! I told you, I'll take care of you."

He grabbed his keys from the dresser. "This is nonsense."

"This is love."

Johnny couldn't control his temper or his mouth any longer. "No, this definitely isn't any kind of love. This is some crazy-ass bullshit. And I'm—"

Before he could get the rest of his words out, Vivana lunged toward him and threw her hefty arms around his shoulders, holding him tightly. "I'm only going to say this one more time. Don't leave!"

"Get the hell off me!" he yelled. Johnny tried to pull away but she held on even tighter.

"I'm not letting you go!" she screamed. "You're mine. All mine!"

"Bitch, your crazy ass better let go of me!"

Vivana slapped him across his face, right in the center of his swollen jaw.

"Dammit!" Johnny yelled. "What the fuck is wrong with you?"

With a move quicker than he could react to, Vivana reached up, cupped her hands around his neck, and squeezed as hard as she could. Johnny was surprised by the strength she possessed because her grip was akin to that of a strapping man. He gasped as she continued her viselike hold, forcing him to struggle for air. She was still completely naked, which left her body vulnerable in strategic areas. He didn't want to hurt her, but he knew he had to use his brute strength before she choked him to death. In a move just as quick as Vivana's had been, he grabbed her hands as tightly as he could and pulled with a force that broke him free of her grip. But in the process she managed to dig her nails into his skin so deep that she drew blood.

Vivana clawed at his flesh like a wild animal. "I got your bitch, muthafucka!" she screamed.

Johnny's first instinct was to give her a firm right hook, just as she'd done to him this morning. But even in this intense situation, he was still hesitant to hit a woman. He tried to grab her hands again, but she was out of control. She clawed and scratched his face even more before ripping the sleeve of his shirt in her violent tirade, damaging his shoulder in the process. His skin felt as though he'd been burned, and he knew he had to get away before this turned into a situation that landed him downtown in the county jail. He grabbed Vivana by her shoulders and pushed her hard until she fell to the floor.

"Urrgghhh," she groaned, landing with a hard thud.

Johnny turned on the heels of his polished loafers as if he was wearing a pair of track shoes and dashed to the door. Vivana sobbed and cursed him from where she lay, still moaning in pain as he made his getaway.

Once he slammed the door behind him, Johnny ran to the elevator as fast as he could and was glad it was empty when he stepped inside. He breathed hard, pressing his index finger against the close button to make sure no one else got on as he rode down the next two floors.

Johnny had thought that this morning's incident had been rough, and completely ratchet. But what had just happened was something he couldn't begin to wrap his brain around. He knew that Vivana was a feisty, aggressive, take-charge kind of woman, which was one of the reasons he'd been drawn to her in the first place. Plus, he knew that those same characteristics could present the possibility of her being a freak between the sheets, which she was. But if he'd known those same qualities served to make her a raving lunatic with a violent streak, he would've stayed as far away from her as possible.

"What the hell have I gotten myself into," he said through clenched teeth. He didn't need a mirror to know that he looked like someone who'd been involved in a street brawl. Not only was his jaw swollen and bruised, he could now add bloody scratches to his face, neck, and shoulders to his list of injuries. He was pissed. "Oh, shit . . . Geneva!" he whispered to himself as he thought about what his wife's reaction to his appearance would be. He was already on shaky ground with her, and he knew this would put him in quicksand. "Damn!"

When he reached the ground floor and the doors opened, he panicked when he heard voices coming at a slow approach. Judging from the sound, they were far enough down the hall that he had time to avoid them. He knew it would look highly suspicious to see a six-foot, two-inch black man with ripped, bloodstained clothing flee an elevator as if someone was after him. Instead of running as he'd done upstairs, he casually walked off, being sure to immediately turn his back to the group of people as he exited.

Johnny breathed with relief when he reached his truck. He climbed inside and sat for a moment, shaking his head, which had begun to pound with a fury. He pulled his visor down and flipped open the lighted mirror to survey the damage. "Sonofabitch!" he hissed. It was worse than he'd thought. "That crazy bitch fucked up my face!" He hit his hand against the steering wheel. "I should've beat her ass when I had the chance."

Johnny's face and neck looked as though a large cat had gone mad on him. The scratches were deep, long, and jagged. The pain of the open wounds was starting to sink in. During his elevator ride down he'd noticed when he pressed the close button that his right hand was also badly scratched, but it wasn't until just now, when he felt another burst of pain, that he realized his left hand had been mauled as well.

He leaned back against his seat and took deep breaths, trying to calm himself and stay focused. With slow and steady care, he reached into his pants pocket and pulled out his cell phone. He didn't want to call Bernard and hear, "I told you so," but at this point he knew he had no one else he could turn to. He started his engine and as soon as his Bluetooth engaged he dialed his friend's number and prayed that Bernard wasn't at Candace's house, or vice versa.

"What up, playa," Bernard said in a happy voice that had become his regular tone.

"Are you home?" Johnny asked as he steered his truck onto the highway.

"Yeah, I'm here. What's up?" Bernard asked, clearly sensing that something was wrong.

"You alone?"

"Yeah."

"Can I swing by?"

Bernard paused for a moment. Johnny could remember there was a time that his friend wouldn't have paused or been hesitant about anything, even if it involved trouble. But his edge was gone, along with his balls, and Candace was holding them both hostage. Johnny wanted to tell him to man up, but he knew he couldn't. "Listen, Bernard, I'm not gonna lie. I'm dealin' with a lot of shit right now."

"Vivana?"

"Yeah, man."

Bernard was silent again.

Johnny breathed hard. "I'm fifteen minutes from your crib. Can I swing through?"

"Come on."

The towering hostas and colorful flower beds that Candace had planted in Bernard's front yard made Johnny sneeze as he slowly made his way to the front door. He winced when he looked at his bloodied right hand as he rang Bernard's doorbell. The night air was muggy and the heat made him feel sick to his stomach. He could hear Bernard coming toward the door and he braced himself for his friend's reaction.

"What the fuck?" Bernard said when Johnny stepped into the foyer.

Johnny felt bad enough about his current state without his friend's comment, but he knew he would have had the same initial reaction if the situation were reversed. He walked into Bernard's living room and sat on the couch while Bernard took a seat in the chair across from him. They were both silent for a moment—Johnny from pure exhaustion and Bernard from temporary shock.

"Vivana did this to you?" Bernard said, shaking his head.

"Yeah, man."

"Damn." Bernard rose from his seat and walked into his kitchen. A few minutes later he returned with a bottle of Grey Goose in the crook of one arm, a half carton of orange juice in the other, and two glasses he'd expertly balanced between his fingers on his left hand. He poured Johnny a drink and passed it to him before fixing one for himself.

"Thanks," Johnny said as he took a long swallow. "This has been one hell of a day."

"I can see."

Johnny looked at his hands and frowned. "I was laying in the bed, chillin', when all of a sudden Vivana pulled out a wedding magazine."

"Get the fuck outa here."

"I couldn't believe it either. She picked out a resort that she wants us to go to. And guess where it was?"

"Aruba?"

"No, Cancun. And get this . . . it's the very same resort that Geneva and I went to on our honeymoon."

"Wait a minute, how did she know where you and Geneva went for your honeymoon?" Bernard let out a deep breath and took a sip of his drink. "What kind of crazy game is she playin'?"

"She was totally oblivious, so I don't think she knew. It's just one of those ironic things."

"Ironic and stalkerish. If she'll follow your ass, she's damn sure capable of some other shit."

"I think it was just a fluke. Vivana likes expensive, high-end things and that resort is five star with all the bells and whistles. Besides, I see how jealous she is, and she'd never want to go someplace where I took another woman. That doesn't even make sense."

"If you say so."

"Anyway, I tried to tell her that I couldn't go. One thing led to another and before I knew it she was goin' ape-shit on my ass. Man, I was fighting for my life."

"I see what you look like, so I'm afraid to ask what state she's in."

Johnny shook his head. "Even though I wanted to knock the shit out of her, I didn't. I was too busy shielding myself. That's why I'm scratched up like I was attacked by a rabid animal."

"She really fucked you up."

"Tell me something I don't know."

"How'd you get out of there?"

Johnny lowered his head. "I pushed her and she fell to the floor. That's when I ran out of the room."

"This craziness is on some reality TV type level."

Johnny couldn't argue because what Bernard had said was true. He'd fully expected to hear his friend say, "I told you so," but he didn't, and for that Johnny was grateful.

"What are you gonna do now?" Bernard asked.

Johnny shook his head. "I'm so spent, I don't even know."

"From this point forward you can't have any more contact with that woman." Bernard looked him in his eyes with a serious stare that Johnny had never seen. "This entire situation has gone way too far. If you don't end it now, it might end you."

If he had heard Bernard make that statement when he woke up this morning, Johnny would've blown it off and told his friend that he was making a big deal out of nothing. But as he sat on Bernard's couch, bruised, bloodied, and humiliated, he had an entirely different view of things. "I hear you," Johnny said. "I'm through with Vivana, and after tonight she probably won't want to have any contact with me, either. It's over and done, and I'm glad."

"You may not ever see her again, but you're gonna have to face Geneva."

Johnny leaned forward and let out a hard sigh. "I know."

"You need to clean up as much of those cuts and scratches as you can before she sees you. Candace has a first aid kit in the bathroom with everything short of a needle in it."

"Thanks. Hopefully I'll look a little better in the morning."

Bernard poured them both another drink. "You're welcome to stay here tonight. But in my opinion, after you get cleaned up you need to go home, face the music, and do what you can to make this situation right."

"Geneva's gonna freak the hell out when she sees me."

"Of course she will. But trust me, you ain't gonna look that much different tomorrow so you might as well get it over with tonight."

"This is so fucked up."

"Yeah, it is. But you've gotta deal with it head-on and be straight up. Geneva's gonna lose it when she first sees you, and then she'll be mad as hell once you explain what happened."

Johnny's eyes got big. "I'm not tellin' her what really happened."

"Johnny, listen to me for once. Come clean with her, and don't try to bullshit your way out of this. The one thing a woman wants from her man is honesty. Even if it hurts, if you're honest with a woman she'll respect you. Don't bullshit Geneva. Tell her the truth and then take the yelling, disappointment, and silent treatment she's gonna give you because eventually, she'll forgive you."

"How can you be so sure?"

Bernard smiled. "There's a lot of things that I don't know, but one thing I do is that your wife loves you."

Johnny had to admit that what Bernard had just said was true. Even through all the neglect, arguments, and mistreatment he'd put

Geneva through, he knew she still loved him. She'd stuck by his side time and time again. He thought about how she'd left work early last week and rushed home to cook his favorite meal so they could have a romantic dinner. He thought about how she'd repeatedly begged him to spend time with her, only for him to disappoint her by never taking her anywhere or showing her any attention. Yet she'd hung in there, trying to make their marriage work. Not once did she raise her voice, let alone cause a public scene, or worse, become violent toward him.

"Johnny," Bernard said, breaking him from his thoughts. "Don't lose a good woman behind a cheap thrill. It ain't worth it, man. I've traveled that road and let me tell you, it leads to nowhere."

Johnny thought about all that Bernard had said, and he agreed with him on everything except telling Geneva the truth. He'd already been lying to her for years, and what she didn't know hadn't hurt her so far, so he planned to keep it that way. With his focus clear, Johnny knew what needed to be done. He finished his drink, then went to the bathroom to clean his wounds and formulate a story that Geneva would believe.

Chapter 16

VIVANA

Vivana lay on the hard hotel floor, stunned and angry about what had just happened. "I can't believe that sonofabitch put his hands on me," she said angrily. She raised her naked body up from the floor and managed to prop herself atop the bed. She rubbed her side and grimaced in pain. It felt as though she'd broken her hip in the spot where she'd landed. "That muthafucka had the nerve to push me down and then walk out the door," she seethed. "Nobody messes with me and gets away with it. Nobody!"

Slowly, Vivana rose from the bed and took measured baby steps over to the chair across the room where she'd set her handbag. She reached inside, pulled out a bottle of ibuprofen, and poured four caplets into the palm of her hand. She put them all in her mouth at once, closed her eyes, and swallowed little by little until each pill slid down her throat. "These things better start working soon," she said. In addition to her hip feeling like she needed a replacement, her head was pounding like thunder. She walked over to where the wine was chilling in the ice bucket and turned the bottle up to her mouth for a long swallow.

Knock, knock, knock.

The sound of a fist pounding against the door startled her, then a smile slowly came to her face. "That must be Johnny. He's coming back to apologize like he did last week." She limped slowly toward the door. "Just a minute, I'm coming."

Vivana ran her fingers through her hair, wiped her eyes with the back of her hand, and licked her dry lips to moisten them. "Baby, I know you didn't mean it. I forgive you," she said as she opened the door.

"Oh, sorry ma'am," the hotel security guard said, averting his eyes away from Vivana's nakedness. "I'll give you a few minutes to get decent." He stepped to the side.

Vivana had been so excited that she hadn't realized she was still naked. She thought it was Johnny knocking on the door, in which case her appearance would've been perfect. But instead of feeling embarrassed that the scrawny, freckle-faced security guard had seen her in this state, Vivana became pissed. "You don't have to give me a few minutes for anything. I'm fine," she said in a huff. "Now what do you want?"

The security guard shielded his eyes away from her and looked down the hall. "Ma'am, you might not be uncomfortable, but I am. Please close the door, get dressed, and open it when you're clothed, because there's a matter I need to discuss with you regarding reports of a disturbance coming from this room."

Vivana stepped back, closed the door, and slowly walked over to where her linen sundress lay on the floor. She reached down and pulled it over her head, calculating how she was going to explain the screams, cries, and whatever kind of noise the other hotel guests undoubtedly heard that had prompted them to call security. She wanted so badly to tell everyone on the floor to kiss her ass and mind their own business. This was between her and Johnny, and she would handle things herself.

Even though she didn't want to, Vivana knew she needed to adjust her attitude. The reality of her current situation was potentially disastrous. She was a black woman, and the part of town she was in was whiter than snow, and add to that, she'd just been involved in a domestic disturbance. Vivana forced a smile to her face as she limped back across the room. She cleared her throat and opened the door. "What can I do for you?" she said to the security guard.

The man walked toward Vivana and stopped a few feet shy of her. "Several guests called the front desk about a disturbance coming from this room."

Vivana smiled. "Oh, there must be a mistake. There's no disturbance here."

The security guard looked directly into Vivana's wild-looking eyes. "There were reports of loud banging, yelling, screaming, and crying, and they indicated the sounds were coming from this room, ma'am. Some of our guests were walking to their rooms and they said they heard a woman screaming when they passed by this door."

Vivana stared right back at him. "I don't know what they think they heard or where they think the sounds were coming from, but what I do know is that it wasn't me. I'm the only person in this room, and I haven't been screaming, yelling, crying, or banging anything."

"When you opened the door you said, 'I forgive you,' and 'I know you didn't mean it,'" the security guard reminded her. "Who were you referring to?"

"No one."

"Ma'am, if someone is trying to harm you . . ."

"I told you I wasn't talking about anyone. I was in the middle of taking a shower before my husband arrives. That's why I, um, opened the door the way I did," she said, feigning an embarrassed blush. "I'm sorry you had to come up here for nothing."

Vivana could tell there was no way in hell the man believed her, but she didn't care. The kindergarten cop had no proof, and she knew that he knew it, too. She wanted him to go away so she could regroup, think, and start putting plans into motion to get Johnny back.

"Okay, ma'am, if you say so. But if the hotel gets any more complaints about disturbances coming from this room, we'll have to take further action."

Vivana closed the door gently instead of slamming it like she wanted to. "I don't have time for these people's bullshit," she said. "I gotta get out of here."

She went into the bathroom, turned on the light, and looked at herself in the mirror. Her hair was a mess and her eyes were puffy and red from crying. "Damn, no wonder he gave me the side-eye," she said, but still didn't care. She reached for the bath cloth near the sink and ran cold water over it before applying it to her face. The damp coolness felt good against her skin. She looked at herself again. "Nothing that a comb and a little Visine can't fix," she said. Then she thought about Johnny, and knew he hadn't fared as well.

Although Vivana had been pissed to high heaven and had tried to choke him, now that she was calm, she felt bad about what she'd done to Johnny. She remembered how mangled his face looked after she clawed him like a bear, and she knew his jaw must feel even worse because her fist had hit him again during their heated exchange. But he'd called her a crazy bitch, and she couldn't allow him to talk to her that way and get away with it. She wanted to teach him not to ever call her out of her name again. "I think I got my point across," she said aloud.

Vivana tossed the cloth to the floor and walked back into the room. She stood at the window for a second and looked down at her car below, and again, she thought about Johnny. With each second that passed, more and more regret surged through her. "All I wanted to do was show him how much I love him," she whispered. "That's why I want us to get away from everything, just the two of us. A romantic getaway is exactly what we need."

Vivana shook her head as she thought about the look that had come over Johnny's face when she showed him the picture of the resort she wanted them to visit. While doing Internet research on him a few months ago, she'd come across his old wedding announcement. Although she was disappointed that the brief text wasn't accompanied by a photo, she saw that he and his new bride had planned to celebrate their honeymoon in Cancun. After the incident this morning she wanted to see how much she could really trust him, so she decided to test him. She pretended that she wanted to go to Cancun, and she hoped that he would be honest and tell her that he'd been, and that, in fact, it was where he'd spent his honeymoon. But instead he lied.

Vivana couldn't understand why he'd lie about something as simple as a vacation spot he'd visited, especially since it was a thing of the past. But then it came to her that Cancun probably brought back too many bad memories of his wife, so she gave him a pass and was prepared to let the small fib slide. But when he reminded her of their "obligations," that was when Vivana started seeing red. Then he added insult to injury by calling her out of her name, and that's when she lost it.

"I'm so sorry about what I did," Vivana whispered aloud, thinking about the beating she'd given Johnny. "I need to make it up to him."

Vivana reached for her handbag and slipped on her shoes. She walked over to the ice bucket and turned the bottle of wine up to her lips again for another long drink. She took the plastic, hotel-issued laundry bag from the closet and placed the half-empty bottle inside. "I've got to put things back on track," she said as she walked out the door.

Once she was in her car, Vivana pulled out her smartphone. She logged onto her BrickHouse account and smiled. "Technology, you gotta love it," she said as her screen lit up, detailing a map with gridlines and red dots. Earlier today after she'd caught Johnny at the apartment building with a strange woman—she now wished she'd remembered to get the woman's license plate number so she could run a trace to learn her identity—Vivana knew she had to find a more efficient way of keeping an eye on Johnny, so she made a visit to a local tech store and purchased a black cloud GPS tracker. The device allowed her to not only track Johnny's vehicle's movements in real time, it left breadcrumbs, indicated by tiny red dots, that pinpointed the locations where he'd been.

Vivana saw that he'd made a stop on the south side of town, which she knew was where his best friend, Bernard, lived. She figured

Johnny needed someone to talk to because he was just as upset and regretful as she was about all that had happened between them today. As Vivana looked at his current location, it showed that he had just arrived at his home. Another smile came to her face. "It makes sense now," she said with excitement. "Johnny probably stopped by Bernard's to ask him if he can stay with him for a while, and now he's going to tell Geneva that it's over and he wants a divorce. I bet he's getting ready to pack his clothes any minute now."

Vivana was so happy she forgot about her sore hip and her throbbing headache. All she could think of was the happiness that she and Johnny were going to experience together once they were both free of the dead weight known as their spouses. She reached into the plastic bag and took another long swallow of wine. "Ahhh, now I feel just right."

With newfound determination Vivana put the key in the ignition of her car, started the engine, and headed home to tell Samuel that she wanted a divorce.

Chapter 17

GENEVA

Geneva felt like a teenager experiencing her first real crush. She was lying in bed, talking to Donetta on the phone, and giggling with each detail she revealed about her conversation with Samuel. "I'm glad you're finally admitting that you're interested in the man," Donetta said.

"It's almost hard for me to believe, but yes, I'm interested."

"Okay, now you know you have to give me the low-down."

"He's so kind and sweet," Geneva said with a smile in her voice that matched the one on her face. "This time last week I would've never thought that I'd feel this way about another man. It's like that love at first sight stuff you see in the movies."

"I've never experienced anything like that, so I wouldn't have a clue."

"Until today, neither had I. But let me tell you, it's real. As soon as I saw Samuel at the open house last week, sparks started flying. We have a natural chemistry that feels so right. I've never felt anything like this."

"And I've never heard you sound like you do right now. This man really made an impression on you, huh?"

"Yes, and as crazy as it sounds, I feel like we're connected. He's easy to talk to and he has a way of making me feel relaxed and comfortable. Oh, and he looks directly into my eyes when he talks to me."

"Honey, that's a good sign. Most brothers totally avoid eye-to-eye combat, acting like it's gonna kill them or something, 'cause they can't tell the damn truth if they mama's life depended on it. They be lookin' all sideways, tryin' to string together some ol' bogus lie."

Geneva felt bad for Donetta because she knew the kind of man that her friend had just described was the kind that Donetta had had the misfortune of being involved with. Donetta's bitter disdain for men was not without irony, given that she was still anatomically a male, and wouldn't complete her gender reassignment surgery until sometime next year. Geneva knew that her friend had a closet full of bad memories and disappointments when it came to relationships. And even though Donetta was salty most times in matters of the heart, she still desired to have someone to love.

"Okay, I know he's nice, and smart and everything," Donetta said, "but do you think he can fuck?"

"Donetta!"

"What?"

"What kind of question is that?"

"A legitimate one. And for your sake, I hope he looks like he can."

"There's no way you can tell if a man is good in bed just by looking at him."

"I disagree. They give you clues, you just have to know what to look for. Take for instance, if he walks with swagger, and especially if he has rhythm when he dances, most likely he can put it down. Did you notice how he walked?"

Geneva shook her head and laughed. "He walks just fine."

"Good, now you need to get him on the dance floor."

"Leave it to you to always be thinking with the wrong head."

"Honey, like it or lump it, sex is what makes the world go round . . . that, and money. But seriously, I asked because you know how it is when it comes to men and screwin'. Either they ain't worth a damn, but they can bring it between the sheets, or they can solve a linear equation but can't find your g-spot if you give 'em a damn GPS."

Geneva laughed. "You're straight-up stupid."

"And I'm right, too."

Geneva had to admit that, although crude in her approach, Donetta made a good point, and Johnny was a perfect example. He was a bad boy, for sure, but over the years he'd given her pleasure that fulfilled her sexual needs and never left her wanting. Conversely, the men she'd dated in the past, who were nice, polite, and gainfully employed but had absolutely no swagger, were the ones who'd left her needing to use her vibrator.

Geneva reached over to her nightstand for the novel she was currently reading. "Donetta, I can't deal with you tonight. I'm going to read the next chapter in my book before I go to sleep."

"Where's Mr. Wrong?" Donetta huffed into the phone. "Is he still out?"

"Yeah, I guess so."

"What do you mean you guess so? Either your husband is or isn't at home."

Geneva sighed. "Honestly, I could care less about where he is or what he's doing. All I know is that I'm going to read my book, fall asleep and then wake up for work tomorrow."

Donetta was silent.

"Are you still there?" Geneva asked.

"Yes, I'm just a little shocked. Normally you get all upset and beside yourself over that Negro, especially when he's out for no good reason. You really feelin' this new man, ain't you?"

"It goes beyond feeling him. I'm feeling myself. For the first time since I married Johnny I'm putting myself first instead of him. I've bent over backwards trying to get that man to do right, to notice me, and to love me. I finally realized that I shouldn't have to beg anyone to be with me."

"Amen to that!"

"Samuel doesn't know it, but he's an important part of what finally opened my eyes. In just the two times we've seen each other he's made me feel more beautiful and appreciated than Johnny ever has."

"Wow," Donetta said. "You sound like a different person. But I like it. This is almost more than my cynical ass can take in one night."

"So does that mean despite the fact that you don't trust love at first sight, you're happy for me?"

"Honey, I'm overjoyed. As a matter of fact, when you see Mr. Wonderful again, ask him if he has any available friends."

"Good night, Donetta."

"See you at the shop in the mornin'."

After Geneva hung up, she opened her book to the page where she'd left off last night. Just as she was about to start the next chapter she heard footsteps coming down the hall. For the first time since she'd been married she hoped that Johnny wouldn't come home tonight, but unfortunately he was there. She didn't want to deal with his lies, moody disposition, or downright funky attitude.

Geneva raised her book eye-level to her face so she wouldn't have to look at him. When he reached the bedroom, he stopped short of coming in and stood at the door. Geneva didn't move a muscle and she hoped he'd do as he normally did, which was avoid her. She continued to read her book in hope that he'd get the hint that she wanted him to go away.

"Um, I'm home," Johnny said in a pitiful sounding voice.

Geneva had wanted to ignore him, but she'd never heard Johnny sound the way he did now, as if he'd just lost his best friend. It prompted her to look up from her book. The first thing she noticed was that he was wearing a shirt she'd never seen before. But as she zeroed in on his face she nearly fell out of bed. She gasped as if she'd just seen a ghost. She placed her hands over her mouth as her eyes grew big at the sight of him.

"Don't panic. I'm okay," Johnny said.

"What happened to you?" Geneva kicked her legs over the side of the bed and stood to her feet. "Oh, dear Lord! What happened?" Her hand flew to her mouth again.

"Geneva, calm down."

"How can I calm down when you walk in here looking like this?"

Johnny slowly made his way over to where Geneva was standing and she became more horrified with each step he took. His handsome face that always felt smooth to the touch was now covered with scratches so deep in some places she could see his pink-colored flesh beneath his skin's surface. She looked down at his right hand, which was holding his bloodstained dress shirt, and saw that his fingers looked just as badly mauled as his face. "Who, or what, did this to you?"

Johnny walked over to his side of the bed and sat down atop the comforter. "I got jacked."

"What?"

"I was carjacked."

Although Amber was a safe town with a very low crime rate, Geneva knew there were some dicey sections where one shouldn't go after dark. She also knew that Johnny made sure he never visited those areas, and being in real estate, he definitely knew where to go and what parts to avoid. When she thought about it, there was a section of town that was known for such activity, and it was one that Johnny specifically avoided. As she took another look at his face, closely examining his injuries, she found his story hard to believe. Although his jaw was badly swollen, most of his wounds were scratches. She knew that carjackers pistol-whipped, punched, and beat their victims, not scratch them.

Then it came to her as if a lightbulb had just been turned on, allowing her to see things clearly. He'd probably been messing around with a woman, pissed her off, and then she scratched the hell out of him. Geneva felt sick to her stomach at the thought. She walked over to him. "Tell me how this happened."

Johnny lifted his head, but he didn't look into her eyes as he spoke. "I don't even know where to begin."

"The beginning is always a good start," she said in a dismissive tone.

"Why're you talking to me that way?"

"What way?"

"All nonchalant like you don't care. I was attacked and I'm sitting here in pain, and you're acting like it's no big deal."

It was hard for Geneva to listen to his pathetic, nonsensical lie. But she surprised herself because even though she was appalled by Johnny's blatant disrespect, she wasn't upset. As a matter of fact, she felt indifferent. She didn't want to see anyone in pain or hurt, but at the same time she didn't feel overly concerned about him, at least not physically. He was strong and he had more lives than a cat.

"Say something," Johnny said, pulling Geneva from her thoughts. "Tell me that I'm wrong. Tell me that you care, Geneva."

"Tell me what the hell really happened to you?"

"I told you, I got carjacked!" he said, raising his voice.

"Don't yell at me," she countered. "Tell me in detail what happened."

Johnny let out a deep breath. "I was at a stoplight in Harris Point, on my way to get my hair cut, when a car pulled up behind me. Two guys got out and stood on each side of my truck. They pulled their guns and told me to get out, and when I did one of them started whalin' on me. It was pretty much a blur after that. It all happened so fast."

His lie was so ridiculous that she didn't feel like punching holes in the story he'd spun. She didn't want to get upset so she went on to a more logical line of questioning. "Did you call the police?"

"No, I didn't. Do you know how many carjackings and robberies happen on that side of town? If I'd called the cops I'd still be there right now, waiting for them to come."

Geneva examined his face again. "Your cuts look like they've been cleaned, and you're wearing a fresh shirt," she said, looking at the bloody one in his hand.

"Uh, yeah. I went by Bernard's."

Geneva tilted her head as she thought about what Johnny had just said. She knew that Bernard had cleaned up his life and was a completely reformed man from the person he used to be. He was now honorable and loyal to his girlfriend, and Geneva knew this from being around him as well as from what his kind-hearted girlfriend, Candace, had told her.

"Okay, so let me get this straight," Geneva said. "You drove to the roughest side of town in the middle of the night to get your hair cut, and you got carjacked, yet they didn't take your truck . . ."

Johnny interrupted her. "Because I fought them off."

Geneva rolled her eyes at his lie, but she found the focus to continue. "Okay, whatever. So after the *attempted* carjacking, instead of calling the police or going to the hospital, you went to Bernard's house, washed your face and changed your shirt."

Johnny nodded his head and continued to avoid her eyes.

"You should be ashamed of yourself for pulling Bernard into your lie."

"I'm not lying! I did go to Bernard's house. You can call him if you don't believe me." Johnny pulled out his cell phone and held it up in front of Geneva. "You know he won't lie."

"I believe that the part of your story about Bernard is true, but I don't believe the rest of it. I've put up with a lot of your foolishness over the years, and I accept responsibility for that because I should've known better, but enough is enough. I've had it up to my neck with your constant lies."

"Geneva, I'm telling you the truth. I was attacked and I could've been killed by a lunatic."

"You just said 'a' lunatic. Not lunatics. I thought you said there were two of them."

"It was, but only one of them attacked me."

"Did he have press-ons or acrylics, because it's clear that someone scratched you up. What's her name?"

Johnny hung his head low. "I'm telling you the truth."

Geneva couldn't bring herself to listen to any more of his lies. She silently walked over to her closet, pulled off her nightgown, and slipped on a pair of jeans and a t-shirt. She grabbed her overnight bag and stuffed it with enough clothes for a few days. She walked back out to the bedroom, bag in hand, and found Johnny still sitting in the same spot where she'd left him.

"Where're you going?" Johnny asked. His voice registered alarm and surprise all at once.

"Not that it's any of your business, but I'm going to Donetta's."

"Why?"

Geneva ignored his question. She walked over to her dresser, opened the top drawer, and pulled out several pairs of panties and bras. She stuffed them into her bag and then headed to the bathroom. It only took her a few minutes to pack the essential toiletries she would need. Her overnight bag was full when she walked past Johnny.

"Answer me, Geneva," he said, standing. "Why're you going to Donetta's?"

She stopped in her tracks and looked at him. "I can't stay here a minute longer. For years I've listened to your lies and put up with your cheating ways, and your total disrespect of me and our marriage. But tonight was the very last straw. I can't, and I won't, do this any longer."

"Geneva, don't leave."

She shrugged her shoulders and shook her head. "Don't leave?" she repeated in exasperation. "Most men who plead and ask their wives to stay can at least say *please*. You can't even beg properly. You're pathetic."

Geneva looked into Johnny's bloodshot eyes. He was staring at her as if she'd just spoken a foreign language, and in many ways she knew she had. They hadn't been on the same page in a very long time, and the reason it was explicitly clear tonight was the fact that she no longer cared. She just didn't give a damn. So without another word, she picked up her handbag, slung her overnight bag on her shoulder, and walked out of the room.

"Geneva, what the hell are you doing?" Johnny yelled down the hall as Geneva headed toward the front door. "Can't you see that I need you? I was attacked tonight. I could've been killed, and all you can do is accuse me of lying. You act like you couldn't care less. What kind of wife treats her husband that way?"

Now she was pissed. She turned around and faced him. "Just stop it! I'm tired, and I don't feel like hearing another word out of your deceitful mouth. You weren't carjacked and you know it. After whatever kind of brawl you got into with whatever tramp who scratched you up, you went straight to Bernard's house to clean up and get your story straight. Then after a few drinks you came home and now you're standing here, still lying through your teeth, trying to make me feel sorry for you. Well, I don't. You asked what kind of wife treats her husband this way? I'll tell you what kind," Geneva said, narrowing her eyes on his, "the kind who's fed up and just doesn't give a damn anymore." And with that she turned, opened the door, and walked out.

Once she was settled into the seat of her car, she called Donetta, quickly explained what had happened, and asked if she could stay at her place for a few days. After she hung up the phone, instead of driving straight to Donetta's house, she pulled into a parking space in front of 7-Eleven up the street. She reached into her handbag, pulled out her wallet, and stared at the business card that Samuel Owens had given her.

"I know this is the right thing to do," she said aloud. She turned the card over and looked at the cell phone number he'd written on the back. Just as she'd had no hesitation in walking out of her house, she opened her text message application. She typed a quick message, pressed send, and then sat back and waited for his response.

Chapter 18

SAMUEL

It was getting late, and Samuel was once again sitting in his den, all alone. But he was anything but lonely. Although he should have been tired after his long day, which included teachers jockeying for elevated status, parents who'd already lodged minor complaints, and new vendors vying for contracts with the school, he was rejuvenated instead. Even with all the challenges in front of him, he still felt as if he was on top of the world, and it was because of Geneva Mayfield.

Samuel opened the carton of chicken lo mein that he'd picked up from the Chinese take-out restaurant near his house. Tonight he was dining as a party of one, but he had a strong feeling that his situation was about to change, and for the better. He reflected on the things that he and Geneva had talked about today, and how they were both ready to make a change.

As he continued to think about Geneva, he wondered what she was doing this evening. He wanted to talk to her and hear her sweet voice that sounded so full of life. He had all her contact information because he'd gotten it from her volunteer application. But he knew that, ethically, he shouldn't call, text, or email her unless there was a very good reason. And although he thought his reason for wanting to speak to her was valid, he knew that until she initiated after hours, non-work-related communication with him, it was wise that he refrained from making the first move. He also reminded himself that even though she was married to a trifling fool, he still was her husband, and he didn't want his call to cause more problems for her.

The fact that he longed to hear and see Geneva reemphasized for Samuel how bad his marriage was. He was in the house he shared with his wife, thinking about another woman, and that could never be good.

On a normal evening, Samuel would have been bothered by the fact that Vivana still hadn't come home at such a late hour, and that she didn't have the decency to call and let him know where she was. But tonight he really didn't care because his thoughts were focused on Geneva. He wanted to know where she was, and how she was doing. He wondered what her evening was like. Had she eaten a good dinner? Was she tired? How did she like to spend her free time—reading a book or watching TV? What did she prefer to sleep in—a cotton nightshirt or silk lingerie?

Samuel found himself smiling as he thought about how exciting it was going to be to discover the answers to all his questions. Suddenly, his thoughts were interrupted when he heard the garage door engage. Vivana was home. He was disappointed for a split second, but that feeling quickly faded and was replaced by a sense of urgency. He knew that if he wanted a new life, he needed to put plans into motion to make it happen now.

Samuel closed the carton of Chinese food that he hadn't touched, took it into the kitchen, and placed it in the refrigerator. He stood by the sink and waited for Vivana to enter the house. He could never anticipate what her mood was going to be, especially of late. Her temperament ran hot and cold, making conversation with her unpredictable at best, and at times, adversarial. But tonight he didn't care, because he was no longer concerned. The only person's actions he could control were his own, and he knew what he needed to do.

When Vivana walked through the door, Samuel had to take a second look because he was startled by her slightly disheveled appearance. If there was one positive thing he could say about his wife, it was that she was always put together from head to toe. Vivana never stepped out of the house without her hair in place, her makeup perfectly applied, and her outfit looking stylish. Samuel couldn't attest to what she looked like when she'd left the house today, but he hoped it wasn't how she looked right now.

Vivana slowly limped past him, as if she was in pain. "Why're you limping?" he asked. "Did you hurt yourself?"

"I fell," she answered in a rushed, flat tone, and headed straight for the refrigerator.

"How and where?"

"You sure do ask a lot of questions."

Normally, a curt remark like the one she'd just made would've sparked an argument, followed by angry words. But tonight Samuel simply shrugged his shoulders and put his fork and drinking glass in the sink without saying a word.

Vivana noticed his change in demeanor right away. "What're you up to?" she asked.

Samuel wanted to throw the same question back at her. Her hair looked as though a bird had laid a small nest atop her loosely spiral-curled weave, and her linen sundress was badly wrinkled and in need of a good ironing. But the most telling thing of all was her face. The precisely applied eye shadow, eyeliner, and mascara that normally framed her catlike eyes was gone, and replaced by tired, puffy looking slits for lids. He could tell she'd been drinking because she smelled of wine. He reasoned that was why she came in walking slow, limping so as not to stumble and fall. The fact that she'd gotten behind the wheel in that state made him shake his head.

But instead of telling her how irresponsible she'd acted or how bad she looked, he took the opportunity to let her know that he'd come to the end of his rope. "Vivana," he began. "We need to talk."

"About what?" she asked as she continued to rummage through the refrigerator in search of food.

"The state of our marriage."

That got her attention, and he could see that for the first time in months she was actually looking into his eyes.

"I'm not happy," he continued, "and I haven't been for a very long time. We come and go, passing each other in the hall like roommates. There's no intimacy between us, and I'm not just talking about the physical. We lost our way, and honestly, I don't know if we ever really found or knew what it was to begin with." He let out a deep breath. "I want a divorce."

Vivana slowly closed the refrigerator door and leaned her weight against it. "So let me get this straight . . . you want to divorce me?"

"Yes. That's right."

A long pause hung in the air as he stared at her while her eyes focused on the floor. "What's her name?" she asked.

"I'm not cheating on you. I'm simply unhappy, and I can't continue to live my life like this."

Vivana shook her head. "Unfuckingbelievable."

Although her words were biting, her tone was calm. Samuel thought it was telling that she was more engaged in this conversation about divorce than she'd been when he'd tried to talk to her about saving their marriage. He folded his arms across his chest and exhaled. "Okay, then we both agree. I guess now it's just a matter of paperwork."

Vivana looked at him as if she was in deep contemplation. But as he stared into her eyes she seemed as though her thoughts were a thousand miles away. She was thinking about something serious, and he was sure that whatever it was, it didn't involve him. Her behavior was further proof that he was doing the right thing. "Do you agree?" he asked again.

Vivana nodded. "Yes, you won't get an argument out of me. But I'm gonna tell you right now, I want half. And I want this house, too."

"Let's leave all of that up to the courts. I'll have my attorney contact yours."

Vivana smirked, but didn't say anything. She gave him a hard roll of her eyes and then limped toward the guest bedroom on the main floor. She slammed the door behind her, putting an end to their conversation.

Samuel walked back out to the den and reclaimed his seat on the couch. He didn't know how to feel about what had just happened and he didn't have time to process it because his phone chirped, alerting him of an incoming text message. He looked at the screen and immediately felt a rush of excitement when he saw that it was from Geneva. But when he read her message he became worried.

Geneva: Hi Samuel, this is Geneva. I hope u r well. I need 2 talk 2 u. R u available 2 chat by txt or talk by phone? Pls let me know.

Samuel instinctively knew that something was wrong because she'd said that she needed, not wanted, to talk to him, which was a big difference. He walked upstairs to his bedroom and shut the door before locking it. Even though he knew that Vivana would be downstairs for the rest of the night, he didn't want to take any chances. He quickly texted Geneva back.

Samuel: Can I call you now?

She responded immediately.

Geneva: Yes

Samuel hurriedly pressed the call button on his phone. She picked up as quickly as she'd answered his text.

"Hi Samuel," she said in a soft, easy voice.

"Hello, Geneva. Is everything all right?"

She hesitated for a moment before she began to speak. "Actually, no. It's not. My husband came home tonight and, well, it was just awful."

"Is he still there?" He figured her husband must be gone, or in another room if she felt comfortable enough to speak freely to him on the phone. But he wanted to be sure.

"I don't know," she responded. "I think he is. I left a few minutes ago."

He knew things must have been bad if she had to leave her house. He felt an overwhelming need to protect her, and his first thought was for her safety. "Are you okay? Did he hurt you?"

"No, it's nothing like that. I'm physically fine. But emotionally . . ."

"Where are you?"

"In the parking lot in front of the 7-Eleven on Popular Street."

It was a good twenty minute drive from where he lived. "I'll be there in fifteen minutes."

"Are you sure?"

The relief he heard in Geneva's voice made him want to tell her that he'd make it there in five minutes flat, but he didn't want to defy the laws of motion or get a ticket for reckless driving, so he tempered his response. "Yes, I'm sure. I'll be there in a few."

"Thank you, Samuel. I'll be waiting."

"Okay, I'll see you soon."

He quickly pulled off his sweatpants and t-shirt in favor of a pair of jeans and a black crew-neck shirt. He walked into the bathroom and grabbed his toothbrush with one hand and his hairbrush with the other, grooming himself as if he was in a speed competition. He wiped his face with a damp cloth and then surveyed his reflection in the mirror. He ran his hand over his thick, black hair, which was cut low and neatly faded on the sides. He rubbed the cloth over his clean-shaven face again, and took inventory of his smooth brown skin.

Samuel would have preferred to be thought of as handsome, like his father was. But he was more than happy to accept the distinction of being cute, as he'd been deemed by many women. He knew that his six-foot, three-inch frame could stand to lose a good twenty-five pounds, especially around his midsection. He remembered that Geneva's body looked like she worked out and her waistline was slim and trim. He turned to the side and sucked in his stomach, studying his side view. "I've got to get back into the gym." But even with a few extra pounds, Samuel knew he still looked good, and was a solid eight on a scale of one to ten.

Samuel hurried down the stairs. The guest bedroom door was shut and he could hear Vivana snoring. He shook his head as he walked into the kitchen and retrieved his keys from the hook on the wall.

Ten minutes later he steered his Mercedes-Benz into the 7-Eleven parking lot right beside Geneva's Toyota Camry. When she looked up and saw him she smiled wide, and he could tell she was happy to see him, which made him feel like he was on top of the world. He rolled down his passenger's side window and motioned for her to get into his car. She nodded.

A few minutes later, Samuel and Geneva were sitting across from each other in a booth in the back of Waffle House, which was the only dine-in restaurant they could find that was open this time of night. After their server brought out their food, Geneva began telling him about what happened once her husband came home.

As Samuel listened, he realized that Geneva's husband was a bigger fool than he'd originally thought. He wondered why a good woman like her had married a louse. But he had to remind himself not to judge because someone could say the same thing about him.

"Johnny has pulled a lot of outrageous stunts," Geneva said, "but tonight was just too much. I had already decided that I was going to ask him for a divorce and tonight made it completely clear that I'm doing the right thing."

"Did you ask him tonight?" Samuel asked, then lifted a forkful of eggs to his mouth.

"No, I didn't. There was too much going on and I couldn't listen to another minute of his lies. When I reached my limit I decided to pack a bag and get out of there as quickly as I could before things escalated any further."

"You did the right thing. Do you have a place to stay?"

Geneva took a small sip of her orange juice. "Yes, my best friend, Donetta, said I can stay with her for as long as I need to. I texted her after you called me to let her know that I'll be a little late getting there."

"Okay, good. I'm glad you have a safe place to stay," Samuel said with relief. Then a thought came to his mind. "Do you think your husband will try to come by your friend's house?"

"No, he doesn't even know where Donetta lives. Besides, he can't stand her. He wouldn't go to her house if his life depended on it."

"Finding out where she lives can be done with the click of a mouse. There's a lot of things a man will do that he normally wouldn't if he's trying to get his woman back."

Geneva was quiet for a minute. "That's a good point," she said. "But he didn't do much of anything to try to get me to stay. I don't think I have anything to worry about with him."

"Sometimes men say and do things that make no sense, especially when it comes to matters of the heart. He might not know how to express the fact that he doesn't want you to leave him, but trust me, he doesn't."

Geneva shook her head. "I know my husband. He's not coming around."

Samuel nodded. "Geneva, I'm a man, and I'm telling you from a male perspective, even though your husband's behavior has been foul and he's neglected you, he doesn't want to lose you. You never miss water until it's gone, and a thirsty person will do whatever they need to in order to get a sip."

"I'll take that under consideration."

"I want you to be careful."

Geneva smiled. "I will be, and thank you, Samuel. I really appreciate you coming out to see me. When I called, I really didn't expect you to be able to talk freely, let alone come meet with me in the middle of the night. Was your wife upset when you left the house?"

Samuel placed his fork on his empty plate. "Not at all. As a matter of fact she probably doesn't even know I'm gone."

Samuel went on to tell Geneva about what had transpired between him and Vivana tonight.

"Wow," Geneva said. "We've both had a crazy night."

"Yes we have."

"Now I'm going to give you the same advice you just gave me. Be careful because you never know what lengths a woman will go to once the reality sets in that she's lost a good man, especially if she's as erratic as you've said your wife is."

Samuel had to admit that Geneva was right. "Point taken. I've learned that you can't put anything past anyone, and that's why I asked if you think your husband might try to come by your friend's house. You never know what a person is capable of until they're pushed."

"I agree with you. But Johnny's ego is much too big to think beyond himself. I truly believe the only reason he doesn't want me to leave him is because of the way it'll look. He doesn't want anyone to think I rejected him . . . He couldn't handle that. It's more about his image than it is about trying to save our marriage. The love between us disappeared a long time ago."

"I told my wife that very thing tonight."

Geneva looked down at the cold food on her plate and then back up at Samuel. "Do you feel a little sad that she didn't try to put up a fight to save your marriage?"

"No, not at all. Do you feel sad that your husband didn't?"

"No, I don't."

Samuel leaned back against his seat. "I think when you get to the point that you're finally fed up, there's nothing and no one that can make you change your mind about what you need to do."

Over the next two hours, Samuel and Geneva's conversation turned from talking about their turbulent marriages to talking about their futures, their hopes, and their dreams.

"I've always wanted to be a father," Samuel confessed. "I just assumed when I married my wife that she wanted kids like I did, especially knowing the profession I'm in. But that was a mistake."

Geneva looked closely into his eyes. "It's amazing how similar our stories are. I assumed the same thing about my husband. I thought that because he never made any objections when I talked about wanting children, he wanted a family, too. But as the years went on, I came to realize that his silence wasn't agreement, it was avoidance, and that in fact he just didn't care."

"It's not too late for you to have children, you know."

"Yes." Geneva smiled. "I know. And the same goes for you."

They let a comfortable silence lay over them as they each thought about how free their future was going to be, and the possibilities that lay ahead. They discovered that they had a lot in common. They both loved the great outdoors. They were both avid readers. They both enjoyed classical music, jazz, and old school hip hop. They both loved Italian food, and their favorite dessert was pound cake. And they both wanted children and a traditional family, sooner rather than later.

Although they were enjoying the evening and could have easily sat in their booth until the sun came up, reality forced their hands. It was nearly two in the morning. Samuel had to go to work in a few hours and so did Geneva.

After Samuel paid their bill, he drove Geneva back to her car where she was parked in front of 7-Eleven. He was still concerned about her safety, so he asked her if he could follow her to her friend's house to make sure she arrived safely. He didn't get out to walk her to the door because she'd asked him not to. "I'm taking your advice," she'd said, "in the off chance that Johnny shows up, I don't want him to see you walking me to the door."

Samuel watched from his car as Geneva stood on her friend's front porch and rang the bell. When the door opened, he initially thought the person inside was a man; the height and build wasn't consistent with that of a woman. Samuel could tell that Geneva said something to her friend about him because the boy-shaped woman smiled and waved in his direction. He waved back as Geneva and her friend closed the door, disappearing inside.

Reluctantly, Samuel drove back home. Along the way he replayed his evening in his mind, trying to make sense of all the twists, dips, and turns that had happened in the span of the time since he'd left work to now.

He was exhausted, but he was also energized by the conversation he'd had with Geneva. He had to laugh about how ironic life seemed to be. Last week after meeting her for the first time, he'd felt silly for constantly thinking about a woman he barely knew. Then this morning after talking to Geneva in the parking lot he knew there was a spark that had developed between them, and now, after spending even more time with her and learning more about her, he realized that his initial feelings weren't silly at all. This felt right, like they were supposed to be together, and they were supposed to meet at this pivotal moment in their lives.

After Samuel peeled out of his clothes and lay down in bed, his mind was still on Geneva. They'd agreed to have dinner this Saturday, and he was already counting down the days. He hoped that between his busy schedule and the nightly chats he anticipated they'd have, the week would go by fast.

Chapter 19

JOHNNY

"She left," Johnny said to Bernard. "She walked out in the middle of the night and didn't even say goodbye." Johnny was sitting in a chair on the other side of Bernard's metal, L-shaped desk, drinking a cup of coffee that Bernard's secretary had gotten for him. "I've never seen Geneva act this way. She was cold, like she didn't care."

"What do you expect?" Bernard said. "The lie you told her was just as bad as how you look, maybe even a little worse, which is saying a lot."

"Thanks for the support."

Bernard shook his head. "I've said it before and I'll say it again. I love you like a brother, but I can't support your mess, and I wouldn't be a good friend if I did."

"Man, I don't need to hear all that right now."

Bernard leaned forward in his chair. "Yes you do."

"I don't need to be kicked when I'm down."

"That's not what I'm doing. I'm trying to help you."

Johnny breathed hard. "Then help me fix this."

"I hate to tell you this, but Geneva's not coming back. She's gonna divorce you."

Johnny placed his coffee cup on the edge of Bernard's desk. "No she's not. She loves me. You even said so yourself."

"Yeah, I did. But that was before you pushed her to the point of no return. Remember what I told you about how women want honesty? Well, you destroyed that last night, and now there's no way Geneva's going to forgive you."

Johnny shook his head. "Yes she will. This is just a rough patch we're going through. She just needs a little time, but she'll come around, and that's where you step in."

"What do you mean?" Bernard asked with skepticism.

"Geneva likes you, and she'll listen to you. I need you to talk to her, man. Convince her that I've changed . . . like you have," Johnny said in a low voice.

"You must be out of your mind."

"Bernard, you're my boy. I wouldn't ask you to do this unless I felt it was necessary."

Bernard shook his head. "You don't deserve Geneva."

"What?"

"You're a lyin' cheat. You don't have a drop of integrity in your body. You don't know how to be honest, and you have no self-control. You need to stop doggin' your wife, let her go, and get some help."

Johnny couldn't believe the insults his friend had just hurled at him. "Man, fuck you!"

"Fuck you!" Bernard shot back. "I'm tryin' to help your stupid ass."

"If you really wanted to help me, you'd stop judging me and agree to speak to Geneva. Whenever you've asked me to do something for you I've always said yes. Now that the shoe is on the other foot all you can do is talk down to me because I still have my balls and you don't."

Bernard shook his head again. "You still don't get it."

"No, I get it, all right. You're punkin' out on me," Johnny said with a huff. "We're supposed to be boys."

"No, we're supposed to be men. And it's time that you started acting like one."

Johnny stood up. "You seem to have forgotten that when Suzanne left your ass I tried to work that shit out for you. I lied and covered for you."

"Which dug me into a deeper hole. What you should've done was talk to me like I'm talking to you. But you were just as blind as I was, and unfortunately, you still are."

"Whatever."

"I told you, the road you're takin' is only gonna lead you to trouble."

"Oh, so now you're a philosopher and shit." Johnny was getting heated and his voice was rising. He looked at the campus officer who'd just passed by Bernard's door. Johnny had visited Bernard's office many times, but today he'd been greeted with stares and whispers when the campus police officers as well as a few admins saw the damage to his face. He wished Bernard's office wasn't in the middle of the campus security and police department, and now that his friend had been elevated to director status, all eyes were on him, making Johnny's situation even more uncomfortable.

"Calm the fuck down," Bernard hissed, lowering his voice as he glanced out his door. "Don't get mad at me. You're the one who came here to my job this morning, without calling me, wanting to cry on my shoulder. You brought your bullshit to my doorstep last night and now you're bringing it to my job, and that ain't cool."

"I can't count how many times you showed up at my office with your problems."

"You work for yourself, there's no one in your office but you. You don't have nosy coworkers lurking outside your door. This is my place of business."

Johnny knew that Bernard was right, but he was so distraught that his emotions were running up and down. For the first time in his life he felt as though he had absolutely no control over what was happening to him. He was used to Geneva begging him for his time and attention. He was used to doing what he wanted, when he wanted, but now everything had changed and he didn't know how to handle it. He calmed himself and sat back down in the uncomfortable office chair in front of Bernard's desk. "My bad," he said. "I'm not tryin' to wreck your work flow. I just don't know what to do and you're the only friend I've got who I trust to help me."

"Brother, you're gonna have to help yourself."

"So it's like that?"

Bernard let out a long exasperated sigh. "Stop it with the pity party, man. You brought this on yourself. You need to let Geneva go and get some help."

Johnny raised his brow. "So now you think I'm crazy."

"I think you need help, and I can say that because I used to be just like you. My life was a mess, just like yours. I was out of control and I had to do something. After I started counseling . . ."

"There you go with that again . . ."

"It helped and I got better. If it hadn't been for the counseling and therapy I got, I don't know what my life would be like right now, and I know I definitely wouldn't have a good woman like Candace by my side."

Johnny had stomached a lot of things that Bernard had said, but he couldn't listen to another self-righteous word his friend had to say. "Candace? That bitch is the reason why you're acting like a punk."

Bernard froze. "What did you just say?"

"You heard me. She's the one with the balls in your relationship. That bitch—"

Johnny couldn't get the rest out because in an unexpected move, Bernard jumped up from his chair, raced around his desk, and punched Johnny in his face, landing a hard blow to the good side of his jaw.

When Johnny felt the force of Bernard's fist connect with his face, a bright burst of pain surged through his mouth. Within seconds the two men were exchanging blows that turned into an all-out brawl. They tumbled over the chair that Johnny had been sitting in, and when Johnny hit Bernard in the stomach, Bernard threw him across his desk, sending Johnny and the computer monitor crashing to the floor.

Even the scream of Bernard's frightened secretary didn't stop the two men from fighting. It took three campus police officers to break the chokehold that Bernard had around Johnny's already mauled neck. Once the officers were finally able to separate the two men, it looked as if a tornado had swept through Bernard's office.

Johnny couldn't believe what had just happened. He felt as though he'd hallucinated a fight scene between him and his best friend, but he knew it was real when he looked across the room and saw that Bernard's lip had been split open and he was holding his hand in an awkward position, as if it was broken.

"This can't be happening," Johnny whispered. He panted hard, trying to catch his breath as a new wave of pain engulfed his body. The cuts to his face that he'd suffered last night had begun to bleed again, commingling with new injuries that included a bloody nose. A large gash accompanied a knot on his forehead, along with a black eye, another blow to his jaw, and soreness that felt much like broken ribs. Johnny's pain was so great he could barely move or understand what the campus officers were saying to him. All Johnny could think about was his pain, and the fact that his best friend had attacked him, all because Johnny had told the truth about Bernard's pushy fiancée.

Johnny looked across the room at Bernard and the man he saw was someone he didn't even recognize. Bernard glared at him with what Johnny could see was something close to hate. He couldn't believe that all this happened because he had the balls to tell the truth about the weak person Bernard had become. "You fucked over our friendship," Johnny said. "And for what . . . a piece of ass?"

Bernard had to be restrained by the officers. "You say one more word about her and I'll kill you," Bernard threatened. "I swear I will. You better get out of here while you still can."

"Bernard, do you want us to take care of this?" one of the officers said.

Bernard shook his head. "Don't waste your time. Let him go. But get him out of here before I do something I'll regret."

Chapter 20

GENEVA

"Here you go. Drink up." Donetta handed Geneva a Starbucks cup. "A double shot of espresso, no whip, just the way you like it."

"Thanks, I need this in the worst way," Geneva said as she took her first sip.

"How many more clients do you have today?"

"Just one, and she should be here any minute. After that I'm outa here to start my weekend. I just hope this caffeine boost helps me keep my eyes open."

Geneva smiled because although she was tired, it was for a good reason. It was Saturday afternoon and she'd been up late every night this week either spending time with or talking on the phone to Samuel. She could hardly believe all the changes that had taken place in her life in such a short amount of time.

Samuel had moved out of his house the day after he and Geneva had met Monday night at Waffle House. He found a small apartment that was actually closer to his job than his house, and conveniently, was only a short distance from where Donetta lived. Geneva found herself looking forward to their late-night talks, which bonded them even closer together. Samuel was unlike any man she'd ever been involved with. His sincere kindness, genuine honesty, and sense of integrity shined through in the way he approached his work, and his life, and Geneva found herself falling hard for him.

"He seems all right," Donetta had said two nights ago when Samuel stopped by the house to visit Geneva. "But everybody puts their best foot forward in the beginning. Give this thing some time."

To the untrained ear, Donetta's words would have sounded doubtful and cautionary. But Geneva took them as a very good sign, especially given the fact that Donetta had been referencing a man. The fact that Donetta had said Samuel was all right was practically the equivalent of deeming him a good man, and her comment about giving things time meant she hadn't dismissed him and was actually giving him the benefit of the doubt. Donetta's sense of people was keen, and although jaded toward the way of distrust, she was usually right.

"I have one more head to whip into shape," Donetta said, drinking her caramel Frappuccino. "And once I leave here I have a hot date with my bed."

Geneva yawned and took another sip of her coffee. "A nice long nap sounds divine, but I'm hoping this coffee will wake me up."

"I bet you are," Donetta teased, and gave her a wink.

Geneva had told her about the dinner date that she and Samuel had planned for tonight. It was something she'd been looking forward to for the last few days.

Shartell glanced at Geneva with an excited smile. "You've come dragging in here every day this week. What's got you up so late at night?"

The three of them were the only stylists left in the salon this afternoon. Geneva and Donetta both looked at each other and then at Shartell. It never ceased to amaze Geneva how unapologetically nosey Shartell was. The woman had no filter when it came to her comments and no boundaries when asking people questions. Geneva knew she had to either ignore her coworker's question or proceed with caution in answering it. But before she could do either, Donetta stepped in.

"What makes you think she's been stayin' up late? She could be tired because of her long list of clients—which by the way, is triple the amount of yours. Geneva keeps her chair jumpin' from the time we open until the time we close. So instead of worrying about how she's spending her time, you should work on building your business and minding it, too."

Shartell glared at Donetta. "Why you always throwin' shade? I was talkin' to Geneva, not you."

"You need to go somewhere and sit the hell down, Shartell."

"And you need to mind your own business, too." Even Shartell knew how crazy her statement sounded, and she had to shake her head at her own self.

Donetta burst into laughter. "Girl, bye!"

"I know, I know," Shartell said, joining Donetta as well as Geneva in more laughter. "But you can't say I'm not honest."

Just then a woman walked up to Geneva nursing a slow limp and a wide smile. She was dressed in a drab t-shirt and capri pants that looked a bit too tight for her full-figured size. She dabbed the sweat from her makeup-free face with a Kleenex, clearly hot from the late summer humidity outside and the climb up the flight of steps leading to the salon. "Are you Geneva?" the woman asked.

Geneva nodded and gave her a warm smile. "Yes, I am, and you must be Cheryl." She extended her hand to her new client. "It's a pleasure to meet you."

"Likewise," Cheryl said.

Geneva took another quick sip of her coffee and spun her stylist chair around. "Have a seat."

"Thank you," Cheryl said. "My knees are killing me. It's so bad that my doctor said I'll probably have to undergo surgery soon." She sat in Geneva's chair and held her handbag in her lap as though someone was going to steal it.

"I can store your bag in my drawer so you won't have to hold it." Geneva watched as the woman looked around the shop. "If it'll make you feel more comfortable I can lock the drawer," Geneva offered.

Cheryl smiled and nodded her head. "Okay, thanks."

Geneva could see that Cheryl's sew-in was high quality Brazilian hair, and whoever had cut it had done a very good job. She placed her hands on the woman's head and could tell that she had a good amount of her own hair under tracks that had become slightly loose. "So tell me, Cheryl," Geneva began, "what kind of style are you looking for today?"

Cheryl smiled and turned in the chair so she could look at herself in the mirror as she spoke. "I want something totally different. I've been wearing this weave for so long and now it's time for a change. I want to go natural. I haven't had a relaxer in over a year, and my hair under this weave is down to my shoulders. I was thinking about wearing it loose, kinda like Traci Ellis Ross's hair. Do you think that would look good on me?"

Geneva nodded. "Yes, I do. Let's go for it."

Geneva began taking out Cheryl's weave, track by track, as the two of them struck up a lively conversation. They talked like they were old friends catching up on each other's lives. Geneva learned that Cheryl had recently gone through a messy divorce from her husband of ten years, and that she'd just relocated to the area from California and was staying with relatives until she could find a job and get on her feet. Geneva admired Cheryl's bravery. She was a woman who'd decided to step out on her own and build a new life, rather than stay in a marriage full of hurt and neglect. It was the very same thing that Geneva had decided to do.

After Geneva finished Cheryl's hair, she wanted to give herself a pat on the back for how well it turned out, despite the unforeseen challenges she'd faced at the onset. Cheryl's natural hair was long, but badly damaged, requiring Geneva to cut it down into a tiny afro so it could grow out even and healthy. Cheryl didn't blink about the drastic change, and had actually welcomed it. After Geneva shampooed, deep conditioned, and cut Cheryl's hair, the woman looked like a million bucks and she said she felt like it, too.

Geneva unlocked her drawer and handed Cheryl her bag from inside. "Doesn't she look great?" she said with excitement, turning to Donetta and Shartell for their expert opinions.

"It's a nice look," was all Shartell said. Donetta simply smiled and remained silent, which Geneva thought was odd.

"Thank you," Cheryl said, looking around at everyone. She patted the short, glistening curls atop her head and admired herself in the mirror, turning at each angle to view her profile. "I love it!" She reached into her handbag and pulled out her wallet, still admiring herself, her eyes glued to the mirror. "How much do I owe you?" she asked Geneva.

"Nothing, it's on the house." Geneva placed her hand on Cheryl's shoulder. "You haven't found a job yet and you're staying with relatives until you get on your feet. I know how that is. Just enjoy your new do and that will be my payment."

Cheryl looked as though she was going to tear up and cry, but she held it back. "This is one of the nicest things anyone has done for me in a long time."

Geneva smiled. "Pay it forward and do something nice for someone when you leave here."

"I sure will." Cheryl hugged Geneva tightly, then made an appointment to see her two weeks from today. "I've got you on my next visit," she said on her way out.

Geneva sat in her chair glad to be finished for the day. It was six o'clock in the afternoon, and she'd been in the shop since six this morning.

"You about ready to leave?" Donetta asked as she unplugged her irons, kicked off her clogs and slipped into her stiletto sandals.

"More than ready. But I'm going to sit here for a few minutes, just so I can rest my tired legs and aching feet."

"You had a long day and you deserve that much. Girl, you did the hell outa some heads today," Donetta said. "That blowout you gave Lataylor was fit for an *Essence* spread."

"*Yaaaasssss!*" Shartell agreed. "That do was the business."

"Thanks. I love it when my clients turn out looking great, like my last one." Geneva thought about Cheryl and she remembered how strangely both Donetta and Shartell had reacted to the woman's appearance. "Is it just me," she said, "or did y'all not like the way my last client's hair looked?"

Shartell spoke first. "I meant what I said. It was a good look."

Donetta pursed her lips and sucked her teeth.

"Donetta, you have to admit, she looked good," Shartell said.

"What's your problem with her?" Geneva asked her friend.

Donetta sat in her chair and crossed her long legs. "I don't like that fake heffa. There's something about her that screams messy-as-hell. Don't you agree?" she said, looking at Shartell.

"Well, now that you put it out there. Yes, I have to agree with you. I don't usually get bad vibes from people, but that chick had trouble written all over her."

"You got that right," Donetta chimed in. "I picked up on it the minute she limped her hefty ass over to your chair."

Shartell nodded. "I overheard some of your conversation, and frankly, she sounded like the kind of person who says things just to sound good. Couldn't you tell?"

Geneva shook her head. "No, not at all. I could see that she's a little vain by the way she constantly stared at herself in the mirror. But I chalked that up to the fact that she was so happy about her new look."

"Vain is being kind," Donetta chimed in. "She watched herself in the mirror of every station she passed when she walked into the salon."

Shartell nodded in agreement. "She sure did, but the thing that got me was the questions she asked you."

Geneva raised her brow. "She talked about herself for most of our conversation, which I think was because it was therapeutic, given her situation. But she didn't ask me many questions at all, so I don't know what you're talking about."

"I do," Donetta answered. "She didn't ask a lot of questions, but the ones she managed to work into your conversation were very personal, asking about your husband and your friends, tryna be all in your business and whatnot. None of your long-time regular clients do that, but this woman who just met you, was in your business."

"We connected on a personal level because we're going through some of the same things." Geneva came short of saying that she was in the same marital situation as Cheryl because Shartell was within earshot.

"Oh, because y'all both goin' through a divorce?" Shartell said.

Geneva and Donetta looked startled, but they knew they shouldn't be. Although they'd been very careful and hadn't let on that Geneva was staying with Donetta, they knew it was only a matter of time before Ms. CIA found out.

Shartell waved her hand. "Don't worry, I haven't said a word to anyone. I like you, Geneva, and I know how private you are. If folks find out your business it won't be from me."

Geneva looked at Shartell with grateful eyes. "Thank you."

"But I'll tell you this," she said. "Folks gonna know real soon because of what your husband did at the college a few days ago."

Alarm ran through Geneva's body. "What happened?"

"He got into a fight with the director of security."

Geneva gasped. "That can't be right. The director of security is his best friend. You must be mistaken."

Shartell looked as though someone had insulted her mother. "When have you ever known me to be mistaken about my information?"

"Never," Donetta said. "Tell us what happened."

Shartell looked at Geneva. "From what I understand, he was already beat up pretty bad when he showed up at his friend's office. They exchanged some words that led to a fight. It took three campus police officers to break it up. Johnny ended up with a fractured jaw and three broken ribs."

Donetta smiled while Geneva shook her head in disbelief.

"My Lord," Geneva said.

"Shartell, you're somethin' else," Donetta said. "Geneva's his wife and she didn't know, so how the hell did you find out so quickly?"

"You know I don't reveal my sources," Shartell said.

Geneva brought her hands to her mouth and shook her head from side to side. "This is just awful. What were they fighting about?"

"Johnny called his friend's fiancée a bitch, not once, but twice."

The sympathy that Geneva had felt for Johnny instantly evaporated. She knew that Candace was a good woman, and that she made Bernard happier than Geneva had ever seen him. But Johnny couldn't stand Candace, and Geneva had heard through the grapevine that Bernard had proposed. She knew that probably hadn't set well with Johnny. Geneva knew that Johnny's disdain came from the fact that he was secretly jealous of Bernard's newfound joy.

Geneva could only shake her head and be thankful that she'd finally opened her eyes to the kind of man she was married to. She made a mental note to remember to have a process server serve Johnny with separation papers first thing Monday morning.

"Damn," Donetta said. "If he was hurt up that bad, I wonder how his friend is doing?"

"He's much worse off than Johnny," Shartell said.

"Oh, no," Geneva gasped, putting her hand to her mouth again. "Is he in the hospital?"

Shartell shook her head. "No, he's at home, probably searching Monster and Indeed.com at this very minute. They fired him the day after everything went down."

"What? He just got promoted to that position."

"And he just lost it. Girl, you know they can't have the director of security fighting on campus. He even threatened to kill Johnny in front of people. Communicating threats like that in this day and time is a no-no. Zero tolerance is real."

Donetta uncrossed her legs and stood. "I don't know the man, but I feel sorry for him. And I can't blame him for wanting to kill that no-good Negro, 'cause Johnny Mayfield ain't shit. Plus he cost that man his job, and a good one at that."

If Geneva thought she was tired before, she was exhausted now. She could only imagine how Bernard felt, and Candace, too. Although she knew she had nothing to do with what had happened, she felt a little responsible. She didn't know if her leaving Johnny had sent him off the deep end, or if he was already at the edge. A sick feeling came to her stomach.

"Don't let that bastard rain on your parade," Donetta said. "Count your blessings that you got out of it when you did. Pretty soon he'll be someone else's problem, if he already isn't."

"That's right," Shartell said. "Keep your head up and enjoy your life."

Geneva knew they were both right, and that she had a lot to look forward to. She and Donetta had been talking about opening a salon together for years, and in the week that she'd been staying with her friend they'd decided to turn their dreams into action. They had an appointment next week with the Small Business Administration to start filling out loan applications. Her personal life was also on the rise, thanks to Samuel, who'd shown her more love and care in a week than Johnny had done during their entire five-year marriage.

Geneva knew that none of the great things that were happening in her life would be possible if she'd stayed with Johnny. From the moment she walked out of her house, her life had skyrocketed to happiness. Johnny was a bad seed, and what happened to Bernard was proof that she needed to keep her distance from him. As Geneva packed up her bag to leave the salon and prepare for her dinner date she made up her mind that she was going to stay as far away from Johnny as possible.

Chapter 21

SAMUEL

Four months later

Just as the season had changed from late summer to late fall, Samuel's relationship with Geneva had blossomed from unexpected attraction to undeniable love. Their relationship not only enriched his life emotionally, he'd physically benefitted as well, the result of a twenty-five pound weight loss. Through diet and exercise, Samuel had slimmed down his once pudgy waistline, increased his muscle mass, and improved his endurance. He'd gone from cute and sweet, to handsome and sexy, and he felt on top of the world with Geneva by his side.

They'd been seeing each other for four months, and it had taken that long for him to convince Geneva to finally come to his place and spend the night. Her initial hesitation was due to the fact that she was technically still married, and Samuel wasn't. But now, after several months had passed, she couldn't wait any longer to share private time with Samuel, outside of Donetta's house.

Samuel sat close to Geneva on his lone couch in his small living room, sipping wine, and eating cheese and crackers that he'd prepared for their first date in his apartment. The room was lit by several cream-colored pillar candles of varying sizes, and the air was filled with the sound of soft jazz that serenaded them from Samuel's extensive iPod playlist.

He was glad that his divorce had happened just as quickly, and without litigation, as his friend, Jerry, had said it would. It also helped that Vivana had wanted to end their marriage just as much as he did, and added to that, she didn't want to challenge the abandonment and alienation of affection claims that Jerry had lodged on Samuel's behalf. After the papers were filed and the thirty-day waiting period was up, Samuel was a free man. But Geneva hadn't been so lucky. Johnny was making things difficult, and refused to agree to the terms Geneva was asking for in the separation agreement she'd filed, which was only her rightful half of their marital assets. Johnny knew she was entitled, but he refused to comply, and that's why they had a court date set for next month.

"This is nice," Geneva said, stretching her legs across Samuel's lap as she sipped from her wineglass. "This was a long week and it feels good to finally relax."

"Yes, and at my place instead of Donetta's."

Geneva smiled and looked around Samuel's sparsely furnished apartment. "The candles are a nice touch."

"I'm glad you like them." Samuel made sure he paid close attention to Geneva's likes and dislikes, and he knew that she loved candles. He enjoyed pleasing her and bringing a smile to her face because of how she made him feel. If his day was stressful or his mood was down, one smile from Geneva would erase whatever was wrong. He loved what she brought to his life, which was balance, support, and happiness.

Geneva had become just as much a fixture at Sandhill as some of the teachers were. Not only did she volunteer with the reading program, she split her time between several other projects and activities. Samuel marveled at how well she juggled it all. She managed to work at the salon during the day, devote time to her business plan of opening a salon with Donetta at night, and volunteer at the school on her days off, all while giving him her undivided attention when they spent time together. She was a good woman, and he felt blessed to have her in his life. Once her divorce became final he wasn't going to hesitate putting a ring on her finger.

Samuel knew that Geneva would be an excellent wife and a great mother. She was a natural nurturer, and it showed in the way she cared for him, her friends, her coworkers, and the kids at school. They both wanted a family, and had already talked about starting one in the very near future. They were just that sure of each other. In all the time he'd been married to Vivana, she'd never wanted to discuss having a family, but he and Geneva had already picked out names and decided on how far they wanted to space their children apart in age.

"Thank you, Samuel," Geneva said.

"For what?"

She smiled and set her wineglass on the coffee table. "For loving me and for doing the little things that make me happy, like filling the room with candles."

"That's nothing," he said, but still appreciated her acknowledgment. "You haven't seen anything yet."

"Oh, really? Then show me."

Samuel's smile widened when he saw a familiar look in Geneva's eyes that he now recognized and welcomed with excitement each time she cast it upon him. It was a tantalizing look that let him know that she wanted him, and it turned him on more every time. He set his wineglass beside hers, rose from the couch, and pulled her up from where she'd been reclined. He brought her into his embrace and kissed her deeply as his hands traveled to the roundness of her behind.

"Mmmm," Geneva moaned as she searched his mouth with her tongue.

It only took a minute for Samuel to feel the stiffness at the crotch of his pants. He pressed his body next to hers, causing her to grind herself against him. He carefully guided her back to his bedroom, which was just as sparsely furnished as his living room, but was replete with glowing candles, and a bottle of champagne resting in an ice bucket on the floor. He watched as she surveyed the room. His small dresser held most of the candles, and was surrounded by a framed picture of the two of them that they'd taken at the state fair a month ago.

Samuel watched Geneva's eyes dance with desire when they finally landed on the single red rose that he'd placed atop the Egyptian cotton sheets that had been pulled back, ready for their enjoyment.

"Oh, baby." Geneva smiled. "This is just perfect."

"Once I close on my new house next month I'll have a proper set-up for you, but I'm glad this will do for now."

Geneva wrapped her arms around his neck and looked into his eyes. "I wouldn't care if you lived in a shack with no running water, as long as we're together, that's all that counts."

Samuel knew that Geneva genuinely meant the words she'd just said. There wasn't a materialistic or superficial bone in her body, and her sincere kindness made him love her even more.

Slowly, he moved her over to his bed, gently easing her down to the mattress with care. He took his time, getting her ready for him. He knew that her ears, along with the small space between her lip and her chin were her hotspots, so he kissed, nibbled, and then licked her soft, fragrance-scented skin until she squirmed beneath him. Within a matter of minutes she'd shed her heavy sweater, he'd pulled off his shirt and khakis, and now he was helping her wriggle out of her skinny jeans. He smiled when he felt the wet spot in the crotch of her floral print panties.

Samuel eased his way down Geneva's naked body as he planted small kisses on her smooth flesh. She let out a sensual moan when he spread her legs and rubbed her inner thighs with his strong hands. When his tongue dipped into her creamy middle he felt his manhood swell and grow harder as he savored her delicious juices. "I love the way you taste," he whispered, which excited both of them.

Samuel enjoyed the way she rotated her hips and jutted her pelvis forward, giving his mouth greater access to her wet mound. He didn't move when she placed her hands around the back of his head and pulled him further into her as he licked, sucked, nibbled, and lapped her like a kitten at a bowl of warm milk. Her moans and groans had him so turned on that he couldn't take it anymore, he had to have her. In one quick move, Samuel eased his body on top of hers.

Over the last few months he'd grown to know exactly what Geneva liked and precisely how she liked it, because again, he paid careful attention. He positioned his swollen head in the same spot where his mouth had been and slowly entered her, taking his time to rotate his hips after each inch he gave her. He took his time going deeper and deeper with slow, hard, movements until he'd filled her up.

Geneva wrapped her legs around his back and held on as he made love to her, moving in and out, back and forth, and side to side. All the while he kissed her as he looked into her eyes. He could feel her hips buck frantically, and he knew that meant she was about to explode. When he felt her arch her back and let out a carnal moan that lingered in the air, he smiled, knowing he'd satisfied her once again. He increased his tempo, thrusting in and out of her, making each stroke deeper than the last. It only took him a few minutes to join her in ecstasy.

Samuel ran his hand up and down Geneva's bare arm as she laid her head on his chest in the afterglow of their lovemaking. This had become one of Samuel's favorite things about making love to Geneva. He enjoyed feeling her body next to his, knowing that she was completely satisfied and relaxed, and that he was responsible for that state.

He'd never been the kind of guy who ran through women like some men tended to do. His sexual experiences in college and as a young man had been good, but nothing to write home about. When he'd married Vivana, he'd expected the hot sex they'd had during their short months of dating to continue, but it had stopped almost immediately after their wedding night, and he'd been in a sexual funk ever since. He'd been nervous the first time he and Geneva had made love because he'd wanted to please her and he hoped he wouldn't disappoint her.

Their first time had been slightly awkward. He'd put so much pressure on himself that he fumbled and stumbled his way through the act. Sensing that his feelings had been bruised, Geneva had wrapped her arms around him, kissed him deeply, and told him to lay back and relax. She whispered lustful, erotic words into his ear, telling him how much he excited her and how much she already loved him, then she slid her body on top of his and eased her way down his shaft, rocking him until she orgasmed with a hard shudder. From that night forward, Samuel had been rocking her world and fulfilling her needs each time they made love.

An hour later they were back on his couch, eating lasagna and garlic bread that Samuel had picked up from their favorite Italian restaurant and had brought back for a quiet, romantic dinner at home.

"I wish I didn't have to go into work tomorrow," Geneva said, munching on the savory pasta.

"Do you have a lot of clients?"

"No, just one, and I think I'm going to have to drop her."

"Why?"

"Because she's becoming a pain."

Geneva went on to tell him about her client named Cheryl, who'd started coming to her a few months ago. Even though Donetta and even Shartell didn't like the woman, Geneva had given Cheryl the benefit of the doubt because she knew she was going through a lot of personal turmoil and was misunderstood.

But over time, Geneva saw that Cheryl had begun to change. She'd become unreasonable in her expectations about her hair. She wanted Geneva to work magic, transforming her look every time she stepped into the salon. Color one visit, twists the next, a blow-out in between, and then finally going back to the weave she'd initially said she was tired of, all while expecting Geneva to know exactly what she wanted, then becoming irritated when her hair didn't turn out the way she thought it should. She'd even been grouchy a few times that she'd come into the salon, saying that her irritability was due to the fact that she was hungry from the low-calorie diet she was on. Geneva found that very odd, especially because it appeared that Cheryl had picked up about twenty pounds in the short time she'd been coming to the salon.

Samuel was concerned because Geneva made a point to leave business at the shop, rarely discussing her clients. But now she was being vocal, with a hint of dislike in her voice. "Do you have her number?" Samuel asked.

"Yes."

"Then just call her and cancel your appointment tomorrow."

Geneva sighed. "It irritates me when clients call and cancel on me at the last minute, so I'd hate to do the same."

"But if she's becoming a problem you really should nip it in the bud."

"I don't know . . ."

Samuel shook his head. He appreciated Geneva's trusting nature and dedication to professionalism, but he also hated to see her stressed. "With all that you've been doing, you need a break. I'm sure your client will understand, and if she gets upset it won't be a bad thing because you're going to drop her anyway."

Geneva nodded. "I know what you mean, and I'm beginning to agree. I'd initially thought Cheryl was just going through a lot, which she is, but her attitude is more than I want to deal with. Every time she comes into the shop it's some kind of drama. She's the pickiest client I've ever had."

"That's saying a lot."

"Yes, it is. When I told all my clients I was going to take tomorrow off, she's the only one who wouldn't change her standing appointment, and insisted that I come in to do her hair."

"That's kind of unreasonable," Samuel said.

"You're right, it is. If I cancel her appointment that means we can sleep in tomorrow."

Samuel reached on the coffee table and handed Geneva her phone. "Call that worrisome woman right now!"

Geneva laughed and dialed Cheryl's number. But to her disappointment it went straight to voice mail. Geneva frowned and whispered, "Voice mail," to Samuel. She left Cheryl a quick message, letting her know that she needed to cancel their appointment and to call back to confirm that it was okay.

Later that night as they lay in bed with Samuel spooning Geneva from behind, his mind took him to the surprise he'd planned for to-morrow, which he would be able to start earlier in the day now that Geneva didn't have to work. He'd made reservations for them at the Roosevelt Hotel, so they could share a romantic weekend of luxury. Samuel had booked the honeymoon package in the presidential suite that included romantic amenities such as champagne, chocolate-covered strawberries, and a rose petal turn-down. He'd even gone by the Godiva store earlier and had them make a custom basket filled with Geneva's fa-vorite chocolates, which he'd carefully stored in the back of his closet shortly before she'd arrived. He knew how hard Geneva worked, and he wanted to pamper her to show his appreciation and love. Samuel drifted off to sleep thinking about how surprised Geneva was going to be when he whisked her away to the luxury hotel downtown.

Chapter 22

VIVANA

Vivana looked at Johnny and felt like slapping him across his face; the same face that, if it had not been for her, would still carry the vicious scars that she now felt he deserved.

After their hotel squabble a few months ago, Vivana had felt terrible about the wounds she'd inflicted upon his face and neck. And to add disaster to an already bad situation, he'd gotten into a violent fight with his best friend the next day, severing their friendship along with a few ribs and Johnny's jaw, which had required wiring for a solid month. Once he healed enough from his injuries, Vivana had used some of the money she'd received in her divorce settlement to pay for two reconstructive surgeries and four skin-resurfacing procedures for him. She'd taken Johnny to the best plastic surgeon in Birmingham to restore his handsome looks to as good as new.

Now, as Vivana looked at her boyfriend, all she could do was wonder how she had fallen so hard, so fast, and so obsessively for someone who seemed not to appreciate her, no matter how much she did for him. It seemed the more she gave, the more he took, and she was beginning to grow weary of always being on the receiving side of zero.

"It only took me thirty-nine days to end my marriage," Vivana huffed as she glared at Johnny, standing over him with her arms folded across her ample chest. "It's been four months and you still haven't even signed the separation papers that Geneva sent you."

Johnny leaned back on the couch and responded without looking her way. "I already told you, I'm not giving up half of this house or half of anything, so I'm willing to wait this thing out for as long as it takes."

"As long as it takes for what? Until she comes back to you?" Vivana asked. "Is that what you want? You want Geneva back?"

"I didn't say that."

"You didn't have to." Vivana looked around the room and wanted to scream. She hated coming over to visit him in the house he'd shared with Geneva, and the fact that some of her belongings were still there, and that he refused to box them up or put them out of sight, made her see red. "Don't you want to be rid of her so you can get on with your life . . . with our life?"

Johnny remained silent.

"Don't you love me?" Vivana asked.

"I had a hell of a long week, and all I want to do is relax tonight, but I can't because you keep pressing me about every little thing."

"Pressing you?" Vivana said incredulously. "All I do is cater to you. I cut my hair and went natural because you said you wanted to see how I'd look without my weave. Then you said you didn't like that look and you thought I should do something to brighten my face, so I changed my hair color. Then you didn't like the color and wanted to see me with long hair again, so I got a blow-out, which you said made my hair look dry, and after that complaint I finally went back to the weave. All I do is try to please you, not press you. I try to be patient with you because every chance you get, you bring up our fight and how much it traumatized you. Well, guess what . . . it traumatized me, too!"

By now Vivana was so mad she was breathing hard. She wanted so badly to tell him about all the other things she'd done to please him, many of which she couldn't speak of for fear that he'd get upset. For instance, she'd tracked him for a month straight through the black cloud GPS tracking device she'd put on his car to make sure he was safe and wasn't getting himself into any unnecessary trouble. That was how she'd come to his rescue at the college the day he and Bernard had gotten into a fight. She'd taken him to the hospital right away, making sure he got the proper care he needed. When he'd asked her what she was doing there, she'd told him that she was interested in enrolling in a computer course that would add to her technical qualifications.

There were other things she'd sacrificed for him, too, but the one that she'd gone above and beyond for was giving up her precious Saturdays in order to sit in Geneva's chair and pretend to be someone she wasn't.

Vivana had wanted to see her competition with her own eyes. She wanted to know what was it about Geneva that had made Johnny want to be with her. It didn't take much time to find her and schedule an appointment. When she first saw Geneva, her initial reaction had been pure jealousy and she had to paint on a fake smile from the time she'd entered the salon until the time she'd left to cover up her envy of and disdain for the woman. Vivana hated that Geneva was slim, yet shapely in all the right places, with a naturally pretty face that looked beautiful once enhanced with makeup. And the woman's syrupy sweet disposition made her want to gag, especially when she refused to take payment for her first appointment. *What a sucker*, Vivana had thought.

But over time, Vivana's jealousy subsided when she realized that there was nothing interesting or exciting about Geneva. She was a run-of-the-mill hairdresser with an annoyingly cheery personality that got on her nerves. She never had any drama to talk about, and she was boring as hell. She could see why Johnny had grown tired of the dull woman, and it gave Vivana more reason to continue to fill his life with the kind of up-and-down thrills that kept things spicy between them. She knew that despite what Johnny said, he loved the heated arguments, occasional shoving, and borderline violent mood swings she engaged in. She knew he liked it because otherwise he would have grown bored with her like he did Geneva, and left her for some-one who could spark his engine.

She was about to launch into another tirade when her cell phone rang. It was Geneva. *Why the hell is she calling me on a Friday night?* Vivana wondered. She'd stored Geneva's number under "Gynecologist" in her contact list, just in case Johnny ever went through her phone log as she occasionally did his. She didn't want to talk to Geneva in front of Johnny, so she pushed the button to ignore. She walked back to the kitchen and listened to Geneva's message.

Geneva wanted to reschedule Vivana's standing appointment to-morrow. Vivana huffed and growled under her breath. "I already told that silly bitch that I wasn't going to reschedule, so what makes her think I've changed my mind?"

"Who're you talking to?" Johnny asked, startling her so much she jumped.

"No one."

Johnny looked at her with skepticism as he reached into the re-frigerator for a beer. But if he felt anything was amiss, he didn't let on.

"I wasn't finished with my conversation with you," she said, con-tinuing their war of words. "When you couldn't find fault about my hair anymore you moved on to my weight, so I started a diet that made me cranky, tired, and about to lose my mind."

"A diet?" Johnny said sarcastically.

"Yes, and what's that tone supposed to mean."

Johnny smirked. "You know as well as I do that you haven't been dieting."

"Yes I have."

Johnny shook his head. "If that's the case, you need to stop because you're the only person I know who goes on a diet and gains weight. And besides, you act cranky, like you're about to lose your mind, on a regular basis."

Vivana was furious. She'd noticed that despite the calories she'd been counting, a few pounds had crept up around her midsection and thighs. But she chalked it up to being big-boned, and the fact that like most women in their mid-thirties, her hormones, metabolism, and body were all changing. "You're a hurtful bastard," she spat out at Johnny.

He shook his head and walked out the kitchen, but she followed him, fussing and cussing with each step.

"Cut it out, Vivana. I've had enough of your mouth and your insults," he said. "If you don't stop right now . . ."

"What're you gonna do?" she challenged.

Just then his cell phone rang and she became even madder. "Who the hell is calling you this time of night?"

He ignored her and looked at his phone with surprise.

"Who is it?" she asked again.

Johnny turned his back and answered his phone without responding to her. She heard him say, "What's up . . . it's been a long time." Then he took a long pause before mumbling something she couldn't hear into the phone. He paused again, apparently listening to the earful that the person on the other end had to say. "That's your problem, not mine," she heard Johnny say in an angry tone. A few seconds went by before he said, "Fuck you!" and then pressed the end button.

Vivana watched as Johnny's chest heaved up and down with anger. The only thing that elicited emotion from him was money and sex. So he must have been talking to a woman who was obviously mad at him. "I can't believe you!" Vivana said. She was beside herself with the fact that he'd had the nerve to answer the phone and talk to another woman right in front of her.

"What the hell's your problem?" Johnny asked.

"Tell me who the fuck you were talking to."

Johnny's eyes narrowed on hers. "Your phone just rang a few minutes ago, and I sat here and watched you switch it to ignore, and then walk into the kitchen right after that. When I came in to get a beer you'd obviously been talking to someone, but I let it go."

"Don't try to turn this on me. I know you were talking to some bitch, now tell me who it was."

Johnny put his beer down on the counter and grabbed his keys.

"Where do you think you're going!" Vivana screamed.

He didn't answer her as he walked out the door, so she ran out behind him.

"Answer me, muthafucka! Where the hell are you going!"

Johnny turned around and glared at her. "I've had it up to here with you!" he shouted.

Vivana saw one of his nosy-ass neighbors out walking her dog, and she wanted to curse her out and tell the woman to mind her own business. But right now she needed to handle Johnny. She walked up to him and slapped him, satisfying the urge she'd had all night. "You better bring your ass back in the house right now."

Johnny lowered his head, and when he raised it, Vivana saw a look in his eyes that she'd never seen before. For the first time since she'd known Johnny she was scared, because she recognized the emotion lurking in his eyes, and she knew exactly what was going to happen next.

When Vivana came to a few minutes later, the nosy-ass neighbor she'd wanted to curse out was kneeling beside her. The woman held the side of Vivana's head, which felt as though it had been hit with a brick. She blinked hard and then closed her eyes after she saw that Johnny's truck was gone.

Chapter 23

JOHNNY

Johnny sped down the street and onto the highway, glancing into his rearview mirror every few seconds. He was on the lookout for blue lights and sirens after what had just happened. He'd known for months that it was only a matter of time before Vivana pushed him to what he'd just done. Tonight was the first time in his life that he'd ever raised his hand to strike a woman. After watching his mother get beaten down little by little at the hands of his father, he'd vowed not to ever physically harm a woman. He'd kept that promise until tonight, when Vivana slapped him.

Johnny steered his truck into the parking lot of the Hilton Hotel, turned off the engine, and sat for a few minutes. He was relieved that he hadn't been stopped by the police, which meant neither Vivana nor his neighbor, Mrs. Lehman, had placed a 911 call. He couldn't figure out why Vivana hadn't called, given that she probably wanted his head on a platter right now. But he knew Mrs. Lehman didn't call because, when it came down to it, the woman couldn't stand Vivana. Vivana had been nasty to Mrs. Lehman on several occasions and had even kicked at the old woman's poodle when he'd gone off his leash one day.

After Johnny settled into his room, he took a hot shower and lay under the sheets in the same t-shirt and boxer briefs he'd worn all day. "How did I get myself into this situation?" Johnny said aloud as he reflected on the last four months of his life.

There were many days when Johnny wished he could push a redo button, and if he could, he would go back to the day he'd met Vivana nine months ago. Since she'd entered his life he'd lost his wife, his best friend, and as of this very moment he stood in jeopardy of losing his real estate business. Amber was the kind of town where bad news traveled fast, and after his infamous fight with Bernard at the college, Johnny had been blackballed in the industry. It had taken some time for Johnny's face to heal, and given the way he'd looked, very few people felt safe touring houses led by a physically intimidating black man with a penchant toward violence and battle scars etched in his face. It didn't take long for his phone to stop ringing and his referrals to dry up, and it didn't matter that he now looked as good as new because the damage had been done months ago. A permanent die had been cast against him that followed him to this day.

What had made matters even worse was that for the first time in Johnny's entire life, women had avoided him. He'd had to go through surgeries, skin grafts, and several resurfacing procedures over the last four months. He'd had to wear bandages and walk around like a mummy half the time, and the other half was spent staying inside to avoid direct sunlight while the strong, topical medications he was prescribed ran their course. It wasn't until five days ago when his final bandages came off, revealing skin as smooth as a baby's bottom, did he feel a semblance of his old self. But he'd lost touch with everyone and everything he'd once known. Geneva and Bernard, along with clients and colleagues he'd known for years now, seemed like distant memories. No one asked about him and his phone never rang.

The only comfort and sense of control Johnny still had came from the monthly payments he received from a few women he'd been blackmailing. Johnny had routinely taken secret pictures and videos of his conquests during his cheating days, and now they were paying off. But even with their money and the money Vivana was giving him, he was still barely making ends meet, now that he was no longer rolling high in the real estate game.

Johnny flipped through the channels on TV until he found ESPN. Normally, he loved watching the game highlights and sports commentary, but tonight his mind was so muddled that he couldn't focus on the screen. All he could think about was the phone call he'd received tonight from the man who used to be his best friend.

When he saw Bernard's number appear on his phone, his initial reaction was surprise. He hadn't spoken to Bernard since that fateful day four months ago. Johnny had wanted to reach out to Bernard on several occasions, but he stopped himself short of calling each time he thought about the way Bernard had initiated the fight that drove a wedge between them. Johnny was hurt that his friend would do that to him. All over a woman.

After Johnny got over the initial shock of seeing Bernard's number, he became hopeful. In the back of his mind he'd been hoping that his friend would come to his senses and apologize so they could restore their friendship. But that didn't happen. Johnny shook his head when he thought about the real reason behind Bernard's phone call.

As soon as Johnny answered the phone Bernard started in.

"What's up," Johnny said in a guarded tone. "It's been a long time."

"I'll tell you what's up, muthafucka," Bernard said, slurring his words. "You're what's up, you no-good piece of shit."

"Whooa," Johnny said. He could tell right away that Bernard was pissy drunk, and it surprised him because Bernard hadn't drank to the point of excess since his divorce several years ago. "I don't know what your problem is, but it's not with me."

"Oh, yes it is," Bernard said. Anger mixed with liquor dripped from his voice. "Because of you I lost my job, my house is in foreclosure, I started drinking again, and tonight Candace gave me back her engagement ring and said the wedding is off. If it hadn't been for your selfish, lyin' ass, I wouldn't be in this situation."

Johnny had to pause for a moment to process the fact that Bernard was actually blaming him for his life falling apart. Johnny was pissed because he wasn't the one who'd thrown the first blow that had led to both their demises. He'd lost a lot behind Bernard's hot-headed, impulsive move. He was so mad he could barely think straight. And added to his frustration, Vivana was looming close by, practically breathing down his neck, demanding to know who he was talking to. He knew he had to end the conversation before he exploded. "That's your problem, not mine," he told Bernard, ready to hang up the phone.

His comment enraged Bernard even more. And what he told Johnny next were words that made Johnny's blood run cold.

"That's where you're wrong," Bernard growled. "My problems are your problems. You caused me to lose everything, and now you have to answer for that shit. I should've killed you when I had the chance. But don't worry, I know how to finish the job. You're a dead muthafucka."

"Fuck you!" Johnny said, and then hung up the phone.

Bernard's last sentence kept repeating itself inside Johnny's head. Never did he think that his friendship with Bernard would come to this. But then again, there were many things in his life that Johnny never thought would happen, but they did.

Unable to concentrate on the TV, and too wound up to sleep, Johnny needed something to relax him. Vivana's drama, along with Bernard's call, had interrupted the ice-cold beer he'd been trying to drink, so he rose from the bed and redressed in the jeans and sweater he'd been wearing. He slipped on his black suede loafers, grabbed his wallet and room key, and headed downstairs to the hotel bar.

"This is more like it," he said as he walked into the elegant looking space. He hadn't gone out much over the last four months, partly because he didn't want to take Vivana with him for worry of how she might act in public, but mostly because it had taken his face so long to heal. But now that he was back to his old self, he had an urge to dip his spoon into whatever tasty treat he could find. It didn't take him long to spot a delicious looking, long-legged beauty who was sitting at the bar all alone.

He knew that wherever there was a beautiful woman, there was likely a man nearby. He took a seat in a lounge chair, ordered a drink, and waited to see if she would remain alone. He noticed that her eyes never left the drink she was nursing and her head didn't turn toward the entrance. Both were signs that she wasn't awaiting company. Johnny finished his rum and Coke and walked over to where the woman was sitting at the bar.

"Is this seat taken?" he said, flashing his brilliant white teeth. He licked his lusciously full lips for emphasis and right away he knew he could have the attractive woman up in his room in a matter of minutes.

She smiled sheepishly. "I'm waiting for my girlfriend to arrive," she said as she blushed.

He checked her ring finger and saw that it was bare. He thought it was rather odd that she wasn't dressed for a night out on the town. He knew that usually when women met up with their girlfriends at a bar this time of night, a trip to the club was next. "Oh, really?" he said smoothly. He was about to tell her to have a good night and be on his way when she smiled and engaged him.

"She texted me and said she's running late," she offered.

"Does that mean I can keep you company until she arrives?"

The attractive woman shifted her slim hips in her seat and smiled. "Only if you buy me a drink."

Johnny gladly obliged.

Her name was Gayle, and she was one of the best looking women Johnny had seen in a long time. Well-groomed, educated, and sophisticated refinement made her extra appealing to his senses. He'd been out of the game for a while, but Johnny was sure that this woman could help him fall right back into place.

He ordered Gayle another Moscato and another rum and Coke for himself. They sat at the bar and flirted shamelessly for another thirty minutes. "Are you sure your friend is still coming?" he asked.

"No, I'm not," she answered. "She said she was on her way, but that was right before you came, and she hasn't texted or called me since."

"Did you have plans to go somewhere after you meet up here?"

"Actually, no. We were going to meet here just to talk because it's close to where we both live, and as you can see it's private and the atmosphere is nice. My friend's had a long week, and she just needs to blow off some steam. That's why I'm surprised she hasn't gotten here by now."

"I hope she's okay," Johnny said, pretending to be concerned, but hoping her friend wouldn't show up so he could take Gayle to his room.

"I guess I should call her because it's not like her to say she's going to do something and not follow through."

Johnny didn't want Gayle to call her friend because more than likely if her friend was troubled, that meant whatever drama she was going through, it was keeping her preoccupied at this very moment. His guess was that her problem involved a man. He swallowed the last of his drink and knew that it was time to seal the deal for a little late-night rendezvous. He slid close to Gayle and looked into her eyes. "I'm really feeling you," he said to her in a slow and sexy voice. "Why don't we continue our conversation upstairs."

Gayle looked a little hesitant. "I'm not sure about that. I, um, I just met you."

"That's true, but as you can tell, I'm a gentleman, and trust me, I know how to make a lady feel like a woman."

Gayle blushed and grinned with seduction as she ate up Johnny's words. But their cat and mouse flirting was abruptly interrupted when a woman walked up on them and glared at Johnny.

"What the hell are you doing here?" Candace said, looking at Johnny as if she'd just seen the devil. Then she turned to her friend, Gayle. "How do you know this low-down son of a bitch?"

Johnny couldn't believe his bad luck. Out of all the women in the world that Gayle could be friends with, Johnny was pissed that it had to be Candace. She was looking at him with a stare that told him there was going to be drama in the quiet, subdued bar.

"What's going on?" Gayle said, looking at her friend.

Candace placed her hand on her hip. "This is the sorry-ass friend that got Bernard fired and ruined our lives."

Gayle gasped. "This is the Johnny that you've been talking about all these months?"

Candace nodded and pointed her finger at Johnny. "Bernard lost everything behind you, trying to defend my honor. He was so happy about his promotion, but because of you it was stripped away before he could enjoy it. His reputation went down the tubes, and after that, every job he applied for turned him down. The next thing I knew he started drinking, his house went into foreclosure, and now he's just a mess," Candace rattled off.

Johnny tried to control his temper, but he was fed up. First Bernard had cursed him out and threatened him, and then Vivana had slapped him, coaxing him into committing an act that he never thought he would do. Now, Candace was coming dangerously close to pushing him over the edge. He knew he needed to leave immediately before things got out of hand. He motioned for the bartender to close his tab, and without another word he rose from his barstool.

"Oh, hell no," Candace barked. "I know you're not gonna leave while I'm talking to you."

Johnny lost it. "Bitch, you better move out of my way."

The bartender stepped in. "Do I need to call hotel security?"

"You might," Gayle said. She hopped off her barstool and stood beside Candace in solidarity.

"Fuck both of you," Johnny said, "I'm leaving."

The bartender stepped in again. "I don't want any trouble in here tonight. Ladies, let him through so he can leave."

Candace lunged at Johnny, but Gayle held her back. "You ruined the only man I've ever loved," Candace sobbed. "Bernard was doing so well. He was attending his counseling sessions regularly and he'd completely changed his life from the drunken sex addict he used to be. I was going to spend my life with him."

"Sex addict?" Johnny said with surprise.

"Don't play stupid," Candace yelled. "You knew about Bernard's struggles, and I knew you were jealous of how he'd turned his life around. It killed you that he and I were happy. I told him months ago to stay away from you because all you were going to do was bring him down. And that's exactly what you did.

"I was late getting here tonight because when I went to Bernard's house I found him drunk, passed out beside some half-naked woman," she said as a small tear rolled down her cheek.

"Oh, no," Gayle said.

"I gave the ring back and called off the wedding."

Gayle placed her hand on Candace's shoulder. "I'm so sorry."

"It's not your fault," Candace said. Her tears turned back to anger. "It's his!"

Johnny balked. "The hell it is! Don't blame me because your man couldn't control his liquor or his dick. If you'd been handling your business at home, you wouldn't be here making a fool of yourself in the middle of this bar."

Candace stopped crying and her voice became colder than the dropping temperature outside. "I—I should kill you," she said, her voice filled with venom. "The world would be a better place without scum like you who continuously hurt others. You better watch your step!"

Her tone and words sent a chill through Johnny that made the hair stand up on the back of his neck, and he knew he had to leave before something really bad happened.

Once Johnny was back in his room he took off his clothes and climbed into bed. His head hurt from the constant bullshit that seemed to plague him. As he lay in the dark he thought about his life and how nothing made sense anymore. He reflected on each chaotic event that had happened over the last few months, and his heart sunk with the realization that the common denominator in all of it was him. As much as he hated to admit it, Bernard had been right. Johnny was at the center of all his problems.

Johnny shook his head, thinking about how, ever since Geneva left him, his life had felt empty. His house was no longer a home. He no longer had a sense of comfort. Through all the lying, cheating, and neglect, she'd stood by him until he'd made it impossible for her to continue on.

Tonight had been a turning point in Johnny's life. When he'd hit Vivana it brought back memories of his mother, which brought back the words she used to tell him long ago, words that he'd buried with her memory. "Son, behind every good man, there's a good woman." For the first time in over twenty years, Johnny wept. He cried in silence for the lost boy he used to be, and for the reckless man he'd become. He cried for the broken pieces he'd created in the lives of the women he'd hurt over the years, and for the best friend whose life he'd ruined with his jealous, selfish ways.

As Johnny drifted off to sleep, he vowed that if he was blessed to open his eyes in the morning, he would look through them with a different attitude and purpose. He knew he needed to start righting some of the wrongs he'd committed, and the first thing he was going to do was go by the salon and apologize to Geneva.

Chapter 24

GENEVA

Geneva sat in her chair at the salon, sipping her white chocolate mocha latte, waiting for her first client to arrive. It was eight o'clock Saturday morning, and the place was already packed with customers. This was the salon's busiest day of the week, and Geneva had hoped she wouldn't have to come in today.

She'd wanted to lie in Samuel's arms this morning, make love to him, and then cook the two of them a big breakfast. But when she awoke before the sun came up and saw that Cheryl hadn't returned her call from last night, she knew she had to come in. Just as she was about to step into the shower and get dressed for work, her phone rang. She looked at the brightly lit screen and was surprised by the contact name that appeared. Councilwoman Harris was calling her.

The councilwoman had canceled her standing appointment a few days ago because she'd been under the weather with a change of season cold. She'd been so sick that she'd forgotten about a city gala she needed to attend tonight, and because she'd missed her appointment, she was in dire need of a wash and blow dry. Geneva told her to come in a half hour after Cheryl was supposed to arrive; that way she could do both their hair in three hours flat and still have time to go home and enjoy the rest of her Saturday.

"I bet that heffa got your message and decided to ignore it," Donetta said, referring to Cheryl. "She's sneaky like that."

"You're probably right," Geneva said with a nod. She spoke her next words in a whisper, just loud enough for Donetta to hear. "This is the last time I'm doing her hair. After I finish her appointment, I'm going to tell her that she needs to find a new stylist."

"Good for you. And if she tries to get funky with you, you know I got your back."

Shartell leaned across her chair. "And so do I."

"You so damn nosey," Donetta said with a laugh.

Shartell smiled. "But you know you love me."

They stopped talking when Cheryl walked into the salon. Even though it was cloudy and dark outside, she was wearing a large pair of fashionable sunglasses. She walked up to Geneva's chair and let out a tired sigh. "By the time I checked my messages this morning I was halfway here," she said with an attitude. "Can you still do my hair or what?"

Geneva thought Cheryl's rude attitude and unnecessary question was nonsensical. "Of course I can do your hair, otherwise I wouldn't be here."

Donetta snapped her fingers. "Hello!"

Geneva couldn't see Cheryl's eyes, but judging from her body language, she knew the woman had rolled them at both Donetta and her.

"Fine," Cheryl snapped. "I want you to take this weave out and cut my hair down to a small natural, like you did the first time I came to you."

Geneva nodded. "Have a seat and we'll get started."

Cheryl sat in Geneva's chair and slowly removed her glasses. Geneva could tell by the look on Donetta's and Shartell's faces, as well as the customers in their chairs, that something was wrong. She spun the chair around and saw that Cheryl's right eye was blackened and swollen almost completely shut.

The saying, "you never know what someone is going through,"

rang out in Geneva's mind, and she instantly felt bad for acting salty toward Cheryl. She'd known that the woman was full of attitude, moody, and obnoxious, and now it looked like she could add abused to that list.

Geneva's thoughts took her back to the first time Cheryl had come into the salon four months ago. She'd been limping and she'd said it was because she needed surgery. But after that day, Cheryl had never limped or mentioned her knees again, let alone the need for surgery. She'd also told Geneva that she'd started seeing a man, but she'd been evasive about the extent of their relationship, which by her tone didn't seem happy.

Geneva gently placed her hand on Cheryl's shoulder. "Are you okay?" she asked.

Cheryl ignored her. "Can you please start taking my weave out. I have somewhere to be this afternoon and you're slowing up my time."

Donetta, Shartell, and their clients all rolled their eyes, but Geneva simply started doing as Cheryl asked.

Once she got Cheryl under the dryer, Councilwoman Harris arrived like clockwork. "I'm glad you're feeling better," Geneva told her as she quickly shampooed and conditioned her hair. "You look great."

"Thank you, Geneva," the modest councilwoman said. "I feel so much better. It's amazing what a little rest can do. This actually taught me a lesson," she said with a smile. "From now on I'm going to take at least one day a month to rest my body and do absolutely nothing unless I want to."

"That sounds like a good plan," Geneva said. She was about to remove the towel from Councilwoman Harris's head and blow dry her hair when Cheryl appeared.

"I'm dry and I need you to finish my hair," Cheryl said as she walked up to Geneva's chair, interrupting their conversation.

Everyone stopped what they were doing and turned their attention to the woman whom the entire salon had grown to dislike. Geneva was starting to get pissed. "Cheryl, please take a seat," she said, pointing to the chair beside her station. "I'll be with you as soon as I finish with my client."

Cheryl put her hand on her hip and rolled her one good eye. "It's not my fault that you double booked us, and I shouldn't have to wait."

Donetta stepped in. "You can either sit down or leave. But either way you not gettin' your hair done right now."

Councilwoman Harris looked uncomfortable as she peeked out from under the towel draped over her head to see what was going on. Geneva could see that one glimpse of Cheryl told the story because the councilwoman turned her head away from the trouble she could see brewing. She quickly offered up her seat. "I don't mind if you finish her up," she said to Geneva as she eased out of her chair, never raising her head to eye level.

Geneva wanted to tell Councilwoman Harris not to move, but the woman quickly scurried away to a seat in the waiting area. Cheryl took the councilwoman's seat, not bothering to say thank you, and that made Geneva furious. She stood silent for a moment, trying to decide if she was going to finish Cheryl's hair or ask her to leave, when she was startled by a voice she hadn't heard in months.

"What the hell's going on here?" Johnny said.

Geneva sucked in a deep breath of air. The last time she'd seen Johnny he was a scratched-up, bruised-up, bloody mess. His injuries had been the type that looked like they would leave permanent scarring. But as she surveyed him now, his face looked as smooth as the day she'd met him.

"Why is my wife doing your hair?" Johnny said, casting his eyes on the woman in Geneva's chair. He looked as if he'd just seen a ghost.

Once again, the entire salon fell silent.

Cheryl's good eye widened and blinked uncontrollably, but her mouth remained closed and she didn't say a word.

"What's going on?" Geneva asked. "Do you two know each other?"

Johnny walked up to within a few feet of where they were standing and looked Vivana in the eye. "You need to start talking!"

Vivana looked at Johnny and broke into tears. "Baby, I can explain."

"Baby?!" Geneva said with surprise. She stepped back from the chair and dropped the bottle of oil she was holding. "Are you two seeing each other?"

"Oh, shit!" Donetta said.

Vivana nodded. "Yes, Johnny and I have been dating for almost a year."

Geneva brought her hand to her mouth and shook her head. "A year?!" she whispered in disbelief. So many thoughts swirled through her head that she couldn't keep them all straight. She looked at Johnny in disbelief. "She just moved here a few months ago. How is it that you and Cheryl . . ."

"Her name's not Cheryl," Johnny said, glaring at the woman sitting in Geneva's chair. "Vivana, I don't know what kind of sick game you're playing but—"

"Vivana?" Geneva repeated. Once again, her mind began to replay scenes from the past few months. Samuel's wife's name was Vivana, and although he'd never described her physical appearance, he'd painted a detailed personal profile that fit Cheryl's character. Geneva nearly lost her balance when she realized that the woman who Johnny had been screwing all these months was the ex-wife of the man that Geneva was in love with. "This is too much."

"Geneva, I can explain," Johnny said.

Vivana jumped up from the chair. "Explain? You don't owe that bitch an explanation. If there's anyone you should be explaining anything to, it's me. Like where the hell were you last night?"

"Bitch?!" Geneva and Donetta both said incredulously.

"I don't owe you anything," Johnny scoffed.

"Like hell you don't. You did this to me," Vivana said, pointing to her face, "and then you left me lying on the ground like a piece of meat."

Geneva gasped. Johnny had done a lot of immoral and despicable things, but she'd never known him to put his hands on a woman. She looked at Johnny with a new level of disdain.

"You provoked me into it," he said defensively. "Did you think I was gonna sit around and let you attack and maul me like you did the first time?"

"She's the one who attacked you?" Geneva said, horrified again. She felt as if she was going to faint.

Vivana was oblivious to their conversation and turned her focus back to Johnny. "I waited up all night for you and you didn't have the decency to come back home, yet you managed to come here this morning to see this trick," she said, pointing to Geneva.

"That's it!" Donetta removed her earrings and reached for an iron out of the stove on her station. She looked directly at the woman she'd known as Cheryl. "If you don't get out of here right now you gonna wish your name was anonymous."

"Come on, Johnny. Let's get the hell out of here," Vivana said. "We can work this out later."

Johnny shook his head. "I'm not leaving with you. I came here to see Geneva."

Vivana tilted her head and looked around at everyone staring at her. She cleared her throat and held her head level. "Don't do this to me," she said through clenched teeth. "I sacrificed everything to be with you. I've paid your medical bills and your mortgage, and I've put up with your bullshit. If you don't leave with me right now, I'll never speak to you again."

"You promise?" Johnny said in a flat tone.

Vivana shook her head. "You're a dead man," she hissed. She stood silent for a few moments, as if Johnny was going to change his mind. But he didn't. She walked up to him and looked into his eyes. "Fuck you. You're gonna regret the day you ever met me."

"I already do," Johnny responded.

Vivana looked as though she could rip his heart out, but instead she slowly turned around without saying another word and walked out of the salon.

Geneva sat in her chair and held her hand to her head. Her heart was beating so hard she thought it would come through her chest. Not in a million years would she have thought that Johnny and the most hateful client she'd ever had were seeing each other.

She was glad that Vivana was gone, but she still had to contend with Johnny. She looked in his direction. "You need to leave," she said. "Go, now."

"I just need a word with you, in private," Johnny said.

"Didn't you hear her?" Donetta said, picking up her hot iron again. "She said leave."

Johnny glared. "No one was talking to you."

Geneva knew that neither her strong-willed friend nor her tri-fling husband were going to back down so she decided to step in. "Johnny, you showed up here unannounced. I don't know why you came and I really don't care. It's clear that you've moved on with your life, so please sign the separation agreement so I can move on with mine."

"We need to talk about that," he said. "Please give me five min-utes."

"We have nothing to discuss."

Johnny hung his head down. "Okay, I understand . . . If you won't talk to me, can you at least walk me to the door."

Geneva was skeptical, but at this point she was willing to do any-thing to be rid of him. Plus, she knew that if he made one wrong move every woman in the salon would pounce on him quicker than he could blink. She got to her feet. "Follow me."

"Don't go anywhere with him," Donetta said. Shartell even nod-ded in agreement.

"It's okay. I'll be right back."

Geneva walked in front of Johnny as he trailed behind her. When they reached the door she opened it and stepped aside so he could leave. "Goodbye." She turned to walk away.

"Geneva," Johnny said in a desperate voice that stopped Geneva in her tracks. "I came here today to apologize for everything I've done to you. I never meant to hurt you."

Geneva had had enough. "I don't want to listen to another word you have to say. You should be ashamed to even show your face. Now leave and don't ever come back here again."

Geneva was about to turn to walk away again when Johnny reached out and held her by her wrist. "Please," he pleaded. "Give me one more chance."

"Let go of me," she said. She whispered a quick prayer that he would do as she asked, because if he didn't she knew that within a matter of seconds, Donetta, Shartell, and a few others would start circling for blood. "Johnny, if you know what's best for you, you'll let go of my wrist, turn around, and keep on walking."

"I've changed. I swear I have. I'm not the man I used to be. And if you give me another chance I'll prove it to you. We had something special and I messed it up. But I love you, Geneva. I always have." He softened his eyes. "You said I didn't know how to beg properly, and you were right. But I know now, so I'm begging you. Please . . . give me another chance."

"You just beat a woman last night, left her on the ground, and never came back home to her. Is that the changed man that I'm supposed to trust? You must think I'm slow."

"She didn't mean anything to me."

"Let go of my wrist."

"Geneva, please. No one is gonna love you like I do."

Geneva shook her head. "You really are full of yourself. I already have a man who loves me."

"What?" Johnny said in a surprised voice.

Geneva quickly looked behind her and saw that Donetta and Shartell were now standing close, there for reinforcement. She was going to give Johnny a piece of her mind and then welcome the help of her friends to usher him off the premises. "That's right," she said, pulling away from his grip. "He loves me, and I love him! And he's more of a man than you'll ever be."

What happened next was a blur. The only thing Geneva remembered was the crazed look in Johnny's eyes, and his arms wrapped around her body before they both tumbled down the salon steps, onto the hard concrete, one flight below.

Chapter 25

SAMUEL

Samuel walked into the packed waiting area of the emergency room at Mercy General Hospital. His mind raced and his hands shook as he searched for Donetta. She'd called and told him that Geneva had had an accident at work, and that she was being rushed to the hospital by ambulance. He'd asked what happened but Donetta had been so upset she could barely speak and he couldn't fully understand what she'd said. He quickly put on his Howard University sweats, grabbed his keys, and headed out the door.

Samuel searched through the maze of people in the waiting room until he spotted Donetta sitting in a chair, biting her nails. He rushed over to her. "Where's Geneva?"

"The doctors are examining her."

"What happened?"

Donetta took a deep breath and told him blow by blow about the chain of events that landed Geneva in the hospital. Samuel shook his head as each detail unfolded. He couldn't believe the irony of it all. His feelings wavered between shock, disbelief, guilt, anger, and all-out rage. "Never in a million years would I have guessed that my ex-wife and Geneva's husband . . ." he sighed, letting his words trail off.

"I didn't see that comin' either," Donetta agreed. "When two danger-ous, deceitful, assholes get together there's bound to be trouble."

Samuel regretted not being more adamant about Geneva cancel-ing her appointment this morning. "I feel responsible," he said. "If I'd gone with my instincts and insisted that she cancel her appointment today, none of this would have happened."

Donetta shook her head. "This isn't your fault. Johnny Mayfield is the bastard who's responsible for this."

Donetta told him that Johnny had flipped out when Geneva said she was in love with another man. He'd reached out and wrapped his arms around her, and that's when Geneva pulled away from him, lost her balance, and fell, taking Johnny down the steps with her. She'd hit the hard concrete with a thud and then passed out.

"She was unconscious the entire ambulance ride over here," Donetta said in a worried voice.

"Did the doctors tell you anything?"

She shook her head. "They rushed her to the back the minute we got here and they told me I'd have to wait."

"I can't believe this is happening."

"Me either. I knew the minute that sonofabitch stepped into the salon that he was gonna start some shit. And what pisses me off is that right after they fell, that muthafucka stood right up and didn't have a scratch on him."

"You're kidding me."

"I wish I was. But don't worry, he's gonna get what's comin' to him 'cause payback is a bitch."

"Where is he now?"

"In hell, I hope."

Samuel leaned forward in his seat and rested his elbows on his knees. He was pissed that Johnny Mayfield had walked away unscathed while Geneva had suffered injuries that were bad enough to send her to the emergency room.

He knew he had to take his mind off Johnny and focus on Geneva. He had to remain optimistic, and that meant he shouldn't worry or think the worst until the doctors fully examined Geneva and determined the extent of her injuries. But no matter how hard he tried to convince himself that everything was going to be all right, his gut told him that more bad news was on the horizon. And if it was one thing this experience had taught him, it was that his gut was always right.

Samuel looked at the clock on the wall in the waiting room and let out a deep sigh. He thought about how at this very moment he and Geneva should've been sipping champagne and eating strawberries and Godiva chocolates in the presidential suite of the Roosevelt Hotel. But instead Geneva was lying on a gurney in the emergency room with injuries that were unknown.

Samuel and Donetta had been waiting more than an hour when Dr. Pauloza came out to talk to them. The petite doctor looked young enough to be carded if she tried to purchase alcohol, but Samuel could tell by her firm handshake and self-assured walk that the woman was as tough as nails.

"Ms. Mayfield had a pretty bad fall," Dr. Pauloza said. "She suffered several lacerations to her face along with a fractured collarbone and two broken ribs."

"Oh, lawd!" Donetta cried out, slightly startling the doctor.

"She also sustained a concussion and swelling of the brain."

Samuel became alarmed. He knew that while painful, the lacerations, fractures, and breaks would heal over time. But a brain injury, particularly swelling of the brain, was cause for concern. "How bad is the brain injury?" he asked.

"The swelling is quite significant . . . seventy percent."

"Jesus in heaven," Donetta said as she fanned herself with her hand.

Dr. Pauloza stared at Donetta. "Ms. Mayfield is getting the best possible treatment we can provide." She reached out and touched Donetta's arm to comfort her as she continued. "We're going to use a pharmacological treatment that reduces swelling by targeting a specific group of negatively charged molecules in the brain. In layman's terms, we're going to use a steady dose of drugs to reduce the swelling. I anticipate that it will subside fairly quickly."

"Will she have any long lasting side effects?" Samuel asked.

"It's hard to say. In most cases no. She seems to be responsive, so that's a good sign."

Samuel nodded with relief.

"We're going to keep her a few days, and we should have a room ready to take her up on the floor in the next thirty minutes. She's in a lot of discomfort, so we're giving her IV pain meds, which has her kind of groggy, but she's conscious."

"Can we see her?" Samuel asked.

Dr. Pauloza nodded. "Yes, I'll take you back, but there's one other thing I need to tell you."

Samuel braced himself because he knew this was it. Dr. Pauloza was going to deliver the bad news that his gut had been preparing him for since he'd arrived at the hospital.

Dr. Pauloza looked at Samuel with compassion and paused, as if the words were stuck in her throat. "I'm so sorry. She was pregnant, and she lost the baby."

The doctor's words echoed in his ears like thunder. He'd been prepared to hear that Geneva might need surgery, or that some of her injuries might leave permanent scarring, but in his wildest thoughts, losing a baby had never entered his mind because he didn't even know she was pregnant.

"Geneva was pregnant?" Donetta said, looking at Samuel.

"This can't be happening," Samuel whispered in a shaky voice.

Dr. Pauloza swallowed hard, empathizing with Samuel's pain. "She didn't know, either. And understandably, she took it hard. We gave her a valium to calm her."

Donetta shook her head and held Samuel's hand in hers.

Samuel's head and heart ached so badly he could hardly breathe. He and Geneva had spent countless hours talking about, and making plans for, the family they hoped they'd have one day. It had been both their desires to have children for as long as they could remember.

Samuel had felt happy every time he thought about his and Geneva's future, raising a family of their own and enjoying life while they did it. Hearing this news felt like a part of his dream had been snatched from him, and it was all at the hands of Johnny Mayfield.

"That sonofabitch!" Samuel yelled in an angry outburst. Samuel wasn't a man prone to raising his voice or speaking harshly, but now he was doing both. "Geneva's in there suffering, we lost a baby, and it's all because of that fucking bastard!" he yelled. "And he's walking around just fine, but he won't be for long. I'm gonna kill Johnny Mayfield!"

Donetta wiped a tear from her eye and looked at Samuel as if she was going to erupt like a volcano. "Not if I kill that muthafucka first!"

Chapter 26

VIVANA

Vivana listened to the engine run as she sat in her car in front of a small brick building where she was parked around the corner from the salon. She concentrated on the humming noise coming from under her hood in her efforts to drown out the memory of what had just happened.

She was so mad at Johnny Mayfield she thought she would explode. It wasn't enough that he'd physically accosted her last night, giving her a swollen, black eye, but he had to go a step further by disrespecting her in front of Geneva and a salon full of women.

Johnny was the last person she'd expected to see in the salon this morning, but he was the sole reason why she'd walked into the shop with an attitude. She was still pissed that he'd hit her and stayed out all night. Each time she called his phone, which she'd done every fifteen minutes for five hours straight, her calls went directly to his voice mail. She'd wanted to kick herself for suspending her BrickHouse GPS vehicle tracking service a few days ago. She'd felt she could stop monitoring Johnny's whereabouts and the monthly fee she'd been paying could go back into her pocket. She didn't see the need to monitor him as closely because he'd been keeping a low profile, mostly staying in the house while his injuries healed. But if she'd been able to track him last night, she would have gone to wherever he was and beaten the shit out of him.

She hadn't slept a wink all night and when she awoke this morning, unable to open her swollen eye, she cursed Johnny for what he'd done to her. She'd thought about canceling her appointment with Geneva when she looked into the mirror and saw her face. But after a few minutes of quick reflection, she decided to go anyway because she didn't want to miss an opportunity to get on Geneva's nerves, and actually, her injury would give her leverage to act out worse than she usually did because she knew Geneva would show her sympathy.

Vivana despised Geneva, she loathed Donetta and Shartell, and she couldn't stand any of the other stylists, or their clients, either. Each time she sat in Geneva's chair, she did her best to make things uncomfortable for her and everyone around in the salon. Vivana enjoyed watching Geneva squirm whenever she made a rude or inappropriate comment, and she felt free in pushing her to the edge because Geneva was one who tried to avoid conflict.

Fucking with Geneva had become the highlight of Vivana's week. But this morning it didn't take much for her to have an attitude, thanks to Johnny. And just when she was ready to really act out, Johnny appeared, sending everything into a nosedive from that moment forward.

"That bastard!" Vivana screamed. She thought about how she'd asked him to leave with her, but he'd refused and even had the audacity to tell her that he'd come there to talk to Geneva. The thought made her blood boil over with anger.

"I'll fix him," Vivana said as she looked at the small brick building in front of her. "And I know just how to do it, too." She turned off her engine and got out of her car. "He fucked with the wrong one this time," she said in a sinister tone as she walked inside the pawn shop.

"It's not over until I say so," Vivana said into the mirror. She was sitting on the stool at her vanity table applying concealer under her

eye. The swelling had gone down but the black ring underneath remained. "If Johnny thinks he can mistreat me, use me, and dog me
out without having to pay, he's crazy as hell."

It had been a week since Johnny had shown up at the hair salon
and humiliated her in front of people she didn't even like. When she
walked out of the salon last Saturday, she'd vowed to never speak to
him again, and so far she hadn't. She didn't want to have contact with
him in any way, ever again. But she knew that was going to be hard
given the fact that she would need to be near him in order to kill him.

She ran her hand across the small black pistol that she'd purchased
from the pawn shop last week right after she'd left the salon. She had
seven whole days to devise a plan to shoot Johnny and get away with it.

"The best time to strike is when they least expect it," she said in a
sly voice. Vivana smiled, filled her gun with bullets, and pointed the
pistol at the mirror. "Bang!" she said, pretending to fire the gun. The
weapon felt good in her hand, and she knew it would feel even better
using it. As she thought more and more about how much fun she was
going to have watching her ex-lover suffer, a brilliant idea popped
into her mind. Since she was going to kill Johnny, she might as well
kill Geneva while she was at it.

Chapter 27

GENEVA

Geneva sat up in bed as Samuel placed a wooden tray on her lap. Sausage, eggs, hash browns, toast, juice, and coffee. He'd gone to Waffle House and gotten her the exact same meal she'd ordered four months ago when he'd come to her rescue. And this morning he was saving her once again, helping her recover from hurt, pain, and a devastating loss.

Today made a week since Johnny had walked into the salon and turned her world upside down in one quick move.

"Baby, try to eat something," Samuel said. He took a seat beside Geneva on the bed. "You've got to build up your strength."

"I'm not hungry," she said.

"I know, but you still need to eat. The doctor said it's important in your healing process." He scooped up a forkful of eggs and placed them at Geneva's mouth. "Please, baby. Eat something for me."

Geneva looked into Samuel's loving eyes and could see that he was hurting just as much as she was. The only difference was that he did a much better job of dealing with it. He'd been a pillar of strength over the last week, encouraging her, nursing her, protecting her, and loving her.

From the moment Geneva had opened her eyes in the emergency room, Samuel had been by her side. He'd slept on a small cot in her hospital room each night, and had come back to visit her during lunch each day. When she was released from the hospital two days ago, he'd brought her to his apartment to recuperate, and had taken the rest of the week off work so he could take care of her.

"Come on, baby," Samuel urged again. He returned the eggs to her plate and picked up a piece of toast. He spread a small amount of strawberry jam on the bread and dangled it in front of her mouth. "You've got to put something in your stomach. Try this toast."

Geneva looked at the food and closed her eyes. She knew she needed to eat, but she couldn't bring herself to open her mouth to do anything except cry, which she'd been doing since last week. She choked back tears when she thought about the fact that she'd lost a child.

She'd known women who'd had miscarriages, but until Geneva experienced it for herself, she hadn't understood the pain and loss it could bring. And what made her situation even harder to accept was that she'd found out she was pregnant and lost it within the same instance. Every time she thought about the chain of events that morning, she felt a pang of guilt and secret shame that was eating her up inside.

She looked at Samuel and shook her head. "I'm so very sorry about what I did."

"What are you talking about?" he asked with concern.

"This is my fault. What happened is my fault . . ."

"Baby, don't say that. What happened to you . . . to us, wasn't your fault."

"Yes it is. If I hadn't walked Johnny to the door, none of this would have happened. I wouldn't have fallen and our baby would still be alive, growing inside my stomach." Geneva burst into tears that she couldn't control. "I purposely told him that I was happy, and in love, because I wanted to hurt him the way he hurt me. But I ended up hurting an innocent, unborn child in the process."

Samuel moved the tray of food to the side, slid next to Geneva, and held her close. "This isn't your fault, and I don't want to ever hear you say anything like that again."

"I lost our baby and that bastard walked away without a single solitary scratch! Not even a limp!"

Samuel's eyes became enraged. "Don't worry. He's gonna pay dearly for what he did, and he won't be able to walk away from what's in store for him. Trust me on that."

His tone sent a chill through Geneva because she'd never heard him sound so hard and almost vicious. She felt even worse because again, she knew this was all her fault. "Lord, what have I done," she whispered.

They stared at each other in silence before Samuel spoke. "You're a good woman and you deserve happiness. Don't let what he did make you feel guilty."

"But I do, and I wish I could go back in time . . . I would do so many things differently," she said in a low voice. "I would've canceled my appointment that morning, too."

Samuel shook his head. "I'm not going to allow you to go down this road, Geneva. We have to move forward from this. When I was sitting in the waiting room at the hospital, I beat myself up with 'would haves.' I wished I would have listened to my instincts from the very beginning about Johnny and Vivana, and I wish I would have insisted that you didn't go into the salon that morning. I even wished I would have come by and brought you coffee, that way I could have intervened. There were so many would haves that went through my mind. But after almost driving myself crazy, I realized that no matter what either one of us would have or could have done, everything happened the way it was supposed to."

Geneva looked at him with questioning eyes. "How can you say that? Do you really think we were supposed to lose our baby?"

"I think we're supposed to face whatever challenge comes our way, and stand strong in our faith that things will work out."

"We lost a child," she whispered.

Samuel nodded and squeezed her hand. "And we'll have another one. This entire experience showed me that even in the face of tragedy, everything is going to be all right as long as we have each other. I love you more and more each day."

Geneva's heart swelled with joy. Just as she was about to sink into more despair, Samuel pulled her out and made her believe that happiness was around the corner. He'd just told her that they would have another baby, and looking into his eyes, she knew they would.

"This bump in the road isn't going to stop us, baby. What God has in store for us is already planned, we just have to have faith and trust that it's going to be all right. I believe it will . . . don't you?"

Geneva smiled. "Yes."

Samuel reached for her tray, picked up the piece of toast, and this time Geneva took a small bite.

Later that night Geneva lay in bed, unable to sleep. But unlike the other nights over the last seven days, her inability to rest didn't stem from sadness. Geneva was wide awake, excited about her future. She was finally starting to feel like her old self again. She'd been down, but she hadn't broken, and she knew that she had a lot to be thankful for. She looked up when she saw Samuel come into the room carrying a hot cup of tea in one hand and a bottle of her medicine in the other.

"Chamomile?" she asked.

"You know it. It'll help relax you."

She smiled and yawned. "Thank you, baby."

Samuel opened the bottle of pills and handed one to her. "Take this. It'll help you sleep."

Geneva looked at the small but powerful pill. She had forgotten about the Ambien that the doctor had prescribed for her. "This medicine, combined with the chamomile, is gonna knock me out," she said.

Samuel nodded. "That's the point. You need a good night's sleep, and this is going to do it."

"You haven't been sleeping well, either," she said. "I'm concerned about you."

Samuel smiled, removed his jeans and t-shirt, and climbed into bed beside her. "Now that I know you're okay, I'm going to sleep like a baby."

Geneva rested her head on Samuel's chest while he held her close. Within a few minutes her eyes felt heavy, and she was glad for the deep sleep that was about to come. She felt safe and loved while she listened to Samuel's slow breathing as he drifted off beside her. This was the first night in seven days that a smile came to her face when she closed her eyes.

Chapter 28

JOHNNY

Johnny placed the cold slice of pizza back in the box, unable to eat it. His life was in shambles and he didn't know how to fix it. "I should've requested a late check-out and stayed my ass in bed," he lamented, thinking about last Saturday morning. Today made a week since the horrific accident at Geneva's salon, and he still couldn't get it out of his mind.

He hadn't meant to hurt Geneva in any way. All he'd wanted to do was tell her that he was sorry, and ask for her forgiveness. But things hadn't played out the way he'd wanted. He had no idea that Vivana would be there posing as a client. Each time he thought about the standing Saturday morning hair appointments she'd kept over the last four months, he had to shake his head. She'd played him in much the same way he'd played women all his life. Lies, secrets, and scandalous behavior weren't new to him, but they took on a different meaning when he was on the receiving end of them.

"This is what it feels like to be shit on," he said, looking around his empty house. For the first time in years he was all alone. Even though his relationship with Vivana had been dysfunctional, tumultuous, and full of drama, she'd filled the void that Geneva had left, but now, even she was gone.

"I guess I'm getting my payback," Johnny said as he walked into the kitchen. He opened the refrigerator and reached for a bottle of his favorite imported beer. He leaned against the counter and took a long swallow as his mind went back to Geneva.

When she left him a few months ago, Johnny knew she was hurt and angry, but he thought those feelings would eventually pass, as they always had. He'd fully expected her to come back to him, and that's why he never signed the separation papers. But as time went on, she didn't return, and now he knew why. He hung his head and mouthed words he never thought he'd say. "My wife is in love with another man."

When Geneva told him that she'd moved on, and that she was actually in love with someone else, a surprising pain had gripped Johnny's chest that he'd never felt before. He wanted her back. He wanted to hold her. So he wrapped his arms around her and set tragedy in motion.

Every time he closed his eyes, the vision of Geneva's body lying limp on the ground plagued him. "I need something stronger than this," he said as he downed his beer. He walked over to the cabinet. "This is more like it." He opened the bottle of Ciroc, put a few ice cubes in his glass, and filled it to the rim with the premium vodka. "Ahhh, that's what I needed." He drank the liquor until his glass was empty, and then filled it again. But no matter how hard he tried to block it out, the vision was still there.

Everything had happened in a flash, but he knew Geneva was hurt the minute they hit the ground because his body had landed on top of hers. She twisted her body as they fell to the ground, and she ended up underneath him, taking the full brunt of his weight. He knew it was bad because she didn't make a sound upon impact. "Geneva!" he screamed frantically. "Geneva, are you okay? . . . Say something!" She didn't move. She was unconscious.

Johnny's heart raced as he watched blood run down the side of her face. He touched her shoulder, which was posed in an awkward position. But before he could further survey the extent of her injuries,

Donetta, Shartell, and a small group of women from the salon had descended upon him. A few of them pushed and kicked him but they backed off when they heard a police siren rushing to the scene. Someone had called the cops just that quickly, and because they were in an upscale part of town, the men in blue had come in record time. Moments later an ambulance arrived and he watched as they placed a still unconscious Geneva on a stretcher.

Johnny wished it had been him instead of Donetta who accompanied Geneva in the ambulance en route to the hospital, but the police refused to let him go anywhere until they got to the bottom of what happened. Luckily for him, they determined from his account, and from that of the eyewitnesses at the salon, that his actions had not been malicious in their intent. Geneva's fall was an accident, and he wasn't at fault.

But Johnny knew he was to blame, and that's why he planned to drink until he passed out; that way he wouldn't have to think about the woman he'd ruined or the unborn baby's life he'd taken. Every time he thought about the threatening, profanity laced text that Donetta had sent him the night of the accident, calling him a baby killer, he'd pick up a bottle to drink away the reality of what he'd done. He was well on his way to doing that again tonight, so drunk he was barely able to hold his glass to his mouth, when he heard a knock at his kitchen door.

It was close to midnight, and he wondered who in the hell could be coming to his house this time of night. As it stood, everyone he knew was avoiding him, including his neighbors. He blinked his eyes and tried to focus on the figure he saw through the sheer valance hanging on the door window. When he finally recognized who it was, surprise and caution filled his muddled mind. He wondered why he was being paid a visit, especially after all that had happened, and all that he'd done. No one visited anyone this time of night without a purpose, and he knew this purpose wasn't good. But he was drunk and he didn't care, so he was willing to take his chances.

Johnny stumbled to the door and opened it. "What're you doing here?"

They stared at each other without saying a word, and it quickly became clear to him that his life was getting ready to end. He was calm when his late night visitor pointed the gun, complete with a silencer on the end, directly between his eyes.

Slowly, Johnny eased back into the kitchen. He knew it was no use to put up a fight, and he actually welcomed what was about to come, because he knew that once he was dead it would be the first time he'd truly be at peace since the day he was born.

It was as if everything was happening in slow motion. He watched as the gun was lowered to his chest, hovering close to his heart. Johnny knew his pistol-wielding visitor was enjoying this, pausing for a moment, no doubt savoring what he imagined was the sweet taste of revenge. Then, when he thought for a brief moment that perhaps his life would be spared, he felt his chest explode. He fell to the floor and he knew it would be over soon.

Chapter 29

GENEVA

Geneva looked out the peephole and was surprised to see two men in suits, flashing their badges, standing on the other side.

"Who is it?" Samuel asked from where he was sitting on the couch.

"I think it's the police," she answered.

He stood up and came to the door with a worried look on his face. "I wonder what they want."

Geneva shrugged her shoulders because she didn't have a clue.

"I'll handle this," Samuel told her.

She looked on as Samuel peered out of the peephole and then slowly opened the door. "How can I help you?"

The detectives introduced themselves, then the shorter, heavy-set one of the two looked past Samuel and directly at Geneva. "We're looking for a Mrs. Geneva Mayfield," the detective said. "We spoke to several people at Heavenly Hair Salon where she's employed and they said we could find her at this address."

Geneva stepped forward. "I'm Geneva Mayfield."

"Are you the wife of Jonathan Nathaniel Mayfield?"

Geneva looked at Samuel and knew there was going to be trouble. "He and I are going through a divorce," she answered. "What's this about?"

When the detective asked if they could step inside, Geneva instantly knew that something very, very bad had happened, and when he told her that Johnny was dead, her body went numb.

"His body was discovered this morning at his residence," the officer said. "It appears that he died of a gunshot wound to the chest."

Geneva clinched Samuel's hand and shook her head from side to side. "Oh my God," she whispered. She looked at Samuel and the expression on his face put even more worry inside her.

"Mrs. Mayfield, we need to know where you were between the hours of eleven p.m. last night and one a.m. this morning?"

"I was here, asleep. I went to bed early last night and didn't wake up until about six this morning."

The detectives both looked at Samuel. "Are you Mr. Samuel Owens?" the other detective asked.

Geneva immediately knew where this was going. If the detectives had questioned her whereabouts with people at Heavenly Hair and the answers had led them here, she knew it was a given that they would have information about Samuel as well. Geneva shifted in her seat when she felt Samuel's hand become clammy inside hers.

"Yes, I am," Samuel answered.

The detective pulled out a notepad and pen and asked Samuel the same question the other officer had just asked Geneva.

"I was here all night. Geneva and I went to bed around the same time and she woke up shortly before I did."

"Were you here all night?" the detective asked.

Samuel nodded. "Yes, I was."

Geneva heard a slight hitch in Samuel's voice. She looked at him and it occurred to her that he hadn't acted surprised when the detectives told them that Johnny was dead. Then she thought about last night. Samuel had given her a cup of herbal tea to relax her and Ambien to help her sleep. She'd rested so well that she didn't move a muscle until she awoke this morning.

It was clear to her that the detective's focus had squarely shifted from her to Samuel, and she didn't like where their line of questions was going. She couldn't sit silent and let this continue. "You don't think Samuel or I had anything to do with Johnny's death, do you?"

The shorter detective who'd first questioned her spoke up. "This is a homicide and we're investigating all leads, and any and all persons of interest."

After more questions about the nature of Geneva's and Samuel's relationships with Johnny, the detectives wrapped things up and told them that they may be called down to the station for further questioning. The detectives left their cards and then walked out the door.

Geneva and Samuel sat on the couch in silence. She wanted him to say something but he remained as quiet as a mouse. She didn't want to think that Samuel had anything to do with Johnny's death. She'd fallen in love with him because he was kind, loyal, and true. He was the most decent man she'd ever known. But she also knew that every person, no matter how decent, had their limit, and once it was tested, anything could happen. Donetta had told her about Samuel's angry outburst in the emergency room, and his threat to kill Johnny.

"Samuel," she began. "Please tell me you didn't have anything to do with Johnny's death."

Samuel took a few minutes to answer before he turned and looked into her eyes. "Baby, I won't lie . . . a part of me takes a little relief in the fact that he's dead. But I didn't do it." He held Geneva close to him. "He got what he deserved, but it wasn't at my hands."

Epilogue

Over the next few weeks Amber was abuzz over the murder of Johnny Mayfield. Little by little the details of his demise were released and more suspects popped up each day.

There were nearly a dozen women whom Johnny had slept with in the last year, and each of them had been wronged by him in some way. Some of them were being blackmailed with compromising pictures that Johnny had taken and threatened to send to their or boyfriends and even their employers, if they didn't pay up. Two of the women had sent him threatening texts, vowing to get even with him. Not a single one of Johnny's conquests had anything good to say about the man. But they had all been one-night stands with airtight alibis, making the hunt for his killer that much tougher.

There were also dozens of people whom Johnny either owed money to, or had been involved in questionable real estate activities with that had gone south, leaving a sour taste in their mouths. But the dollar amount of his offenses had been low. Their weak motives and strong alibis had put them in the clear.

Then there were those who the detectives considered persons of considerable interest. The list consisted of a half dozen people, and they all had clear motives and good reasons for wanting to kill Johnny.

Geneva, Samuel, Vivana, and Bernard were at the top of the list. They'd all suffered great pain, either emotional, physical, or financial, from their involvement with Johnny. Unlike the other suspects, their motives were strong but their alibis were weak. Then next in line came Donetta and Candace, whose known hatred of Johnny and public threats made against him put them high on the list of people who wanted to make him push up daisies.

Gossip swirled around them all, and it seemed every person in town had a theory about who killed Johnny.

The investigation dragged on for several months until the day the murder weapon was recovered. When the detectives charged Vivana Owens with the murder of Johnny Mayfield, no one was surprised. No one, that is, except Vivana herself.

Vivana was adamant that she didn't kill Johnny. "I was framed," she'd said. Vivana refused to take a plea deal, and against the advice of her attorney, she took the stand in her own defense during the trial. She admitted that not only did she want to kill Johnny, she wanted to do away with Geneva as well. But someone got to him before she could, and therefore made her hesitant about carrying out revenge against Geneva.

After the prosecution finished with Vivana, it left very little doubt in anyone's mind that Johnny's ex-lover was guilty of the crime. After only an hour of deliberation, a jury reached a unanimous guilty verdict.

After the trial, as Vivana was transported from the county jail to a state correctional facility, she still maintained her innocence. "I didn't kill that son of a bitch. I was framed!" she was quoted in a jailhouse interview.

What people in Amber didn't know was that as guilty as Vivana appeared to be, there was someone living among them who was even guiltier.

Vivana had been telling the truth all along, and the one person who knew that she was innocent was the same person who murdered Johnny Mayfield in cold blood.

Councilwoman Charlene Harris felt a sense of relief the night she killed Johnny. She'd exacted revenge, not only for herself but for the countless other women whom Johnny had harmed in some way, just as he'd done to her.

After Charlene had separated from her husband she'd come out of her shell and was ready to enjoy life. She'd cut her hair, changed the way she dressed, and transformed herself into a happier version of the woman she used to be. She decided that she needed a fresh start. She wanted to create new memories going forward, and she couldn't do that living in the past. She decided to move out of the large, cold-feeling house she'd shared with her cheating husband, in favor of downsizing to a condo that would fit her newly single lifestyle.

She'd been referred to Johnny Mayfield by a friend who'd raved about his services. Charlene had no idea that Johnny was her hairstylist's husband. Geneva never spoke about her personal life, and when Charlene had met Johnny he hadn't been wearing a wedding band, and he'd even told her that he was single. His subtle seduction excited her, and made her feel more desirable than she had in years.

Before Charlene knew it, she was having passionate, wild sex with Johnny, and she'd enjoyed every hot, unadulterated minute of it. His youthfulness brought out the vixen in her that made her feel sexy and free. But that feeling was short-lived when Johnny's crazy mistress showed up and caused a scene that was reality TV–worthy. After narrowly escaping with her body bruised but intact, Charlene swore to herself that she'd never act impulsively again.

She thought that dark day was behind her until a month later when she received a letter at work from none other than Johnny Mayfield. He'd said he'd fallen on some hard times and he needed money. He gave her a number to call with an area code she didn't recognize, and later found out was a burner phone. When a week went by without her contacting him, he called her job and asked her for money. Charlene had balked. "I don't understand why you're calling me," she'd told him. "Your financial problems are not my concern."

"They are very much your concern," he said in a voice that made it known that he was up to no good.

There had been a video camera set up in the closet of the vacant condo unit where Johnny had taken Charlene for their morning tryst. The camera was positioned directly across from the bed and had captured every illicit act the upstanding councilwoman had performed on him, and had received in return. Johnny threatened to upload the sex tape on porn websites and then mail copies to her children, friends, fellow council members, and, last but not least, the attorney representing her husband in their pending divorce.

Fearful that Johnny would make good on his threat, Charlene paid him hush money—in cash—every month. She hated being held hostage and she felt angrier and angrier each time she had to pay him, wondering when his blackmail scheme would ever end. Then one Saturday morning she got her answer when the house of cards came crashing down.

She'd made a last minute hair appointment with her stylist on an early Saturday morning, and had been completely mortified when she saw Johnny's mistress approach Geneva's chair, demanding to take the very seat Charlene was sitting in. Even though the woman's hair was shorter and she had a blackened eye, no doubt a result of her own violent temper, Charlene still recognized her. But she was glad that the crazy woman was so preoccupied with Geneva doing her hair that she overlooked Charlene altogether. Charlene quickly ducked away to the waiting area, glad to lay low until the coast was clear. But she got another shock when she saw Johnny Mayfield walk through the door.

A light went off and illuminated what had been going on.

The man who'd been blackmailing her for months was her stylist's husband. Johnny had been so engrossed in the drama involving him, Geneva, and Vivana, that he hadn't noticed Charlene in the seating area when he first came in.

Not to her surprise, a terrible scene ensued. Charlene felt awful about what happened to Geneva, and when she realized that not only had Geneva been badly injured, she'd also lost the baby she was carrying, Charlene had had enough, and flew into a rage. She'd put up with a whoring, cheating, no-good husband for three decades, and she refused to let another woman suffer at the hands of a trifling, no-good man.

Charlene had stayed up late each night for a week, plotting Johnny's demise. On the night that she planned to kill him, she left her Mercedes in her garage and opted to drive the old Camry she used for weekend errands. She parked several blocks away from Johnny's house and walked quickly through the back alleys so she wouldn't be spotted. She walked up to Johnny's kitchen door and knocked. She couldn't believe how easy it had been, or how good it felt to pull the trigger of the pistol and watch her blackmailer fall to the ground.

Charlene thought about how she'd gotten away with murder as she sat behind her desk in her large office in City Hall. She was glad to put the murder of Johnny Mayfield behind her, and with Vivana Owens safely away in prison, she knew she was in the clear. But her eyes got big and her blood ran cold when she looked at the message that appeared from a blocked number on her cell phone.

Unavailable: You're a murderer

Charlene's eyes widened and her mouth went dry. It took a few minutes for her to decide if she was going to respond. Finally she began to type.

CH: Who is this?
Unavailable: I'm the person who has proof that you murdered Johnny Mayfield

Charlene dropped her phone as if it was wired with explosives. She sat behind her desk and for the first time since Johnny's murder, she no longer felt at peace.

SECRET INDISCRETIONS

Trice Hickman

ABOUT THIS GUIDE

The questions that follow are included to enhance your group's reading of this book.

Discussion Questions

Thank you for reading *Secret Indiscretions*! I hope you enjoyed the story, and if you did, please spread the word and tell your friends to get their copy too!

Here are some questions I believe will enhance your reading experience and spark some interesting dialogue. If you're a member of a book club I'd love to join you at your monthly meeting, in person, by phone, or by Skype! If you're interested, please visit my website at www.tricehickman.com, and we'll make it happen!

1. Johnny and Geneva and Samuel and Vivana were couples who were polar opposites, yet they ended up together. What qualities do you think drew these mismatched couples to each other?

2. Very early in the story it was clear that Johnny was cheating on Geneva. But like many women, Geneva held out hope that he wasn't. Why do you think Geneva overlooked and put up with a cheating husband for as long as she did?

3. Johnny was a man who had a loving and loyal wife at home who loved him, yet he cheated on her anyway. What do you think were some of the reasons he was unfaithful?

4. An article published in the *Journal of Couple & Relationship Therapy* suggested that 45 to 55 percent of women and 50 to 60 percent of men engage in extramarital sex at some time during the course of their marriage. Given these statistics, and from your own observations of society, do you believe that monogamy is natural?

5. They say, "Once a cheater always a cheater." Do you believe this is true? Why or why not?

6. Geneva and Samuel experienced an instant connection when they met, and became deeply involved shortly thereafter. Based on the details of their relationship, do you think it will last? Why or why not?

7. There were several characters in the story who became involved because of physical attractions. On a scale of 1 to 10, how important do you think physical attraction is in a relationship?

8. Who was your favorite character and why? Who was your least favorite character and why?

9. Did you correctly guess who killed Johnny?

Don't miss the thrilling conclusion to Trice Hickman's
Dangerous Love series

Deadly Satisfaction

Available in February 2016!

The elegantly sleek interior of G & D Hair Design was alive with chatter, laughter, and gossip. Even though G & D was a high-end salon situated in the trendy arts district of town, the owners, Geneva Owens and Donetta Pierce, made sure their establishment was as down-home and welcoming as sweet potato pie, which they often served their customers. And on this particular Saturday morning the salon was extra busy. It was the weekend before Thanksgiving, and as Donetta said, "Every woman in town is tryin' to get her style on this holiday."

Every stylist's chair, shampoo bowl, and hooded dryer was occupied, and even more women were patiently waiting in the lobby, sipping flavored coffee at the complimentary beverage station. Geneva and Donetta had worked hard to overcome many battles, and now they were reaping the rewards with their thriving business.

"I've been doing hair for nearly twenty years, and this is the busiest holiday turnout I've ever seen," Donetta said. "You'd think we were giving away weaves up in here."

"Everyone wants to look good when they visit with their families," Geneva said with a smile as she reached for her flat iron.

"Speak for these other women," Shartell Brown huffed as she sat in Donetta's chair. "As for me, I'm gettin' fly for me, myself, and I.

My family is on my last nerve and I'm glad I only have to tolerate them once a year."

Donetta made a *tsk*ing sound as she measured a track of hair for what would become part of Shartell's freshly styled weave. "Girl, why're you stressing about your family? Shoot, if they know like I know, they'll stay outa your way before they end up in one of your columns, or maybe even that new book you're writing."

Shartell smiled slyly. "That's not a bad idea. Real life is much more exciting than fiction."

"That's just flat-out wrong to use your family like that," Donetta said. "Even I wouldn't do that."

"Honey, it's called being shrewd."

"How 'bout it's called being a cold-hearted bitch?" Donetta quipped. "You need to sit back and be quiet before you end up having to do your hair your damn self, 'cause you know I barely like you."

Geneva laughed. "You two talk so much junk."

"Donetta knows she loves me," Shartell said with a chuckle. "I might be a bitch, but I'm not a phony."

Everyone within earshot nodded in agreement with what Shartell had just said. Shartell Brown, who had once worked as a stylist with Geneva and Donetta several years ago, and had been nicknamed Ms. CIA, because she was a known gossip with intel on everyone in town, was now a respected news and entertainment columnist as well as a bestselling author. Shartell had risen to prominence thanks to the most salacious and talked-about murder case the town of Amber had ever seen. Two years ago, Johnny Mayfield, Geneva's late husband, had been murdered in cold blood inside his home, and the list of suspects had been as long as a hot summer day. But thanks to Shartell's contacts, inside information, and her uncanny ability to find out the word on the street before it ever hit the pavement, she'd helped the police solve Johnny's murder and cement a new career for herself in the process.

Geneva shook her head. "Shartell, you should rejoice that you're blessed to have family to spend the holidays with. I'd give anything to share a meal with my mother again, God rest her soul."

Shartell pursed her lips. "That's because your mother was probably just as nice as you are, Ms. Pollyanna," she teased. "But my mama could drive Jesus to drink hard liquor, and my four siblings . . . let's just say that if the devil needed extra disciples, he'd come looking for them and their badass kids."

"Shartell!" Geneva chided. "That's an awful thing to say."

Donetta threaded her weave needle and nodded her head. "No it's not. Especially if it's true, which I'm sure it is."

"Thank you," Shartell said, reaching up to give Donetta a high five.

Geneva adjusted her smock as she spoke. "You two are the most jaded human beings I know. Where is your optimism?"

"We're realists," Donetta said, hand on her slim hip. "Hell, I know exactly what Shartell's talking about. My family drives me to the bottle every holiday, and that's why I'm not foolin' with them this year."

"Donetta, your aunt is gonna have a fit if you don't go over to her house to celebrate with her and your cousins."

Donetta smirked. "She'll just have to have one because my back-stabbing relatives won't see my face in the place this year. I refuse to go over to my aunt May May's and listen to all their bullshit. I got my life to live and I'm doin' just fine without them."

"I'm truly sorry to hear that," Councilwoman Harris spoke up from Geneva's chair. "I'll say a prayer for both of you, that you and your families will find peace."

Charlene Harris was one of Geneva's favorite and most loyal customers. She was a pillar of the community, and much like Geneva, she was a woman who'd mastered the art of reinventing herself. Two years ago she'd decided to end her three-decades-old marriage and started a new life. She updated her look and style, but kept the same classic grace and comportment that commanded respect and attention from all who knew her.

Geneva smiled. "You understand what family is all about, and I know you can't wait to see your children when they come to town," she said.

Charlene beamed with pride. "Yes, Lauren's flying in tomorrow morning and Phillip will be here later tonight."

"I know you're proud of them," Geneva said as she worked her flat iron through Charlene's razor-cut bob, putting the finishing touches on her hairdo.

"Yes, I am. Lauren is in her first year at Johns Hopkins and Phillip just finished clerking for Washington, DC's state's attorney. I couldn't be more proud of them because they're both accomplishing their goals, but more than that, they're genuinely great people, and that's what's most important."

Geneva nodded. "Yes, it certainly is."

"Amen to that," Donetta chimed in, along with Shartell. "Not everybody has the opportunity to pursue their dream or maintain the dedication to keep at it until they accomplish it. Trust me, I know."

Geneva looked at her co-owner and best friend and smiled. She knew that it was a topic near to Donetta's heart. In two months she was going to have her final gender reassignment surgery that would make her transition into an anatomical woman complete. It had taken Donetta many years, tremendous sacrifice, and at times heartache to pursue her long-held dream of living life the way she'd always wanted to.

"Your words speak so much truth," Councilwoman Harris said with a nod. "Life is a journey filled with many different paths to get to one destination."

"And the best way to get there is in a pair of Jimmy Choos," Donetta replied with a wink.

They all laughed at Donetta's joke, but suddenly the room fell silent when Shartell looked up at the fifty-inch television screen hanging on the wall and gasped. Every eye was glued to the face on the screen that put panic in each of their hearts for very different reasons.

Geneva stood frozen in place while Donetta reached over her, grabbed the remote, and turned up the volume. The "Breaking News" caption rolled across the screen with a photo of Vivana Jackson above it. Although her last name had changed from Owens, back to her maiden name Jackson, and she looked a bit haggard, there was no mistake that the woman on the screen was a murderer. A hush came over the entire salon as they listened to news that left their mouths hanging open with questions.

Vivana Jackson had been convicted of murdering Johnny Mayfield, and was serving a fifty-year sentence in the state prison. But according to the information coming out of the news reporter's mouth, Vivana had enlisted the help of a local attorney who'd taken her case pro bono, and had found evidence that suggested she was innocent of the crime for which she'd been convicted. Her attorney was set to appear before a judge in the next two weeks to present the evidence. The reporter concluded by saying they planned an exclusive jailhouse interview with Vivana that would air tonight.

Everyone remained silent while their eyes fell on Geneva, who was still frozen in place.

Donetta looked at Geneva. "Are you okay?"

Geneva shook her head. "No, I'm not." She took a deep breath. "I need to go home."

From that moment forward, the salon was filled with gossip, speculation, and theories about the murder case that had rocked Amber. Johnny Mayfield had done so many people wrong that the list of suspects in his murder had been long. Half the town believed that his scorned ex-lover had done it, while the other half believed Vivana's claim that she'd been framed. There were only three people who knew that Vivana was innocent. One of them was dead, and the other one was Johnny's real killer, Charlene Harris. But now there was a prominent local attorney who believed in Vivana's innocence, too, and was determined to prove it.

Later that night, nearly everyone in Amber was held captive in front of their televisions as they looked at Vivana's defiant face and listened to her lawyer's self-assured words. "I've uncovered evidence that corroborates my client's claim that she was framed for the murder of Jonathan Mayfield," Vivana's attorney said. "I can't go into detail now, but when I present the evidence to the judge next month it will be clear that Ms. Jackson, previously known as Mrs. Owens, was not only framed, but the real killer is still at large."

Just as in the salon in the morning, people throughout town were abuzz with chatter and speculation. But there were a few people who were more than a little concerned, including Geneva, Donetta, Shartell, and especially Councilwoman Harris. Each one of the women knew that in the weeks to come, this would be a holiday that they would never forget.